Praise for Kristin Harmel's books!

The Art of FRENCH KISSING

"Overflowing with bubbly fun, filled with delicious romance and madcap adventures, and, toujours, intoxicating with the magic of Paris . . . Like a bottle of champagne . . . You'll drink it down in one glamorous gulp."

—Julia Holden, author of *One Dance in Paris*

"A sweet, funny tale about losing love and finding yourself. Set against the backdrop of the most romantic city on earth, THE ART OF FRENCH KISSING takes us on an exciting whirlwind of glitz, glamour, and celebrity scandals—with a side order of reinvention."

—Johanna Edwards, author of *The Next Big Thing*

"I'm a big fan of Kristin Harmel, and THE ART OF FRENCH KISSING is my favorite of her novels."

—Melissa Senate, author of *See Jane Date*
and *Love You to Death*

"*Très magnifique!* I loved this book and you will, too! . . . A sweet and adorable page-turner that will make you long for the City of Light."

—Brenda Janowitz, author of *Scot on the Rocks*

"A fun, lively story that made me fall in love with Paris all over again."

—Lynda Curnyn, author of *Bombshell*

more . . .

THE BLONDE THEORY

"Entertaining." —*London Free Press*

"Rush out and pick this one up. You'll be glad you did. So entertaining that I won't be surprised if this one ends up on the big screen." —NightsandWeekends.com

"With a smart heroine willing to date as a bona fide ditz, there are plenty of laugh-out-loud moments . . . the true joy comes when Harper drops the silly blonde act and gives the shallow men she meets a piece of her mind."

—*Romantic Times BOOKreviews Magazine*

HOW TO SLEEP WITH A MOVIE STAR

"Hilarious." —*Cosmopolitan*

"Hilarious . . . deliciously entertaining."

—Sarah Mlynowski, author of *Milkrun* and *Monkey Business*

"We recommend *How to Sleep with a Movie Star.*"

—*New York Daily News*

"Forget the movie star! For a really good time, take this hilarious book to bed instead."

—Jennifer O'Connell, author of *Dress Rehearsal* and *Insider Dating*

"Kristin Harmel dishes with disarming honesty and delivers a sparkling, delightful story about the push and pull between being average and being a celebrity."

—Laura Caldwell, author of *The Year of Living Famously* and *The Night I Got Lucky*

ALSO BY KRISTIN HARMEL

The Art of FRENCH KISSING

KRISTIN HARMEL

NEW YORK   BOSTON

5 Spot
Hachette Book Group USA
237 Park Avenue
New York, NY 10017

Visit our Web site at www.5-spot.com.

5 Spot is an imprint of Grand Central Publishing.
The 5 Spot name and logo is a trademark of Hachette Book Group USA, Inc.

Book design by Stratford Publishing Services, a TexTech business

Printed in the United States of America

First Edition: February 2008
10 9 8 7 6 5 4 3 2 1

Library of Congress Cataloging-in-Publication Data

Harmel, Kristin.
    The art of French kissing / Kristin Harmel. — 1st ed.
        p. cm.
    Summary: "A novel about a woman's quest to find love while working to rein in a rowdy pop star in Paris"—Provided by publisher.
    ISBN-13: 978-0-446-58143-1
    ISBN-10: 0-446-58143-7
    1. Young women—Fiction.   2. Singers—Fiction.   3. Paris (France)—Fiction.   I. Title.
    PS3608.A745A78 2008
    813'.6—dc22

                                                                2007030664

Acknowledgments

A special thank-you to Lauren Elkin, my wonderful friend who first lured me to Paris and has let me sleep on her futon each time I've been tempted to return. She's also a great writer, and I was fortunate enough to have her give me early feedback on this book. Thanks as well to Amy Tangerine (extremely talented superstar designer and fantastic friend), who is a great cheerleader and one of the people whose opinion I trust wholeheartedly on early drafts. A thousand thank-yous to Gillian Zucker, my trusted friend whom I admire greatly as both a person and a professional (and who lets me call her second bedroom home when I'm in LA!). I owe you a drink (or several dozen) at Katsuya!

Thanks, as always, to Mom, Dave, Karen, Dad, and the rest of my fantastic family. I truly think I'm related to some of the warmest, most wonderful people in the world.

I owe a huge debt of gratitude to my fabulous editors Karen Kosztolnyik and Rebecca Isenberg for helping beat this novel into shape, and to my wonderful agent Jenny Bent (and her assistant, Victoria Horn) for listening to me ramble about all the ideas that pop into my head. Thanks also to my film agent, Andy Cohen, whom I'm happy to call my friend; to all the folks at Hachette, especially

Elly Weisenberg (congratulations!!!), Emily Griffin, Caryn Karmatz Rudy, Brigid Pearson, Laura Jorstod, Celia Johnson, and Mari Okuda; and to my UK editor, Cat Cobain. And as always, thanks to my first editor, Amy Einhorn.

I'm also fortunate enough to have met some of the nicest writers in the entire world. Thanks especially to Sarah Mlynowski for being so generous with her time and advice; to Alison Pace for giving me a New York couch to sleep on and taking me on walks with the fabulous Carlie; and to Sarah, Alison, Lynda Curnyn, and Melissa Senate, for the friendship and support you've all provided. Thanks also to the wonderful writers (and wonderful women) Jane Porter, Laura Caldwell, Brenda Janowitz, Johanna Edwards, Megan Crane, and Liza Palmer.

Thanks to my many wonderful, amazing friends, especially Kristen Milan, Kara Brown, Kendra Williams, Wendy Jo Moyer, Megan Combs, Amber Draus, Lisa Wilkes, Ashley Tedder, Don Clemence, Michelle Tauber, Willow Shambeck, Melixa Carbonell, Josh Yang, Courtney Jaye, Marc Mugnos, Ryan Dean, Wendy Chioji, Brendan Bergen, Ben Bledsoe, Jamie Tabor, Andrea Jackson, Lana Cabrera, Joe Cabrera, Pat Cash, Adam Evans, Courtney Harmel, Janine Harmel, Steve Helling, Emma Helling, and Cap'n. Thanks also to my Mediabistro.com students.

And thanks to you, the reader, for coming along on this journey with me! I love your e-mails, so keep 'em coming! *Mille fois merci!*

Chapter One

Our wedding was supposed to be in September.

I'd already been to my final dress fitting. I'd chosen my bridesmaids, picked out my flowers, and booked a caterer. The invitations were printed up and all ready to be mailed. We'd chosen a band. We'd talked about what we would name the kids we'd have someday. I'd filled pages and pages with scribbles: *Mr. and Mrs. Brett Landstrom. Brett and Emma Landstrom. Brett Landstrom and his wife, Emma Sullivan-Landstrom. The Landstroms.* I could already envision the future we'd have together.

And then one day, it all fell apart.

It was a hot, muggy Tuesday evening in April, and I'd left work at three so that I could make a special dinner for Brett to celebrate our one-year anniversary of moving in together. I cleaned off our patio table, bought fresh flowers, and cooked his favorite meal—grilled chicken stuffed with artichokes, sun-dried tomatoes, and caprino cheese, served over angel-hair pasta with homemade marinara sauce. *Perfect*, I thought as I poured a glass of Chianti for each of us.

"Looks good," Brett said, strolling out through the sliding glass doors to the patio at six o'clock. As he stepped outside, he loosened his tie and unbuttoned the top button on his shirt, which of course made him look even sexier than usual, in a haphazard way. It was a good sign, I thought, that I found him just as attractive as I had the day I'd met him. I hoped he felt the same way.

I beamed at him. "Happy anniversary," I said.

Brett looked baffled. "Anniversary?" He raked a hand through his dark, wavy hair. "Anniversary of what?"

My smile faltered a bit. "Moving in together," I said.

"Oh." He cleared his throat. "Well, happy anniversary to you, too." He folded his six-foot-two frame into the chair closest to the sliding glass door and took a sip of wine. He swished it around in his mouth for a moment, nodded approvingly, and swallowed.

I smiled, sat down across from him, and passed him the salad bowl, which was full of chopped lettuce, olives, pepperoncinis, tomatoes, freshly squeezed lemon juice, and feta cheese. He sniffed it approvingly before spooning some onto his plate. "Greek," he said, his hazel eyes crinkling at the corners.

"Yes," I said with a smile. "Your favorite."

I was determined that I'd be better at this—cooking, cleaning, and basically being a domestic goddess—after we were married. Brett's mother (who, mind you, didn't work and employed both a cook and a maid) had already reminded me several times, with a stiff smile on her face, that her son was accustomed to having dinner on the table when he got home from work and a house that was neat, tidy, and virtually spotless. I knew the subliminal message was that I wasn't quite up to par.

Evidently, I was supposed to be a full-time housekeeper and a full-time cook at the same time I balanced my full-time job.

"So," I said after a few minutes of dead air between us. Brett had begun eating already and was making *mmmmm* noises as he chewed. I hesitated for a moment. "Have you had a chance to work on your invitation list yet?"

All I needed from Brett was a list of the names and addresses of the family members he wanted to invite, and I'd already asked him four times. I knew he hated planning things and looked at our wedding prep as a burden, but considering that I had booked the minister and the band, gone to all the caterer tastings, met five times with the wedding planner, and picked out the invitations all by myself, I didn't think I was being too demanding.

"Not yet," Brett mumbled, his mouth full of chicken.

"Okay," I said slowly. I tried to remind myself that he was busy at work. He had just started on a big case, and he put in longer hours than I did. I forced a smile. "Do you think maybe you can get it to me by Sunday?" I asked sweetly, trying not to sound like I was nagging. "We really have to get those invitations in the mail."

"About that," Brett said. He ran his fork around the edges of his plate, picking up the last strands of pasta and taking one last big bite before pushing the plate toward the center of the table. He took another long sip from his wineglass, draining it. "I think we need to talk."

"About the invitation list?" I asked. I thought we had already agreed that we would include everyone we wanted to invite. After all, my father had promised to pitch in as much money as he could, and Brett's parents were, to put it mildly, loaded. They lived just fifteen minutes from us in Windermere, the Orlando suburb where Tiger Woods and some of the *NSYNC guys owned sprawling mansions. The Landstrom estate was just as grand, and they had already announced that money was no object in planning the perfect wedding for their only child.

"Not about the list," Brett said. He drummed his fingers on the table. "About the wedding."

"Oh." I wasn't totally surprised. Brett and I had been through some minor disagreements over things like whether we'd have the ceremony on the beach in St. Petersburg or in his parents' huge backyard (I had deferred to him, and we were planning a garden wedding), and whether we were going to have a traditional vanilla cake or a cake with a different flavor in every layer (we'd gone with plain vanilla, which Brett's mother had practically insisted on).

"What is it?" I asked. "Is it the seating? We can go with the plush folding chairs if you want. It's not really a big deal." I'd been partial to white wooden benches, which I thought would look beautiful in his parents' rose garden. But it wasn't about the location or the cake or the seating, was it? What was important was that I was going to spend my life with Brett.

"No." He shook his head. "The benches are fine, Emma."

"Oh," I said, somewhat stunned. It was the first time he had deferred to my opinion without an argument. "That's great. So what did you want to talk about, then?"

He glanced away from me. "I think we should call the wedding off," he said.

I was sure, at first, that I'd heard him wrong. After all, he'd said the words nonchalantly, as if he just as easily could have been telling me that the stock market was down or that there was rain expected in the forecast the next day. And after dropping his bombshell, he simply reached for the wine bottle, refilled his glass, and glanced inside at the TV, which had been strategically turned so that he could see the Braves game through the sliding glass door while we ate.

"What?" I asked. I shook my head and forced an uncomfortable laugh. "That's so weird. I could have sworn you just said we should call the wedding off."

"I did," Brett said, glancing at me and then looking away again, back to the Braves. He took another sip of his wine and didn't elaborate. I felt the blood drain from my face, and my throat went dry. I gulped a few times and wondered why all of the air had suddenly been sucked out of the space around me.

"You did?" I finally asked, my voice squeaking a bit as it rose an octave.

"No offense or anything, Emma, but I don't think I love you anymore," he said casually. "I mean I love you, of course, but I don't know if I'm *in* love with you. I think maybe we should go our separate ways."

My jaw dropped. I mean, it actually felt like it came unhinged and fell open on its own.

"Whaaaa . . ." My voice trailed off. I couldn't seem to get my mouth to cooperate with me. I was so shocked that

I could hardly form words. "What?" I finally managed. "Why?"

"Emma," Brett began, shaking his head in that condescending manner he seemed to have adopted when talking to me lately (it was the same way his father often talked to his mother, I'd noticed). "It's not like I can explain why I feel the way I do about things. Feelings change, you know? I'm sorry, but I can't control that."

"But . . . ," I began. My voice trailed off again because I hadn't the faintest idea what to say. A thousand things were racing through my mind, and I couldn't seem to get a handle on any of them. How could he have stopped loving me? Had our whole relationship been a lie? How would I tell my parents that the wedding was off? What was I supposed to do now?

After an uncomfortable moment, Brett filled the silence. "You know, Emma, it's for the best, really. You didn't want to stay in Orlando anyhow."

My jaw dropped farther. "But I *did* stay in Orlando!" A little flash of anger exploded inside me all of a sudden. "I turned down that job offer. For *you!*"

Just three months earlier, I'd been offered the job of my dreams—as the head of PR for a new alternative rock label under the Columbia Records umbrella in New York. I'd talked it over with Brett, and he'd told me in no uncertain terms that he would never consider moving; his life always had been—and always would be—here in Orlando. So I'd reluctantly turned down the job (after all, I was engaged, and my fiancé should come first, right?), and as a result, I was still working the same less-than-fulfilling job as a PR coordinator for Boy Bandz, the thriving Orlando-based record label whose latest creation, the boy band 407, had just landed at number four on the *Billboard* Pop Charts with their song "I Love You Like I Love My Xbox 360."

"Well, Emma, that was your choice," Brett said, shaking his head and smiling slightly, as if I'd said something childish. "You can't really blame me for choices you've made in your life."

"But I made the choice for *you*," I protested. My head felt like it was spinning. This couldn't be happening.

"And I'm supposed to marry you out of a sense of obligation?" he asked. He stared at me. "Come on, Emma. That's not reasonable. We make our own choices in life."

"That's not what I'm saying!"

"That's what it *sounds* like you're saying," he said. He looked almost smug. "And that's not fair."

I stared at him for a long moment. "So that's it, then?" I managed to say. "After three years?"

"It's for the best," he continued smoothly. "And don't worry; you can take as long as you want to move out. I'm going to go stay with my parents to give you some time."

I gaped at him. I hadn't even considered that I'd have to move out. But of course I would. That's what happens when people break up, isn't it? "But where will I go?" I asked in a small voice, hating how desperate and unsure I sounded.

Brett shrugged. "I don't know. Your sister's?"

I shook my head once, quickly, pressing my lips tightly together. No way. I couldn't stand the thought of having to slink up to Jeannie's door and admit that I'd lost Brett.

Eight years my senior, she was married to the passive, mousy Robert, and they had a three-year-old son who was the most spoiled child I'd ever seen. I couldn't bear to think what she'd smugly say about Brett leaving me. *Failure*, she would call it. *Another failure for Emma Sullivan.*

"Well, I don't know, Emma," Brett said, sounding exasperated. He raked a hand distractedly through his hair, which was starting to grow too long. *He needs a haircut*, I thought abstractly for a millisecond, before I realized that it would no longer be my responsibility to remind him of such things. "You could go stay with one of your friends," he said. "Lesley or Anne or Amanda or someone."

Hearing their names—the names of three of the girls who were meant to be my bridesmaids—sent a jolt through me.

Brett blinked at me a few times and looked away. "Obviously you understand why you need to move out."

I felt sick. I couldn't believe he was doing this.

"Because it's *your* place," I said through gritted teeth. I could feel my eyes narrow. It had been a point of contention between us for the past year. Brett, with his bigger salary, had made the down payment on our MetroWest Orlando house. Each month, we split the mortgage payment, but Brett was the only one with his name on the deed. The few times I'd complained that the arrangement didn't seem fair to me—after all, I was paying half the mortgage but earning no equity—Brett had smiled and reminded me that once we were married, all of our assets would be shared anyhow, so what was the point in worrying about something so inconsequential now?

It had all sounded so reasonable at the time.

"Right," Brett responded, not even having the decency to look embarrassed. "We'll figure something out about the mortgage, Em. I'm sure I owe you some money since you've made some contributions over the last year. I'll talk to my father and see what we can do."

I gaped some more. *Contributions?*

"Anyhow, I'm sorry, sweetheart," Brett continued. "This is really hard for me, too, you know. But in all honesty, it's not you. It's me. I'm sorry."

I almost laughed. Really. And perhaps I would have if I wasn't currently absorbed in fantasizing about stabbing him with the knife I'd used to cut the bread.

"You'll be okay?" Brett asked after a moment of silence.

"I'll be fine," I mumbled, suddenly furious that he would even ask, as if he cared at all.

I hadn't known what else to do the next morning when I awoke alone in an empty, king-size bed that was no longer half mine. I was numb; I felt like I was in the middle of a bad dream.

So I did what I did every morning: I got up, I showered, I blew my hair dry, I put on my makeup, I picked out a sensible outfit, and I went to work. At least there was solace in routine.

The offices of Boy Bandz Records were in a converted old train station in downtown Orlando, just a block from Brett's law firm. Sometimes we would run into each other on Church Street as he went to get lunch at Kres with a colleague or I went to pick up a greasy slice of pizza from Lorenzo's. I prayed that I wouldn't run into him today. I didn't think I could handle it.

I sat down at my desk just before eight thirty and stared numbly at my computer screen. It was as if I had lost all ability to function. I had a million things to do today—a press release about the 407 boys, a CD mailing for O-Girlz (the girl band our company's president, boy-band impresario Max Hedgefield, had just launched), several media calls to return—but I couldn't imagine doing something as banal as work when my life had just fallen apart.

Just past ten, Andrea, my boss, stopped by my desk. I had just put in my third series of Visine drops that morning, in an attempt to mask my bloodshot eyes. I hoped that the tactic was working. I knew how the emotionless Andrea despised it when her employees brought their personal problems to work.

"Great job with the 407 account," she said. They were named 407 because Max Hedgefield—whom everyone called Hedge—had apparently run out of silly phrases to string together and had thus resorted to using the area code for Orlando, the birthplace of modern boy bands.

"Thanks," I said, forcing a smile at her through blurry eyes. I *had* done a good job, and I knew it. One of our 407 boys had decided to come out of the closet the week their album was released, and I thought I had handled the resultant media storm gracefully. Thank goodness Lance Bass had blazed the way for boy-loving boy banders everywhere. Danny Ruben, the out-and-proud lead singer of our band, had been welcomed by the media with open arms, and as a result of all the publicity, 407's album had climbed the charts even more quickly than expected.

"We need to talk about something," Andrea said. She looked down at her left hand and examined her perfectly manicured fingernails intently.

"Okay."

Maybe, I thought with a little jolt of hope, *I'm about to be promoted*. After all, I certainly deserved it. I'd been with the company for four years, and although I was running the 407 and O-Girlz accounts by myself, I was only a PR coordinator. I'd heard rumors lately about a company reorganization, and I had my fingers crossed that I was next in line to move into a PR managing director position, which came with a substantial pay bump.

"Emma, sweetie," Andrea chirped, glancing now at the perfect nails on her right hand, "Hedge has decided to downsize a little bit, so I'm afraid we're going to have to let you go."

I could feel my vision cloud up, despite the Visine.

"What?" I must have heard her wrong.

"Don't worry!" she went on brightly, glancing away. "We're offering four weeks' severance, and I'd be happy to write you a nice letter of recommendation."

"Wait, you're *firing* me?" I asked in disbelief.

Andrea looked back at me and smiled cheerfully. "No, no, Emma, we're *laying you off*!" she said, carefully enunciating the last three words. "It's a totally different thing! I'm very sorry. But we'd appreciate it if you could have your desk cleared out by noon. And please try not to make a scene."

"A . . . a scene?" I stammered. What did she think I was going to do, throw my computer at the wall? Not that that would necessarily be a bad idea, come to think of it.

She leaned forward and lowered her voice conspiratorially. "You're just so well liked around here, Emma," she said. "It would be bad for company morale if you create a scene, you know. Please, for the good of Boy Bandz. We truly are sorry we have to let you go."

I tried to wrap my mind around what she was saying. I felt numb, like someone had just smacked me across the face.

"But . . . why?" I asked after a moment. My stomach was tying itself into strange, tight knots. I worried for a moment that the granola bar I'd eaten on the way to work was about to make a reappearance. "Why me?"

Andrea looked momentarily concerned and then flashed me a bright smile. "Emma, dear, we're just downsizing," she said. "It's nothing personal, I assure you. You're very overqualified for your current position, and there's simply no room for growth here. Besides, I'm sure you'll find another job in a jiff! I'm happy to be a reference for you, of course."

I didn't bother reminding her that Boy Bandz was the only record label in town. Or that it would now be impossible to walk back into Columbia Records in New York after I'd already rejected their more-than-generous offer three months ago. All of a sudden, my life was completely falling apart.

"Oh," I said finally. I wasn't sure what else to say. It seemed my brain was working in slow motion.

"Out by noon, Emma," Andrea repeated. "Please, no scenes. And again, I'm sorry."

I opened and closed my mouth, and when no words came out, I forced myself to nod at her to acknowledge my comprehension.

I didn't panic. I wanted to, but I didn't. Instead I numbly cleaned out my desk, went home, and cried for the rest of the day.

When I woke from a troubled half slumber the next morning, exhausted and confused, I tried my best to pull myself together. I logged on to the computer, went to OrlandoSentinel.com, and searched for PR jobs. There were eleven posted, and foolishly optimistic, I applied for all of them, faxing my résumé from a nearby Kinko's and dragging back home around noon, feeling useless and confused.

In the next two weeks, which I mostly spent holed up in the house, refusing to talk to any of my friends, I was called in for six interviews. Unfortunately, I burst into tears during five of them (not that this was normal for me in the slightest; I blame it on the post-Brett trauma). In the sixth interview, the one in which I hadn't cried, I knew I wasn't going to be hired when the man interviewing me asked why I wanted to work as a PR rep for J. Cash Steel, and I couldn't come up with a single reason because, well, I really didn't *want* to work for a steel manufacturer.

Brett called three times in the two-week period, asking me in a monotone voice if I was okay. I was confused by his uncharacteristic concern until he finally revealed his *real* reason for calling at the end of the second week.

"Look, I know you lost your job, Em," he said. "And I'm sorry to hear that. But I'd love to move back into my place. Any idea when you might be ready to move out?"

I'd called him a name that my mother had once washed my mouth out with soap for using. Then I slammed the phone down so hard that it cracked.

That afternoon, I finally picked up the damaged (but still functioning) phone to call my three best friends, the girls who were supposed to be my bridesmaids. They hadn't called since I'd split from Brett, but I hadn't called them, either. I hadn't wanted to talk about it. I knew they'd be shocked to hear that he'd left me, and I was looking forward to being consoled by them.

At least they'll stand by me, I said to myself before I dialed Lesley's number. *At least I can count on them not to hurt me.*

Wrong again.

"I feel terrible telling you this," Lesley said after she'd mentioned casually that she'd known about the dissolution of my engagement since last week, "but I thought you'd want to know."

"Okay . . ." I waited for her to go on, wondering why she hadn't called or come by if she'd known for a week that Brett and I had split.

"Well . . . maybe I shouldn't tell you," she said quickly, her breath heavy on the other end.

I sighed. I didn't have the energy to play games.

"Whatever it is, Lesley, I'm sure it pales in comparison with everything else in my life right now." After all, what could be worse than having your engagement broken off and then being fired the next morning?

"Well, if you're sure . . . ," Lesley said, her voice trailing off. She paused. "All right then. I don't know how to tell you this, so I'm just going to say it. Amanda has been sleeping with Brett."

Okay. So clearly *that* could be worse than having your engagement broken off and then being fired the next morning.

I opened my mouth to say something but no words came out. I suddenly felt like my whole chest had been hollowed out. I couldn't breathe.

After a moment, Lesley spoke again. "Emma?" she said. "Are you there?"

"Urghrhgrgh," I gurgled.

"Are you okay?"

"Uhrhghrh." I couldn't seem to formulate words.

"Listen, Emma, it's not like you two were still together when it happened," Lesley said quickly. "Amanda says the first time they hooked up was three nights after Brett moved out. I think he just needed a place to stay, you know? And one thing led to another."

I felt sick. For a moment, I really thought I might throw up.

"You knew about this?" I asked in a whisper after swallowing hard a few times. "Did Anne know, too?"

"Well . . . yes."

"How long have you known?"

Silence.

"Lesley, *how long*?"

"Since last week."

"I'm going to kill her," I breathed, suddenly hating Amanda with every bone in my body.

"Emma, don't say that," Lesley said sweetly. "After all, you have to admit, it was over between you and Brett."

I couldn't even find the words to respond. I gagged on the sour taste that had risen in the back of my throat.

"You're *defending* her?" I whispered once my vocal chords worked again.

"No, no, not exactly," Lesley said quickly. "I'm just saying to look at it logically. It's not like Brett *cheated* on you with her or anything."

"But—" I started to say.

"Really, Emma," Lesley interrupted. "Anne and I have talked about it, and we don't think Amanda has done anything wrong. I mean, it's a sticky situation, but I'm sure you'll feel better about it in a week or two, once you've had some time to think about it. Let's all meet for dinner this week, and we can talk about it. I know Amanda would love to see you."

I was aghast. "I have to go." I hung up before Lesley could hear me cry.

I called my sister, Jeannie, next, illogically hoping for some sort of consolation. Six years earlier, our father had moved to Atlanta with his twenty-years-younger new wife, and three years ago, our mother had moved to California with her twenty-years-older new husband, so Jeannie was the only family member I had close by. Unfortunately, we were as different as night and day, and Jeannie's idea of a good conversation was one in which I was nearly reduced to tears thinking of all my shortcomings.

Perhaps this time, though, she'll comfort me, I thought. *After all, isn't that what sisters were for?*

"Seriously, Emma," she said instead after I'd explained everything. I could hear her three-year-old son, Odysseus, yelling something in the background, and she sighed loudly. "Brett's just going through a *thing.* It's perfectly natural before a guy gets married. It's just cold feet."

"Jeannie, did you hear what I told you?" I said slowly, not quite sure that she was understanding me. "He's *sleeping* with one of my *best friends*!"

"Emma, you're overreacting." She sighed. "You *always* overreact. Robert got cold feet before our wedding, too, but I talked some sense into him. Men just need a little persuading sometimes."

"But, Jeannie—"

"Emma, really, you need to stop being so high-maintenance," interrupted my sister, the most high-maintenance person in the world. "And do your best to persuade him to take you back. You're almost thirty, for goodness' sake. You're running out of options. I was married at twenty-three, you know."

"Yes, you keep reminding me." Disgusted, I hung up and picked up the phone again to call the only remaining close friend I had—Poppy, whom I'd roomed with in London during a summer internship eight years earlier. She had relocated to Paris three years ago to work for Colin-Mitterand, an international entertainment PR company based in France, and last year she had gone freelance and opened her own boutique firm. Now, I knew, she had been hired to do PR for KMG, an international record label based in Paris.

I crossed my fingers before dialing the last digit of her phone number. If she couldn't be supportive, I didn't know where else to turn.

"Your friend Amanda did *what*? That horrid little tart!" she exclaimed in her clipped British accent after I had explained everything.

I breathed an enormous sigh of relief, and the beginnings of a smile tugged at the corners of my mouth. "You have no idea how relieved I am to hear you say that."

"You don't need a friend like that!" Poppy said hotly. "Nor the others, for that matter. How dare they stand up for her?"

I felt a surge of relief. "You're right," I said.

"And frankly, sweetie, Brett never sounded like much of a winner, either," she continued. "He always was a bit of a spoiled mummy's boy. Good riddance! Now you can focus on your work!"

"Not exactly," I mumbled. I took a deep breath and closed my eyes. "I was fired."

"What?" Poppy's voice rose an octave. "Fired?"

"Well, laid off," I said. "But it's basically the same thing."

"Oh, bollocks," Poppy said. She paused. "Listen, Emma. We're going to figure things out for you, yeah? I promise. I have an idea. Let me see what I can do. I'll call you back tomorrow, okay, luv?"

I felt momentarily buoyed by her enthusiasm, but there was a part of me that didn't want to let her off the phone. After all, she seemed to be the only sane, supportive person in my life at the moment.

She called back the next day, as promised.

"Look, Emma, I think I have the solution to all your problems," she said cheerfully.

"Okay . . ." I blew my nose, wiped my tears, and put the cap back on the carton of Blue Bell mint chocolate chip ice cream I'd been eating. I was grateful no one was there to see me consuming my fourth pint of ice cream that day. I felt a bit sick all of a sudden.

"I talked to Véronique, my liaison at KMG, and I have some good news for you," she went on, obviously oblivious to my ice-cream stomach pangs. "I haven't told you yet, but KMG hired me specifically to do British and American press for the English-language launch of Guillaume Riche's first album."

"Guillaume Riche?" I repeated, surprised. Guillaume Riche was, of course, the big French TV star who was best known for his high-profile romances, including reported flings with some of the top actresses at the US box office and a yearlong romance with British supermodel Dionne DeVrie, which had ended last year in a dramatic breakup that had been splashed across the cover of celebrity rags everywhere. I'd just read last week in *People* magazine that he was launching an English-language recording career, but I'd had no idea Poppy was involved. "Poppy, that's great!"

"Yes, well, it seems his personal publicist has quit, which

leaves me solely responsible for him through the launch of his album," she went on quickly.

"That's amazing!" I exclaimed. I felt a swell of pride for my friend, who was obviously doing quite well for herself. Unlike me.

"Right, but our big press event in London is just five weeks away, and I could really use some help," she said. She paused and took a deep breath. "I persuaded Véronique that with your experience and connections, you'd be the perfect temporary addition to my team, and she has approved some extra money in the budget for it. So how about it, Emma? Can you come over for a month or so and help me with Guillaume's launch?"

"Come to Paris?" I repeated. I dropped my ice-cream spoon, and it clattered loudly to the ground.

"Yes!" Poppy said gleefully. "It will be such fun! Just a little something to get you through while you look for another job. And I can help you get over Brett!"

It sounded tempting. But there was a gaping hole in her logic. "Poppy, I don't even speak French," I reminded her.

"Oh, pish posh," she replied. "It's no matter. I'll translate for you. And besides, you're working on Guillaume's English launch. I'll have you dealing mostly with British, Irish, American, and Australian journalists. It should be a piece of cake for you!"

"I don't know . . ."

"Emma, listen to me." Poppy was suddenly all business. "You've lost your fiancé. You've lost your friends. You've lost your job. Do you really have anything else to lose by coming over here for a bit?"

I thought about it for a moment. When she put it that way . . . "I guess you're right," I mumbled.

"And let me tell you, Emma, there's no place better to get over a wanker like Brett than in Paris," she added.

And so, a week and a half later, there I was, on a jet bound for a city I'd only spent a week in a decade ago to work with an old friend I hadn't seen in ages.

Unfortunately, it never occurred to me to ask a single additional thing about Guillaume Riche or why his personal publicist had quit so close to his album launch. If I had, chances are I never would have boarded that plane.

Chapter Two

The jet glided into Paris's Charles de Gaulle airport an hour ahead of schedule, which I took as a good sign. On the approach, I'd strained to see out the window, sure that I would catch a glimpse of the Eiffel Tower or Notre Dame or even the winding Seine River, all landmarks that would mark my visit. Instead, all I could see were strangely geometric pastures and a low-hanging mass of dense, gray clouds that obscured everything as the plane approached the airport. It was disconcerting; this was not the France I remembered. Where were the glittering monuments and the picturesque rooftops?

I'd brought my *Fodor's Exploring Paris* and my *Frommer's Portable Paris* with me on the plane, with the intention of reading both of them cover-to-cover during the eight-hour flight. It had been eight years since I'd been to Paris; I'd taken a weeklong trip there with Poppy at the end of our internship when we were twenty-one. However, between the overweight businessman in the window seat, the airsick woman on the aisle jostling me constantly in my middle seat, and the fact that I was moderately scared of flying, I couldn't focus on my guidebooks.

Instead, I thought about Brett.

I missed him. And I hated myself just a little bit for feeling that way.

If I was going to be honest with myself (and let's face it, what did I have to lose at this point?), I'd realize that he and I were probably never meant to be in the first place.

We'd met three years ago during a Saturday '80s night at Antigua, a club in downtown Orlando's Church Street district. I'd been vogueing to Madonna with Lesley and Anne when a tall, dark-haired guy leaning against the bar caught my eye. He was cute, he had an enticing smile, and he was staring right at me. When "Vogue" faded and "Livin' on a Prayer" began pumping from the speakers, I'd mumbled an excuse to the girls and made my way casually to the bar.

"Hey!" Brett had shouted over the din as I landed next to him, pretending, of course, that I'd randomly chosen that very spot to order my vodka tonic.

"Hey," I'd responded casually, my heart thudding as I noticed for the first time what beautiful hazel eyes he had. *Take my hand, we'll make it I swear,* Jon Bon Jovi belted out in the background, his chiseled face giant on the video screens around the room.

"Can I buy you a drink?" he asked. I hesitated and nodded. He smiled, his cheeks dimpling. "I'm Brett," he said.

"Emma," I said, taking his hand.

He shook my hand up and down slowly, never breaking eye contact. "You're beautiful, Emma," he'd said. There was something about the way he said it that made me believe he meant it.

After we talked for half an hour and he met Lesley,

Anne, and Amanda, he'd asked me if I'd come next door with him to the rooftop bar Lattitudes. We had stayed there, at a table under the moonlight, sipping vodka tonics (we had the same favorite drink), discussing movies (we both thought *Shawshank Redemption* and the indie film *Primer* were two of the best films we'd ever seen), swapping concert stories (we'd both been to the last three Sister Hazel shows at House of Blues), and talking about what we wanted in our futures. We seemed to have so much in common, and the way he gazed intently into my eyes and then smiled slowly made my heart flutter. By the end of the night, I was smitten. We went out on our first date the next night, and a month later, he called me his girlfriend for the first time. It felt perfect.

He was everything I thought I wanted—cute, successful, funny, good with people. My family loved him, and his parents grudgingly seemed to accept me. I thought we went together like peanut butter and jelly. Evidently, I hadn't considered that one of my best friends would one day worm her way into the sandwich.

"Passeport, s'il vous plaît." The gruff voice of the stern-looking customs agent behind the glass cut into my thoughts. Somehow reminiscing about Brett had carried me off the plane and toward the immigration control area, like flotsam on the sea of arriving passengers.

"Um, yes, of course," I stammered, fumbling in my bag, past the two unopened Paris books, past my pink iPod loaded with Five for Fighting, Courtney Jaye, and the Beatles, past the laptop computer I'd purchased with my holiday bonus last year. Finally, my fingers closed around the thick navy jacket of my gold-embossed American passport, and I pulled it out triumphantly. *"Voilà!"* I exclaimed happily, hoping the agent would appreciate the use of my limited French vocabulary.

He didn't look impressed. He simply grunted, opened my passport, and studied it closely. My hair was shorter in the photo, just above my shoulders instead of just below, and since the picture had been taken in the winter, the blond strands were a few shades darker than they were now, in early May, which in Florida meant I'd already had two good months of sun. My current tan was a bit deeper and my freckles were a bit more pronounced. And of course, thanks to four weeks of unlimited cartons of mint chocolate chip (hey, it's how I cope, okay?), I was a good ten pounds heavier than I'd been when the photo was taken. But my general dishevelment was the same. In the picture, I knew, my lipstick had worn off, my lips were cracked, and my hair looked like I'd been caught in a wind tunnel. I suspected I didn't look much better today, having just stepped off a transatlantic flight.

"You are visiting?" the guard asked after a moment, his voice so thick with a French accent that it took me a full ten seconds to decipher what he'd said.

"Oui," I said firmly, although it occurred to me a moment after the word was out of my mouth that I wasn't, in fact, a visitor. I was here to work. I wondered if I should tell him.

"For how long?" he asked, remaining stubbornly English speaking.

"Five weeks," I replied. Suddenly the length of time sounded very long to me, and I had a strong urge to turn back around and make a dash for the departure gates.

The French guard muttered something unintelligible, stamped my passport, and handed it back to me.

"You may enter," he said. "Enjoy your visit to France."

And then I was in, being swept along in another tide of people into a country I hadn't seen in years, to start a new life I wasn't prepared for at all.

"Emma! Emma! Over here!"

I spotted Poppy the moment I passed through the doors on the far side of baggage claim, dragging my two giant purple suitcases behind me.

"Hi!" I exclaimed, feeling even more relieved to see her than I'd expected. I hoisted my laptop case and hand-bag up on my shoulder and dragged my enormous load of luggage toward her in what felt like slow motion. She was grinning widely and waving like a maniac.

"Welcome, welcome!" she said, clapping her hands excit-edly before rushing forward to embrace me. Her shoulder-length, red-streaked dark hair was pulled back in a ponytail, and she was wearing a little too much makeup—which was pretty much how Poppy always looked. Three inches taller than me, she had a wide, ear-to-ear smile, rosy cheeks, enormous sea-green eyes, and curves she liked to describe as "voluptuous."

Today she was dressed in a bright purple blouse, a black skirt that looked several inches too short and a size too small, and a pair of forest-green ribbed tights. She was currently giving me the signature Poppy grin, and I couldn't help but smile back, despite my exhaustion.

"Let me help you with your bags, yeah?" she said.

With relief, I gave up one of the giant purple rollers to Poppy, who began lugging it toward the airport exit, her face promptly turning beet red from the strain.

"Emma, what on earth do you have in here?" she exclaimed after a moment. "A body?"

"Yep," I said. "I've stuffed Brett into my luggage to dispose of him properly over here."

Poppy laughed. "That's the spirit! Give the tosser what he deserves, then!"

I smiled wanly, wishing that I felt as resentful toward Brett as Poppy evidently did. Clearly I had lost my self-respect, along with my job and fiancé.

As Poppy and I piled into a sleek black taxi and began to make our way toward the city center, I began to relax, soothed by the rhythm of her chirpy cadence. Somehow, being here with someone so familiar made the whole experience feel that much less foreign, even as everything around me was entirely unfamiliar. Gone were the Fords and Hondas and Toyotas I was used to back home. Instead the highway was a confused and honking mass of tiny smart cars, compact Peugeots, and boxy Renaults as it wove through suburbs that didn't resemble anything I remembered about Paris.

Instead of quaint neighborhoods, rooftops with flowerpot chimney stacks, and windowsills framed by flowers, there were factories with smokestacks and enormous, characterless modern apartments with tiny balconies. Clotheslines hung with brightly colored T-shirts and jeans dotted the land-scape, interspersed with hundreds of makeshift antennas. This wasn't quite the charming France I had envisioned.

"We're not into the city yet," Poppy whispered, perhaps catching my worried expression.

"Oh. Right." I felt moderately appeased.

But then our cabbie, who was mumbling to himself and driving at what seemed like the speed of light, shot off the highway, and the industrial skyline of the eastern suburbs suddenly gave way to my first glimpse of the Gothic tow-ers of Notre Dame off in the distance.

It was the first time it had hit me—*really* hit me—that I was in Paris, a continent away from the only life I'd ever known.

I gasped. "It's beautiful," I said softly. Poppy squeezed my hand and smiled.

A few minutes later, as we emerged from a crowded thoroughfare, the rest of the Parisian skyline came into view, and my breath caught in my throat. In the evening light, with the sky streaked with rich shades of sunset pink, the Eiffel Tower was a soft outline against the hori-zon. I could feel my heart thudding against my rib cage as our taxi wove its way farther into the city, around pedes-trians, past stop signs, through streets soaked with history and tradition.

As we crossed the Seine, I could see the sprawling Louvre museum, the looming Conciergerie, the stately Hôtel de Ville. The fading sunlight melted into the river and reflected back a muted blend of pastels that seemed to glow from beneath the surface. It was, I thought, the most beautiful thing I'd ever seen.

"Welcome to Paris," Poppy said softly.

Already, I felt a bit like I was coming home.

"So what's Guillaume Riche actually *like*?" I asked once I had settled my bags into the tiny second bedroom of Poppy's small apartment, where I'd be staying for the next several weeks. She had misled me *slightly* when she'd said that her place was a "spacious two-bedroom flat." In fact, it couldn't have been more than five hundred square feet, and in the room that would be mine, I could stretch my arms out to the sides and touch both walls at once. Its one saving grace—and it was a huge saving grace—was that it was a mere two blocks from the Eiffel Tower; if you looked out the living room window, you could see the graceful iron structure rising upward behind the apartments across the courtyard. My throat felt strangely constricted each time I caught a glimpse of it.

"Oh, Guillaume? He has quite a lovely voice," Poppy said vaguely. "Would you like a café au lait?"

"I'd love one," I said with a smile. Poppy walked over to her tiny, crowded kitchen area and busied herself with a bright red espresso maker that hissed and spewed steam when she pressed down on the handle. "So he's talented? Guillaume Riche?" I tried again. "I've never heard him sing."

"Oh, yes, he's quite good, really," Poppy said hurriedly.

"Would you like cinnamon on top? Or whipped cream perhaps?"

I had a nagging feeling that she was purposely avoiding my questions. "I think it's really cool that you're working with him. He's huge right now," I said, making a third attempt to bring him up. "I heard a rumor he was dating Jennifer Aniston."

"Just a rumor," Poppy said promptly.

"How can you be so sure?"

Poppy shot me a sly grin. "Because I'm the one who started it. It's all about building buzz."

I stared at her, incredulous. "And the rumor that he wanted to adopt a baby from Ethiopia, like Angelina and Brad?"

Poppy smiled sheepishly. "I started that one, too," she admitted.

"But that's why the press have started calling him *Saint Guillaume!*" I exclaimed. "It's not even true?"

"Not at all," Poppy said, winking at me.

"So what *can* you tell me about him?" I asked as we walked into the living room and settled side by side onto the sofa with steaming mugs in our hands. "Is he as perfect as he always seems in the magazines? Or have you made that up, too?" The sofa was lumpy, and I could see water stains on the ceiling, but there was something about the window box of yellow daisies and the quaint rooftops across the miniature courtyard outside that made the apartment seem much more luxurious than it probably was. I took a sip of the café au lait Poppy had made.

"Er . . ." Poppy seemed to be at a loss for words, quite

a rare condition for her. "Yes, he's wonderful," she said finally. "Do you fancy a croissant with that café au lait? I picked some up this morning from the patisserie on the corner."

"That sounds great," I said, suddenly realizing how hungry I was. Poppy hopped up from the sofa and disappeared into the kitchen, where I could hear the rustling of a paper bag.

I stood up while I waited for her to come back and studied the tall bookcase against the wall, which was overflowing with more than forty of what appeared to be self-help books. I read a few of the spines: *How to Make Men Lust After You, Forty Dates with Forty Men, Boys Love Bitches, Love Them and Leave Them.* I shook my head and smiled. Poppy had always gone overboard on things. I'd had no idea that self-help dating books were her new obsession.

"This is quite a collection you have here," I said to Poppy as she returned with a pair of delectably flaky-looking croissants on a pale pink plate.

Poppy glanced at the bookcase and smiled proudly. "I know," she said. "They've changed my life, Emma."

I raised an eyebrow quizzically. "Changed your life?"

"It's amazing," she replied, her eyes sparkling. She reached out and grasped one of my hands as we sank back into the couch. "After Darren . . . well, let's just say I went a little nuts."

I nodded sympathetically. Darren had basically been Poppy's Brett. They'd dated for three years, and when he'd broken up with her four years ago, she'd gone into seclusion for two months, refusing to talk to anyone. I hadn't entirely understood what she was going through at the time, but now . . . well, let's just say that going into seclusion for two months didn't sound like such a terrible plan.

"This book got me through," she said excitedly, leaping up from the couch and pulling a tattered pale green volume from the shelf. She handed it to me, and I glanced down at the cover. I blinked a few times, registering the words, and then stared at it incredulously.

"*Voodoo for Jilted Lovers*?" I read the title aloud, still gazing at the cover, which featured a photograph of a male doll with dozens of pins sticking out of the general area of his crotch.

"Yes!" Poppy beamed at me and clapped her hands together. "It was perfect. Every night before I went to bed, I would stick a new pin in my Darren doll. It made me feel so much better!"

"You had a Darren doll?"

"Oh, yes!" Poppy enthused. "I still have it, in fact!" She vanished into her room for a moment and reemerged with a little doll, no bigger than her hand, that was dressed in jeans and a green shirt and had a thick shock of yellow hair and a smattering of freckles. "Whenever I think of him, I simply insert a pin somewhere that's bound to hurt."

"You do?" I asked. While I looked at her skeptically, Poppy cheerfully pulled a pin from a mug on her desk and stuck it into the Darren doll's belly.

"There!" she said. "See? Now wherever he is in the world, I'll wager he's having a sudden and inexplicable bout of indigestion!"

Poppy looked quite pleased with herself as she held up

the Darren doll for me to see. "Anyhow," she continued, "after that, I started thinking, perhaps some of these other books out there would help me, too! And, Emma, I am a whole new woman."

"Oh. Well, that's, um . . . interesting."

"Emma, it's wonderful," Poppy bubbled on. She put the poor Darren doll down and reached for another book on her shelf. "Like in this book, *How to Date Like a Dude*, Dr. Randall Fishington explains how to chuck men before they chuck you. It's amazing. And in *Secrets of Desirable Women*," she continued, reaching for another book and handing it to me, "the authors explain how to make a man want you by acting like you have no interest in him at all. I thought it would be total rubbish, but, Emma, it completely works!"

"It does?" I asked.

"Emma, I've discovered the secret to successful dating." Poppy paused dramatically. "The worse you treat these wankers, the more interested they'll be. If you blow them off, they'll wonder what makes you so special, and they'll fall directly in love with you. And the best thing about dating like this, Emma, is that *you* always get to chuck the guys before *they* chuck you. You never get hurt!"

"Well, I guess that sounds good," I said uncertainly.

"Listen, Emma," Poppy said. She knelt in front of me and smiled. "I'm going to change your life this month. I'm going to teach you everything I've learned. You're never going to think of Brett again."

Chapter Three

After I showered, changed, and had a second cup of coffee, Poppy and I went out to have dinner at one of her favorite restaurants.

I'd forgotten just how dazzling Paris could be. In the wake of a month that had stopped my life in its tracks and shattered much of what I believed in, I was, perhaps, in dire need of something magical. Maybe that's why I found myself rooted to the spot for a whole minute after Poppy and I emerged from the underground Métro at the Saint-Michel stop.

"It's so beautiful," I breathed, staring up in wonder.

Beside me, Poppy put an arm around me and smiled. "It's the most beautiful place in the world," she agreed.

Night had fallen, and we were standing in the shadows of the Notre Dame Cathedral, surely one of the most stunning spots in the city. In the darkness, the church glowed with an ethereal light, both soaring Gothic towers lit from somewhere beneath so that they appeared to shine from within. Between them, a huge circular stained-glass window shone with muted blues and pinks. The illuminated building seemed to go on forever, with a spire rising from its middle and curved, leglike supports rounding out the back end. The light from the church spilled onto the surface of the river and across the water to the sidewalk on which we stood, bathing everything in a pale glow that made all of this feel a little like a dream.

"Wow," I said softly.

"That's an understatement," Poppy bubbled. "Wait until you see where we're eating."

She led me a block down the quai to a café on the Left Bank, just across from Notre Dame. Its yellow-and-green neon letters spelled out CAFÉ LE PETIT PONT, and its umbrella-covered terrace overlooked Notre Dame across a narrow sliver of river.

"It's one of my favorite restaurants in Paris," Poppy said as we waited at the entrance to be seated. "I never grow tired of this view."

Indeed, I kept pinching myself throughout dinner, convinced that I couldn't possibly be sitting nonchalantly in a Parisian café, sipping Beaujolais, eating the most delicious coq au vin I'd ever tasted, and looking out on the fabled Notre Dame Cathedral. Only a month ago, I'd been eating at a patio table with Brett, thinking that I had everything in life I could possibly want. It suddenly felt like the world I had lived in before was very small.

After toasting to my new life in Paris with the last of our bottle of wine, we ordered espresso and apple crumble and giggled our way down memory lane, reminiscing about our summer in London eight years earlier and filling in the gaps of our lives since then. We'd stayed in touch, but there had been lapses here and there—particularly on my side, I was ashamed to admit.

"I guess once I started dating Brett, I let a lot of things sort of fall to the wayside," I mumbled, avoiding Poppy's gaze. "I'm sorry."

"It's in the past," she said. She reached across the table and gave my hands a squeeze. "And so is Brett. Good riddance."

I tried to smile, but it was harder than it should have been to get the corners of my mouth to cooperate. I took a deep breath.

"So tell me about Guillaume." I changed the subject, hoping that Poppy would be less hesitant than she'd been at home. After all, it had been a long time since I'd worked with a bona fide celebrity. By the time the Boy Bandz boys made it big, I already knew them for the pimply-faced, spoiled, hormonal kids they were, which sort of reduced their charm factor for me. I was looking forward to working with someone whom *People* had named one of the sexiest men alive and whom 67 percent of *Glamour* poll takers had said reminded them most of a real-life Prince Charming.

"Yes, right, okay," Poppy said, nodding and looking away. "We're all very excited about him; he sings in both English and French, and his music makes him the perfect crossover artist. He's sort of Coldplay meets Jack Johnson, with a side of John Mayer and the influence of the Beatles, all with that delicious French accent."

"Poppy, that's great!" I exclaimed. It was just the kind of project I'd dreamed of during all those years of pushing flavorless teen groups. "He sounds wonderful."

"Well, that's the way we're marketing him," she said, finally smiling and meeting my eye. "He's supposed to be KMG's next big thing, the deliciously sexy up-and-coming French star. The higher-ups here have decided that they'll be pushing him hard to the British and American markets. Everyone already knows his name because of the whole Dionne DeVrie thing—and of course the Jennifer Aniston rumor has helped enormously—so it's perfect. Together, you and I will be handling his English-language launch, with a big kickoff event in London in just under four weeks. I've been working my bum off for the last two months on this."

"Wow!" I said. "This all sounds so exciting."

"It will be," she said with a nod. "It's a big deal, really. We're flying lots of press in from the States. Basically, KMG's big rollout plan this year is to make Guillaume Riche the next big worldwide superstar, starting with the UK and America. It's up to me and you to make that happen."

"It is?" I asked. I blinked at her a few times. The responsibility sounded huge.

"Don't worry, yeah?" Poppy added hastily. "Everything's already in place. Everyone loves him already because he's a TV star over here, of course, and because of his reputation as one of Europe's hottest bachelors. In fact, we organized a poll of fifty British women and fifty American women just last week, and when asked to name the sexiest Frenchman they could think of, ninety-two percent of them said Guillaume Riche!"

"And the other eight percent?" I asked.

"A few said Olivier Martinez, a few named Gérard

Depardieu, and one woman, who seemed a bit off her rocker anyhow, kept declaring her love for Napoléon," Poppy said, grinning at me.

I laughed.

"Plus," she continued, "the press think Guillaume's a saint. Along with that whole Ethiopian adoption rumor, we've had him doing lots of charity work in the last five months, and the newspapers and TV shows have started to pick up on it. In the last month alone, he's been featured three times in *Okay* magazine and made *Hello*'s list of Europe's most eligible bachelors—after he and Dionne broke up, of course. The whole Saint Guillaume thing has really caught on."

"So how come he's not releasing an album in French?" I asked.

Poppy shrugged. "Over here, the French love English-language music, so they'll embrace the fact that he sings in English. This way, we can launch him to the UK and America at the same time we're launching his French music career. It's like killing two birds—well, a lot of birds, really—with one stone. It's the Americans and the Brits that drive the world's taste in music. Plus, he grew up speaking English, so he'll be ace in interviews. His father spent some time living in the States before Guillaume was born, I gather."

"Well," I said, "he sounds perfect. I don't even know how to thank you for giving me this job."

"No matter," she said, glancing away. "I really need the help for the next four weeks, believe me."

We lingered over the apple crumble while a jazz trio began to play inside. The smells, the sounds, the feel of everything here was so different from what I was used to. I could almost forget that somewhere, thousands of miles away, Brett even existed.

I fell right asleep that night, thanks to my jet lag. When Poppy gently shook me awake the next morning at eight thirty, I felt disoriented, and it took me a moment to remember where I was.

"Wake up, sleepyhead," she said softly, smiling down at me as I blinked at her with bleary eyes. "It's Monday morning! Time to get up for work."

I groaned. "It's too early!" I moaned. After all, with the time difference, my body was telling me it was two thirty in the morning.

"Sorry," Poppy apologized. "But you're on the French clock now. Rise and shine!"

I dragged myself out of bed, muttering words that Poppy wisely ignored. By the time I had showered, put on a suit and some makeup, and appeared in the tiny kitchen forty minutes later, she had a flaky apple tart and a mug of cappuccino waiting for me.

"Eat up," she said, nodding at the pastry. "I popped by the patisserie on the corner while you were in the shower. You're going to have a full day, and you'll need the energy."

"Thanks," I said, my eyes widening as I sunk my teeth into the flaky tart. "This is incredible."

"Yes, well, be careful with them or you'll gain ten pounds in a month," Poppy said. She smiled sheepishly and patted her stomach. "Yes, I confess, I speak from personal experience."

I laughed.

"Er, Emma?" Poppy asked tentatively. "Would you be insulted if I offered a suggestion on your outfit?"

"Um, no?" I responded hesitantly. I glanced down at my outfit—a charcoal skirt suit with a crisp pink blouse—and wondered what was wrong with it.

Poppy nodded, gazing at my clothes. "Your suit?" She shook her head. "Much too New York–boardroom. This is a city that dresses up—but the women here do it much more subtly, and in a much more feminine way."

"Oh," I said, feeling suddenly foolish. This outfit had made me feel powerful and successful in Orlando. Did I not look feminine? I thought the slender cut accentuated my hips. "But what am I supposed to wear, then?"

"Give me a moment," Poppy said with a smile.

In ten minutes, she had re-outfitted me in a pair of slender black pants I hadn't had a chance to unpack yet as well as a pale pink blouse with a lacy collar from her own closet. She also loaned me a slim black tortoiseshell headband, which I used to pull back my somewhat unruly blond hair.

"*Voilà!*" she said, standing back to admire her work. "Now we just need to tone down your eyeshadow and make your lips and cheeks a little rosier, and you'll have transformed into a Parisian woman before our very eyes!"

Poppy's finishing touch was a slender scarf, which she tied expertly around my neck beneath the collar of the shirt. I had to admit that when I looked in the mirror, even *I* was surprised at the image looking back at me.

"I *do* look kind of French," I said in surprise.

"You look lovely." Poppy beamed at her handiwork. "Shall we go?"

Poppy's office was located in an old building that looked as though it could have been a series of upscale apartments a century ago. It was directly in back of the Musée d'Orsay, an impressionist museum she promised I'd like more than the enormous Louvre once we had a chance to go. Even from the outside, the museum was impressive. Poppy, reveling in her role as impromptu tour guide, explained that it had been a train station until right around World War II. I could indeed imagine Parisians a century ago bustling in and out of the long, ornate building that stretched for several blocks along the Seine. Two giant glass clocks glowed the hour, casting pale pools of light onto the sidewalk below.

"Here we are," Poppy said as we entered the old office building behind the museum. We walked down a narrow hallway and stopped at a broad, gold-leafed door halfway down. She inserted a key in the lock, jiggled it a few times, and pushed. I followed her into the office as she flicked on the lights.

"Oh," I said in surprise as the room lit up. I guess I'd assumed that if Poppy owned a PR firm that handled someone as big as Guillaume Riche, she'd have a bigger office. Instead the room we'd just entered had barely enough space to contain the two big desks that faced each other. One, clearly Poppy's, was overflowing with paper-work, photographs, and a few self-help books.

The other desk was a bit smaller and had a hard-backed stationary chair instead of a plush rolling one. There was an eight-by-ten black-and-white Eiffel Tower photograph pinned to a corkboard beside it, and a computer monitor sat on the desk, but other than that, it was empty.

"We can go shopping this weekend to decorate it," Poppy said as I took in the bare space. She nudged me and added, "We'll be out shopping for your new clothes anyhow."

I smiled and rolled my eyes at her. Evidently, Poppy had already decided that the wardrobe I'd brought with me was entirely useless.

"I had a business partner for a while, you know," she said softly after a moment, glancing at the bare desk and then looking away. "But she's gone."

"What happened?" I asked. It was hard to imagine that anyone would walk away once they'd landed the Guil-laume Riche account.

"I'll tell you later," Poppy said quickly. "But it doesn't matter. For now, it's just me and you, Emma. Did I men-tion I'm really going to need your help?"

The first three days of work went smoothly. Véronique, our liaison at KMG, was out of town on business until Thursday, so I wouldn't get to meet her until the follow-ing week. Nor would I get to meet Guillaume—although

I spent several hours drooling over his chiseled features and muscular physique in the hundreds of photos in Poppy's database. According to Poppy, he was holed up in a hotel room somewhere in Paris, writing his next album.

"You'll meet him before the junket," Poppy assured me. "KMG doesn't like us to bother him while he's creating."

That week, I had to read over some KMG company literature, sign a bunch of employment papers (I was being paid through KMG's small American branch to avoid the French employment laws), and help Poppy write a press release about the upcoming release of Guillaume's first album, *Riche*, which we were describing (somewhat cornily) as a "lyrical ode to Paris and the power of love."

Poppy also caught me up on the plans for Guillaume's London launch, for which she and I would be solely responsible. It sounded amazing. One-hundred-plus members of the media would be flown into London from the United States, Great Britain, Ireland, Australia, and South Africa—as would a few high-profile English-speaking music reporters floating around continental Europe. At London's five-star Royal Kensington Hotel, Poppy and I would host a two-and-a-half-day media junket—complete with a welcome reception, a surprise live performance, and five-minute interviews for every reporter—to officially launch Guillaume Riche and his debut album to the English-speaking world.

Guillaume's first single was due to hit airwaves next week, so there would be plenty of buzz built around the star by the time the junket rolled around.

"Emma, this guy is gold," Poppy said on Tuesday as we

laid out photos. We were trying to select two to send out with the advance press packet. "Millions of women are already in love with him."

In fact, I'd half fallen in love with him myself by the time we were done poring over his pictures. As I already knew from the dozens of photos I'd seen of him in *People*, *Hello*, and *Mod*, he had dark shaggy hair, deep green eyes, broad shoulders, and the kind of perfectly chiseled features that you expect to see on Michelangelo statues, not real human beings. Women all over the world were going crazy for him, and his breakup with Dionne DeVrie had only excited the public appetite. But would his sound measure up as Poppy had claimed?

Thursday afternoon, I had my answer. Before we left work for the day, a courier delivered our first copy of the "City of Light" single, hot off the press, and we popped it into the CD player at Poppy's desk excitedly. It would be Poppy's first time hearing the final recorded version of the single, but at least she'd gotten to sit in on some of Guillaume's studio sessions, which was why she was so awed by him already.

It was my first time hearing Guillaume at all.

The song, which he had written himself, was hauntingly beautiful. Poppy was right—it was reminiscent of Coldplay and Jack Johnson, with perhaps a little James Blunt thrown in—but there was no doubt that Guillaume Riche was in a class all by himself.

"Oh, my God," I said, gazing at Poppy in wonder when the song finished. "We really do have a star on our hands."

I'd never felt something so strongly in my life. It suddenly made sense that KMG was willing to invest so much in Guillaume. His voice was incredible, the lyrics were gorgeous, and the melodies were so pretty that they gave me goose bumps. It was a totally new sound, familiar yet ultimately like nothing I'd heard before.

That night, Poppy took me to a bar in the fifth arrondissement called the Long Hop. It was, she explained, a bar that catered to Anglos like us. But, Poppy added with a smile, it was always populated with lots of Frenchmen, too.

"It's classic," she told me as we walked through the entryway beneath the fluttering flags of our homelands. "They think we British and American girls are so gullible, we'll fall for their smooth talk. But don't be fooled, Emma. They're just as bad as men anywhere else."

I gave Poppy a look and didn't bother reminding her that I obviously wasn't here to pick up any guys, French or otherwise. Surely she knew I was in full-on mope-about-Brett mode.

Inside, the Long Hop was dark and smoky, with a hardwood bar framed with a list of chalk-written drink specials, a pool table in the back, a stairway to a small second level, and a room full of twentysomethings packed in like sardines. Vintage beer posters and signs decorated the shadowed walls, and blond, study-abroad American girls in jeans and heels tried desperately to look more French by tying scarves around their necks while talking to Frenchmen, who were, amusingly, trying desperately to look more American in jeans, Nike and Adidas shirts, and sneakers. Music—mostly in English—pumped from the speakers, making it hard to hear. Half of the dozen flat-screen TVs around the room were tuned to soccer matches, the other half to a rotating mix of concert footage and music videos. The Eagles' "Hotel California" ran effortlessly into Fergie's "London Bridges," which pumped seamlessly into Madonna's "Material Girl."

"Let's find a place to sit!" Poppy shouted over the music. "There are a lot of hot guys here!"

I hid an amused smile and followed her around the room, where she unabashedly looked guys up and down and returned their glances with a confidently sexy stare. I couldn't imagine ever being able to look at guys that way again. Not that I was sure I ever had. It sounded strange, but it was hard to remember what going out had been like before Brett.

"According to *Smart Woman, Stupid Men,* you have to exude confidence to attract confidence," Poppy whispered as we walked. I shook my head and tried to hide my amused smile.

We settled on a ledge near the dance floor, and right away Poppy excused herself to get us drinks. She returned—after five minutes of flirtation with a tall, floppy-haired blond bartender—with a gin fizz for herself and a Brazilian lime-and-sugarcane concoction called a caipirinha for me.

"To your visit to Paris!" Poppy said cheerfully, holding her glass up. "And to you discovering the art of French kissing!"

I held my glass up and clinked it against hers uncertainly. "What exactly are you talking about?" I asked after we had both taken a sip. I tried not to feel insulted. "Things may not have worked out with Brett, but Poppy, it wasn't because I didn't know how to kiss!"

Poppy laughed. "No, no!" she said. "I don't mean *actual* French kissing. I mean kissing Frenchmen!"

That didn't clarify things at all. "What *about* kissing Frenchmen?" I asked. I was starting to get a bad feeling about this.

"Well," she said dramatically, leaning forward and lowering her voice, "I've decided that the best way in the world to get over an ex is to date as many Frenchmen as possible and chuck them before they chuck you!"

"You're telling me that you want *me* to date a bunch of Frenchmen?" I repeated incredulously. I looked suspiciously at her glass. What was in that gin fizz of hers anyhow?

"Exactly!"

"And then dump them?"

"Precisely!"

"And this is supposed to make me feel better?"

"Voilà!"

I took a deep breath. Clearly I wasn't getting through. "Poppy," I began patiently. "In case you've forgotten, I just got out of a three-year relationship with a guy I was engaged to. And I'm only in Paris for five weeks. I'm not exactly looking for another boyfriend here."

"Who said anything about a *boyfriend*?" Poppy wrinkled her nose at the last word, as if it were somehow distasteful.

She paused for a moment and intently studied a tall dark-haired guy in a striped, collared shirt and designer jeans who passed us by without a glance.

"I thought *you* did," I said, confused. I focused on pretending that I didn't notice the very attractive dark-haired guy in the striped shirt giving me the eye. Or the blond guy nursing a Guinness in the corner who was staring at me. Or the muscular black guy shooting pool near the dance floor who kept glancing my way and smiling.

"Boyfriends are more trouble than they're worth," Poppy said with a shrug. "Who needs them? I'm just talking about a lovely date or a good snog, Emma."

I couldn't imagine that any of the men at this bar would want to snog me—or do anything else with me, for that matter. "I'm not exactly Audrey Tautou," I said, rolling my eyes. In fact, with my somewhat stringy blond hair, wrinkle-rimmed blue eyes, and less-than-lithe figure, I was pretty much the polar opposite of the doe-eyed brunette gamine.

"Oh, rubbish." Poppy waved dismissively. "You're gorgeous. Besides, just by virtue of your Americanism, you're fascinating to these men, you know. We Anglos are quite different from French girls, you know. And guess what? These Frenchmen? They are rather fascinating, too."

"They are?" I asked, casting a glance at one cigarette-smoking slender guy, dressed head-to-toe in charcoal gray, who was giving Poppy—or rather her on-display cleavage—the eye.

"Absolutely," she confirmed. "They are nothing like those duffers back home in our countries. They know how to treat women. They wine us, they dine us, they actually fall in love with us without getting all effed up because their friends think they've no bollocks. They speak romance as a second language. If you're going to get back on the horse, Emma, these are the guys you want to saddle up with."

"But I don't *want* to get back on the horse," I said stubbornly.

"Sure you do," Poppy said. "You just don't know it yet. And there's no better place to start than right here."

Chapter Four

An hour later, Poppy was deep in conversation with the cigarette-puffing guy in head-to-toe gray while I was being chatted up by a sandy-haired French guy named Edouard.

"Ah, I know Floreeda!" he had exclaimed when I told him where I was from. His accent was thick and his speech, slow and careful. He blew smoke out of his mouth, took another drag of his cigarette, and grinned widely. "Ze land of Meeckey Mouse, *oui*?"

"Er, yes," I said, stifling a cough. "But there's lots more to Florida than that."

"I know!" he said, his broad smile growing even wider. "Beaches everyvhere! *Le jus d'orange!* Sunshine every day!"

More cigarette puffing from him. More coughing from me.

"Um, something like that," I said, neglecting to mention the storms every summer afternoon or the fact that in Orlando, I'd been forty-five miles from the closest beach, or the fact that I drank Tropicana, not fresh juice from some mystical grove out back. I imagined it was much like the fact that many Americans envisioned all of France as one big baguette-eating, beret-wearing country sur-rounding the Eiffel Tower.

"So, you would like to see Paris *avec moi?*" Edouard asked carefully, resting his right hand on the banister behind where I stood and leaning forward in a way that was clearly meant to be seductive but seemed more like an invasion of my personal space. Not to mention my personal lung capacity. "I can give you ze tour, *non?*" he asked with another giant exhalation of smoke. He grinned again.

I coughed. "Um, no thank you," I said, taking a discreet step backward. Unfortunately, the whole bar seemed to be swirling with smoke, so stepping out of Edouard's cloud just meant stepping into someone else's. I took a long sip of my third caipirinha of the evening and reminded myself to be polite. "I just got here today," I added. "It will take me some time to settle in."

"So Saturday, maybe, heh?" he pressed, leaning closer. "I take you on a peecnic, perhaps? Paris, it is such a roman-tic city."

I stared at him for a moment. This was so different from an American conversation, where the guy would have asked for my number, strolled casually away, and failed to call for three days—all as a means of expressing interest in me.

"Maybe another time," I said finally.

"So, I can to have your phone number?" he persisted.

I paused. "Um, why don't you give me yours?"

He frowned. "That is not normal."

I shrugged, not quite knowing what to say.

He hemmed and hawed for a moment but eventually scribbled his number on the back of a gum wrapper and handed it to me.

"I hope you will to call me, pretty lady," he said.

I forced a smile, took the gum wrapper, and excused myself, backing out of his haze of smoke as he stared after me, seemingly confused that his advances hadn't been successful.

I walked back over to Poppy, who cheerfully informed the gray-clad guy that we'd both like another drink. As he hurried away, she leaned in and whispered to me, "So? How'd it go with that guy you were talking to? Any snogging potential?"

I shrugged. "He had bad breath. And he smoked the whole time I talked to him."

Poppy laughed. "You'd best get used to that in this city," she said.

"Great," I muttered. Now I could add lung cancer to my list of things that would go wrong because Brett had broken up with me.

"Don't take things so seriously," Poppy chided.

I made a face at her. "I think I'm ready to head home whenever you are," I said after a moment, glancing around at the burgeoning crowd of cigarette-smoking Frenchmen on the make and the giggling American girls batting their eyelashes at them.

"No," Poppy said simply.

"*No?*" I was sure I'd heard her wrong. "What do you mean?"

"I mean that you're not going home until you've made a date for tomorrow night." She fixed me with a firm stare.

"What?" This hadn't been in my plans for the evening. Or for the foreseeable future, for that matter.

"Were you paying *any* attention to me earlier when I told you about Frenchmen?" she asked, raising an eyebrow.

"All I remember is something about horseback riding," I said crossly.

Poppy laughed. "I believe you're referring to getting back on the horse."

"Whatever," I mumbled.

"Look, Emma, if you're going to stay with me this month, I'm not going to let you sit around and mope about Brett." Poppy was suddenly very serious. "You have to get back out there. In *Secrets of Desirable Women*, Dr. Fishington writes that your chances for finding love decrease by six percent for every week you refrain from dating after a breakup."

I stared at her for a moment. Although I didn't believe in her self-help mumbo jumbo, I couldn't help doing the calculations in my head. It had been four weeks since Brett and I broke up. By Poppy's inane theory, that meant that my chances at love had diminished by almost a quarter.

"That's ridiculous, Poppy," I said, wishing I felt as confident as I sounded.

"Emma, French guys are the best," Poppy continued, ignoring me. "It will build your self-esteem. Besides, when's the last time you've just been on a *date* that you didn't intend to turn into a relationship?"

I opened my mouth to respond but thought better of it. I considered her question for a moment. Even before Brett, every guy I'd dated had turned into a boyfriend, at least for a few months. In fact, I couldn't even remember a time when I'd gone on a series of meaningless first dates. But wasn't dating supposed to be all about finding Mr. Right?

"You've just been racing into relationships, haven't you?" Poppy continued, evidently reading my mind. "The French call it the quest for *l'oiseau rare*—the rare bird, the perfect man. You were like that the summer we lived together, too," she added triumphantly.

I stared at her. Was she right? I'd gone out on exactly two first dates that summer. One, with a British guy named Michael, had resulted in us having drunken sex at the end of the night and me falling head over heels for him, which scared him away inside of five weeks. The next date I'd had, with a banker named Colin, had resulted in a three-month relationship that he finally broke off after I'd moved back to the States, citing the difficulty of doing long distance.

"So?" I mumbled.

"So . . . ," Poppy said, drawing the word out. "Maybe you need to simply *date* without trying to make it a race to girlfriend status."

I opened my mouth to protest, but nothing came out.

"You're at your sexual peak, you know," she added.

"Um, what?" I asked, wondering how this was relevant.

"Yes." She nodded with confidence. "According to *Sexy Time* by Dr. Boris Sudoko, a woman's sex drive peaks

between twenty-nine and thirty-five. Now, I'm not suggesting you sleep with anyone. But there's no better time
in your life to feel attractive and sexy. Frenchmen are the
best remedy for heartbreak."

"You realize you're insane," I muttered.

"Yes, of course." Poppy thought for a second. The guy
in gray was on his way back, balancing three drinks and
smiling at Poppy.

"Look," she said. "What if I see if this guy Gérard has a
friend that he can set you up with? And the four of us can
meet tomorrow for a drink? Not a date, just a drink."

"You know I don't want to," I said.

"And you know that's mostly irrelevant."

I made a face at her and was about to respond when
Poppy's cell phone began ringing to the tune of Gnarls
Barkley's "Crazy."

"Bollocks," Poppy cursed. She blushed and, casting a quick
look at the approaching charcoal-clothed guy, scrambled
for the phone, which was sticking out of her purse. *"Allô?"*
she answered, sounding very French. I watched as the color
drained from her face. She spoke a few more sentences in
rapid French and hung up, looking distressed. "Bollocks!"
she exclaimed again, slamming her fist down on the bar in
frustration. The guy in gray glanced at her, set two of the
drinks down, and hurried away, shaking his head.

"What's wrong?" I asked with concern.

"It's work," she said tersely. She reached for a drink and
took a big swig. "We have to go."

"Work?" I repeated in disbelief. I checked my watch.
"But it's almost one in the morning!"

"Well, technically we're on call all the time." She made a face. "That's what happens when you run your own agency."

I just stared at her. "What on earth could we possibly have to do at one a.m.?" At Boy Bandz, I'd been "on call" two nights a week, but there had never been a middle-of-the-night incident I'd had to respond to. Our boys were usually tucked away in bed by eleven, probably with their night-lights on.

"It's Guillaume Riche," Poppy said tightly, leaning forward and lowering her voice. "Véronique from KMG just called. There's apparently been, er, an incident."

"An incident?" I asked.

"Véronique didn't explain," Poppy said. "She just said we needed to get to her office immediately. We need to do some damage control."

Damage control? I opened my mouth but didn't have time to respond before Poppy grabbed my hand and dragged me toward the exit.

Chapter Five

"*Merci*," Poppy said quickly as the cab screeched to a halt in front of KMG's office building, which was just a few blocks from her own office in the sixth. She thrust a handful of bills and coins at the driver and piled quickly out of the cab. I scrambled after her, trying to compose myself. I was afraid I was failing miserably. I was exhausted, confused, and utterly disheveled. I was fairly confident this was not the best way to make a good first impression on Véronique, who, according to Poppy, was currently waiting to brief us inside.

As I hurried a pace behind Poppy toward the building, the enormous brick-colored front door flew open, and in the entryway a slender, dark-haired woman in inky black skinny jeans, a crisp white blouse, and a pile of pearls stood framed there, her arms crossed over her chest.

She said something in rapid French, her voice low-pitched and confident, then, glancing at me, she seemed to realize that she needed to translate.

"You are late!" she exclaimed, her French accent thick as strong espresso and her words coming in sharp staccato. "Where is Marie?" She glanced at Poppy and then back at me. "And who are you?"

"Um, I'm Emma," I replied nervously. I took a step forward and extended my hand. "Nice to meet you."

She looked at my hand but didn't shake it. I stood there for a moment, feeling foolish, then lowered my arm back to my side. I wondered what I had done to offend her in under ten words. Poppy patted me on the shoulder.

"Emma, this is Véronique, our boss," she said smoothly. "Véronique, this is Emma, the new publicist I've mentioned to you."

"Well," Véronique muttered, looking at me with what appeared to be suspicion. She looked back at Poppy. "Marie is not responding to my calls," she said crisply.

"Marie quit last month, remember?" Poppy said wearily. She glanced at me. "Marie was my business partner," she said softly. "The one I mentioned to you. You're sort of, er, replacing her." I suddenly realized that there must be more to Marie's departure than Poppy had initially led me to believe.

"*Quoi?*" Véronique said sharply. "Well. This is *monstrueux*. This means that you and the new girl must take care of this on your own!"

"What exactly is happening, Véronique?" Poppy interrupted.

She heaved a weight-of-the-world sigh and rolled her eyes. "Come with me," she said.

The moment Véronique turned her back to walk back into the building, Poppy shot me a look of concern and shrugged. *Guillaume*, she mouthed. I shook my head, not understanding yet what the handsome rock star could have done in the middle of the night to leave Véronique so panicked. After all, Guillaume was practically a saint, wasn't he?

We followed Véronique down a long corridor into a big open-floor-plan office that looked out of place in such an old building. I'd expected ornate, tiny rooms that had belonged to businessmen centuries earlier. Instead the room felt oddly reminiscent of the Boy Bandz offices back home.

Fluorescent lighting, just as unflattering here as it was stateside, poured over a dozen desktops, which were separated by cubicle walls into work spaces almost too small to turn around in. The desks were white and modern looking, and the swivel chairs looked like they had come straight out of Ikea—not at all the ornate antique desks and chairs I had anticipated. The walls were decorated with twenty-by-thirty framed posters of the bands on the KMG label. I glanced at each of them, familiarizing myself with the names. Le Renaissance. Amélie Deneuve. Jean-Michel Colin. Jacques Cash. TechnoPub. République de Musique.

"Where's Guillaume Riche's poster?" I whispered to Poppy as we hurried to keep up with Véronique.

"He's not up there yet," Poppy explained. "His album cover won't be final for another week. Then we'll add him to the wall. Believe me, it will be quite the distraction. He's shirtless on the cover."

I raised an eyebrow. That sounded like nice workplace scenery.

We followed Véronique into her office, where Poppy and I sank nervously into side-by-side chairs without taking our eyes off her. She was standing before us with clenched fists, looking as if steam might begin shooting from her ears at any moment.

"This is a disaster," she said, staring first at Poppy, then at me. "Your *Guillaume* is at it again. You must take care of him! What are we paying you for?"

Poppy sighed, and I looked at her in confusion. I was feeling more and more out of the loop by the moment. Just then a phone rang in the outer room, and Véronique made a face.

"Don't move," she said, fixing us with a glare, as if we might be tempted to climb out a window in her absence. "I'll be back in a moment."

She hurried out of the office. I turned to Poppy.

"What exactly is going on?" I demanded.

Poppy averted her eyes. "Oh, yes, Guillaume Riche," she said with forced casualness. "There *may* have been a few things I forgot to mention about him."

"A few things?" I repeated slowly.

"Er . . . yes," she said, still not meeting my gaze. "Guillaume sort of has a, um, certain propensity for getting himself into trouble."

"Trouble?" I was starting to get a bad feeling about this.

"Er, yes," she said. "You might say that. All sorts of messes."

"For example?" I prompted.

Poppy sighed. Her eyes flicked to me and then away again. "He's gotten locked in a wine cellar in the south of France," she said quickly. "He's gotten trapped in the dolphin tank at the aquarium in Brittany; he even tap-danced through the prime minister's backyard in the middle of the night. He's a bit batty, you might say."

"But . . . I've never read about *any* of this!" I exclaimed.

"Good," Poppy said with a wry smile. "That means I've been doing my job. Most of the stories were reported in some capacity, but my old colleague, Marie, used to do a wonderful job of coming up with logical explanations for everything."

My heart—and my hopes of an easy stay in Paris—were sinking like a stone in the Seine. "But I thought you said he was some kind of saint!"

"That's not *quite* what I said," she replied, eyes down. "What I said was that's how KMG has decided to market him. They did a ton of research with focus groups and all sorts of psychological studies and found that women in our target audience are getting tired of the stereotypical rock-'n'-roll bad boy. The market is ripe for something new. Our research showed that positioning Guillaume as a nice guy, the kind of guy you want to take home to your mother, was the best way to make him an international star."

"Except he's *not* exactly a nice guy?" I filled in flatly.

"No, it's not quite that," Poppy said quickly. "He's nice enough. He's just . . . well, let's just say he has a screw or two loose. Which doesn't *exactly* fit with the image we're trying to project.

"So far," she continued, "we've managed to spin all his little mishaps to make them look like innocent mistakes.

The press hasn't caught on. But he can't seem to stop getting himself into trouble."

Before I could reply, Véronique bustled back into the room, a handful of papers in her hand.

"Faxes from just about every reporter we've ever had contact with," she said sharply, holding up the stack. Poppy and I exchanged glances. "They all want to know what Guillaume is doing."

"What *is* Guillaume doing?" Poppy asked, quite sensibly, I thought.

"You mean you don't know?" Véronique demanded. She mumbled something in French that sounded a lot like an expletive. "Well, I'll tell you then! He's shut himself in a hotel room up in Montmartre with four girls—all of them seemingly underage—and a pile of drugs. It seems a room-service waiter called the press, and they're there in droves, waiting for him to come out and get caught."

Poppy swore under her breath and stood up quickly.

"I expect you to take care of this," Véronique continued sharply, thrusting a piece of notepaper at Poppy. "Here's the information about where he is. If Guillaume Riche gets arrested—or winds up looking like he's coaxing young girls into getting high—it's going to be KMG taking the fall. And you'll both be out of a job."

"I can't lose this job, Emma," Poppy said, white-faced, as we sat in the back of a cab on the way to Montmartre, the bohemian quarter of historic Paris that sat atop a small hill and was famous for its miniature windmills and winding roads. She knocked on the divider separating the driver from us. "Can you go any faster?" she asked loudly. The driver cursed back at her in French and threw his hands in the air. Poppy sighed, leaned back in her seat, and closed her eyes.

"Poppy, everything will be fine." It was disconcerting to see my normally cool, calm, and collected friend so shaken. "I'm sure that whatever is happening with Guillaume isn't that bad. We'll work it out."

She opened her eyes and stared at me bleakly. "You don't know Guillaume," she said. "He's a complete disaster."

I shrugged. "I'm sure you're exaggerating."

Poppy shook her head. "No, I'm not. That's why Marie quit last month. She'd finally had enough. She was great at this, though. Every scrape he got into, she somehow talked him out of. All I had to do was basically translate whatever nonsense she said and keep the English-speaking journalists happy."

"So you never had to talk him out of anything yourself?" I asked.

Poppy looked away. "I'm crap at inventing stories, Emma, I really am. I begged and pleaded with Marie to stay, but she was sick of this and sick of being yelled at by Véronique. I don't know how I'm going to handle this on my own."

"You're not on your own," I said softly. I took a deep breath. "Look, I'll help you."

Poppy glanced at me. "You think you can make something up to talk Guillaume out of this?"

I paused. "Well, I've had to talk the boy-band guys out

of some ridiculous situations in the past," I said. There was, for example, the time Robbie Roberts was arrested for shoplifting three pairs of women's panties. Or the time Justin Cabrera was caught naked with his young, blond high school math teacher. Or the time Josh Schwartz was caught smoking pot with the rabbi at his little sister's bat mitzvah.

Poppy nodded slowly. "I just don't know what I'd do if I lost this job. I'd have to close my agency."

"That's not going to happen," I said more firmly than I felt.

"You're my only hope," she said bleakly. I could see her blinking back tears. We rode in tense silence for a moment. "Oh, no," she moaned softly as our taxi turned a corner and pulled up at a red light. "It's worse than I thought."

My eyes widened as I took in the Hôtel Jeremie, which looked more like a paparazzo cloning factory than a hotel. Spilling out into the street, a whole gaggle of nearly identical-looking disheveled men toting large cameras with complicated-looking flashbulbs stood jostling one another.

Even with the cab windows rolled up, I could hear their excited chatter, the clamor of a group of hungry wolves waiting for the kill.

The light changed, and the cab started moving forward again, closer to the hotel, closer to the hungry pack of predators. Poppy groaned and closed her eyes.

"Can you take us around to the back entrance?" I suddenly asked the driver. My mind was spinning, and I had no idea what sort of situation we'd find this Guillaume in, but it suddenly occurred to me that if we were going to have to explain his way out of things, it might be better if we weren't seen entering the building. We could be his alibi—but only if we could make it look like we'd been there all along.

"Comment?" the driver asked, still appearing as if he was going to turn into the hotel drive, therefore mowing over several paparazzi (which didn't sound like such a bad idea at the moment).

Poppy quickly translated my request into French. The cabdriver snorted and said something back.

"He says there is just one entrance," Poppy said, turning to me worriedly.

"Impossible," I said. "There has to be a service entrance in the back. Tell him to just drive around the building and we'll find it."

Poppy hesitated for a moment, opened her mouth as if she was going to say something to me, then shrugged. She spoke quickly to the driver, who glared at me for a moment in the mirror then, shaking his head, twisted the wheel sharply to the left and turned down the side street just before the hotel.

"Voilà!" the cabbie said, screeching to a halt at the curb of a dark alleyway. *"Vous êtes contente?"* He smirked at me in the rearview. Obviously, sarcasm translated.

"Yes, very content, thank you," I chirped back. Poppy shot me a look and paid the driver. He screeched away the moment we tumbled out of the cab into the darkness.

"Why did you want to find the back entrance?" Poppy

asked as we made our way toward the hotel. "Shouldn't we just go in and face the music, so to speak? No point in delaying the inevitable."

"We may need to claim that we've been with Guillaume all along, and therefore the things he was accused of can't possibly have happened," I said slowly. "If that's the case, we can't be seen arriving."

Poppy was silent for a minute. "You know," she said. "That just might work."

We found a back door that was slightly ajar and made our way into what appeared to be the hotel kitchen.

"Is there anything else I need to know about Guillaume?" I asked as we hurried through a silent, dimly lit space filled with massive refrigerators, industrial-size stoves and ovens, and a series of prep stations, toward a small sliver of light behind a doorway that I figured was the hotel lobby. "Other than his apparent clinical insanity?"

Poppy chose to ignore the last half of my statement. "Just that he's actually pretty nice once you get past all the craziness," she said, hurrying along after me. "And wildly talented." She paused and added, "I know this must feel ridiculous to you."

"That's an understatement." I stifled a cry as I smashed my hip bone against the edge of a counter that I hadn't seen in the dark.

"But believe me, Emma, he's going to be so big!" Poppy enthused. "He really has it all!"

"Including a mental problem," I muttered as we slipped out of the kitchen and through the darkened dining room, which was closed and silent at this late hour. We silently hurried toward the lobby, keeping our faces turned away from the press mob and trying to look casual. But as soon as we rounded the corner and saw the elevator all the way across the room, we groaned in unison.

"We'll never be able to get to it without the reporters seeing us," I said.

Poppy nodded and rolled her eyes. She looked around for a moment. "There's a stairway over there."

I darted after her. She pulled open the heavy doorway, and we both slipped inside.

"I hope you're in shape," she said as we began to climb. "Guillaume is in the penthouse suite on the twelfth floor."

"The twelfth floor?" I groaned, craning my neck to look up at stairs that seemed to go on forever. "I didn't think the French built tall buildings."

"Evidently, they made an exception here," Poppy said drily. "It's where Guillaume always stays when he's writing music."

Six minutes and a dozen excruciating flights of huffing and puffing later, we emerged to find the maroon double doors at the far end of the hall flanked by two enormously beefy, stern-looking men, one of whom had a Salvador Dalí–style mustache that looked designed for twirling, quite an odd sight on a man who could probably snap me in half if he so desired.

"Thank God," Poppy said, still panting from our climb. "Edgar and Richard are here!"

"Who?" I asked, gazing skeptically at the two strange-looking giants who stood between us and our errant rock star. This was getting weirder by the moment. But Poppy was already striding down the hall toward the enormous men, smiling and saying something in rapid French to the Dalí-mustached man. He stared at her for a moment, impassively, then reached out and pulled her into a bear hug. She exchanged a few words with the other beefy guy, who also broke into a grin and reached over to muss her hair.

"Emma," Poppy said, finally pulling away from him and smiling at me. "This is Edgar." I reached out hesitantly and shook his massive hand. "And this is Richard," she added, gesturing to Edgar's mustacheless twin.

"Nice to meet you." I shook his hand, too, and then looked to Poppy for an explanation.

"Edgar and Richard are two of KMG's bodyguards," Poppy explained, beaming. "I had no idea they were here! This is fantastic!"

Edgar said something to me in rapid French, and I shook my head.

"Je ne parle pas français," I recited—one of the only French phrases I had memorized, the one that meant "I don't speak French." "Sorry."

"It eez not problem," Edgar said, shaking his head and speaking in slow broken English. "I taked ze English in ze school. I just tell Poppy that no *journalistes* enter here. Me and Richard, we, how you say, we block ze way."

"Well, thank you," I said.

"Merci beaucoup!" Poppy beamed. She turned to me. "We're in luck!"

I raised an eyebrow at her. Somehow, even with this latest turn of events, *luck* didn't seem like the proper word to apply to a situation that involved standing on the twelfth floor of a hotel outside a crazed rock star's room, while a gang of hungry reporters waited for us downstairs.

"So, Edgar, can you tell us what is happening?" Poppy asked.

"*Oui*," he said, nodding solemnly. "After dinner, Guillaume bring four, how you say, er, young ladies to *la chambre*, er, ze room," he began.

"You were with him?" Poppy asked.

"*Oui*," Edgar confirmed. "KMG ask us to stay with him tonight. But he keep losing us." The man rolled his eyes. "Now, *on est dans un beau pétrin*."

"What?" I glanced at Poppy for clarification.

"It's an expression that means 'We're in a fine mess now,'" Poppy translated softly.

"You can say that again," I said.

Edgar looked at me strangely and shrugged. "Okay. Eef you wish. *On est dans un beau pétrin*."

I took a deep breath and reminded myself to be careful using English expressions. "Edgar," I said. "Can you tell us what happened once they got to the room?"

Edgar nodded. "The music, it go on," he said, glancing at Richard, who was staring impassively forward. "And we hear ze laughter from ze room. Guillaume, he order ze food in ze room, and *le serveur* who deliver ze food, he notice ze girls. *Les journalistes*, they arrive twenty minutes later, so we think it was *le serveur* who call them."

"Did any of the paparazzi make it up here?" Poppy asked.

"*Oui*," Edgar responded. "But we make them to go away. Now they wait like—how you say—vultures, down ze stairs. They wait to catch Guillaume and his girls to leave."

"Do you know what they're doing in there now?" I asked, nodding toward the door. Edgar and Richard exchanged glances.

"*Non*," Edgar said slowly. He glanced nervously at Poppy.

"It's okay, Edgar," she said. "Emma works with me. She's going to try to help get Guillaume out of this. You can be honest with her."

Edgar stared at Poppy for a moment then turned to look at me.

"There are drugs," he said slowly. "But there are always drugs. Guillaume, he does not do ze drugs. He never do ze drugs. But the girls, they do ze drugs. Guillaume, he is just crazy. He does not need ze drugs to be crazier. As we say in French, *il est marteau*. And I think he make ze love with ze girls."

"*All* the girls?" I asked, incredulously. I wasn't sure whether to be disgusted or mildly impressed.

Edgar laughed. "I do not know. Is that not what ze rock stars do?"

I cleared my throat. "So Guillaume *isn't* on drugs. But the girls might be?"

"*Oui.*"

"Which ones?" I asked. "Which drugs?"

Edgar glanced nervously at Poppy again. "*La cocaine*," he said finally.

"We're going in," I said suddenly. Edgar looked at me in surprise.

"We are?" Poppy asked. I sighed and looked at my watch. It was now two thirty in the morning.

"Yes," I said, trying to sound confident. Edgar and Richard glanced at each other then at Poppy, who shrugged as if to say, *I guess we'll just have to follow the whims of the crazy American.* That's right. They would.

I raised my hand to the door and knocked. Nothing happened. I waited a moment, cleared my throat, and raised my hand to the door again.

"There's no answer," Poppy pointed out helpfully a moment later, after I'd stood staring at the doorway for what felt like a small eternity, willing some sort of reaction from inside.

"Yes, I see that," I said and knocked again. Still no reply, although I could have sworn that the decibel level on the blasting music went up a notch or two.

"Bon, je vais frapper à la porte," Edgar said. "Let me try knocking, Emma." He pronounced my name *Ayma*, but as far as I was concerned he could call me Bob as long as he figured out how to get Poppy and me into Guillaume's suite.

Edgar pounded on the door so hard that I feared it might actually come crashing off the hinges. Still no answer. So he pounded again, even harder and more violently this time. A moment ticked by, and then inside, the music suddenly screeched to a halt.

"Qu'est-ce qui se passe?" came a slurred male voice from inside.

Edgar shouted something in rapid French through the door. To me, he whispered, "I told him to open ze door, because there are two more ladies who want to join his party."

"Good plan," I said.

A moment later the door opened, and framed in the entry stood the most beautiful man I'd ever seen.

"Meet Guillaume Riche," Poppy muttered.

I know it's not polite to stare, but I figured that the dark-haired Adonis in front of me was probably used to it. Six feet tall or so; with his thick, dark, shaggy hair, emerald-green eyes, and perfectly chiseled face, Guillaume was literally breathtaking. As in, I had to take several deep breaths in order to pretend that I was annoyed at him, not attracted to him. He was a thousand times hotter in person than in any photo I'd ever seen. It didn't help me that he was wearing only low-slung jeans, unbuttoned at the top, and that his shirtless physique was absolutely perfect.

"Ah, Poppy!" he exclaimed, his eyes lighting up as he focused on her. "You have come to join my party!" He turned his gaze to me and studied me intently before grinning again. "And you have brought a friend, I see!" he added.

I continued to stare dumbly at him, marveling at the fact that his English was much cleaner and less accented than I would have suspected. Had he been able to pronounce his *r*'s correctly, and had he not drawn out the ends of the words *Poppy, party,* and *see* so dramatically, I would almost have been able to believe that he was American instead of French. I hadn't expected such English proficiency.

"Emma, meet Guillaume Riche," Poppy said hastily, nodding at him, then at me. "Guillaume, this is Emma."

"Ah, Emma, you are beautiful!" Guillaume replied with a wink that made me blush. He reached forward and planted a kiss on each of my cheeks, French-style. "Just my type!" He took my hand in his and kissed it.

"I didn't bring her to add to your harem, Guillaume," Poppy interrupted. He looked questioningly at her and then back at me. "She's your new publicist."

Guillaume looked back at me, still clutching my hand. I forced a smile. He studied me for a moment more, then grinned sheepishly.

"Right!" he exclaimed. "I knew that. I meant she was just my type of publicist. Really, Poppy. You always suspect the worst."

"Right," Poppy muttered. "I'm sure that's entirely unfounded."

"So, uh, what exactly is going on here, Guillaume?" I asked, putting my hands on my hips and trying to sound tough. But Guillaume just looked amused.

"I'm having some drinks with a few friends, Emma," he announced brightly, wobbling just a bit as he said the words. "It's totalleeeee innocent."

"I'm sure," Poppy said, glaring at him and then poking her head into the hotel room. I followed her gaze inside, where four girls, who looked like they could be in high school, were flitting around in various stages of undress. One was sniffing and wiping at her nose, which seemed to support Edgar's assertion about the cocaine. My heart sank. Guillaume followed our eyes and shrugged.

"We were just playing a little bit of strip poker," he added. He arched an eyebrow. "I'm winning. Good for me!"

"Yes, excellent for you," Poppy said, glancing past him to glare at a wispy blonde wearing just white panties and a matching cami, who glided through the room toward the bath.

"Don't they have underage laws here?" I whispered. Poppy nodded.

"Oh, sweet Emma, they are not underage!" Guillaume exclaimed, having apparently overheard. "I wouldn't be that foolish! I checked all of their IDs before inviting them here!"

I just stared at him, dumbfounded, until Poppy took over.

"Damn it, Guillaume!" she exclaimed. "You know we're launching your album in less than four weeks! You *know* how much KMG has invested in you. Do you know how many photographers and reporters are in the lobby waiting to destroy your perfect image?"

"So it's good publicity!" Guillaume exclaimed brightly, wobbling a bit as he said it. He glanced at me, seemed to have trouble focusing, then shook his head and looked away. "All press is good press, right?"

"Wrong," Poppy said firmly. "You *know* we're trying to portray you as Mr. Perfect. Clearly, you're determined to make sure I fail miserably at that task." She sighed and looked around the room. *"Allez-y!"* she said, making eye contact with each of the girls and clapping commandingly. "Let's go! Everybody out!"

She spoke a few sentences in French to the girls, who

suddenly looked worried and scrambled to put their clothes back on.

"What on earth did you say?" I whispered.

"I told them we had called the police, and they're on their way," she said. "Sentences for drug use in France are pretty severe."

"Poppy!" Guillaume exclaimed, watching dejectedly as the girls scrambled to get dressed. "You are ruining my fun!"

She fixed him with a glare. "One of these days, Guillaume, you are going to get into a mess we can't get you out of."

Guillaume shrugged sheepishly. Then he turned to me and winked, as if I were his conspirator.

I swallowed hard and tried to look annoyed instead of smitten.

Chapter Six

Ten minutes later, Poppy and I were riding an elevator in silence toward the ground floor with Guillaume wedged between us. Edgar and Richard had helped sneak the girls down the back stairs and out the service entrance by disguising them in bellboy outfits Edgar had found in a storage closet on the eleventh floor.

"I don't see why I can't just sneak out, too," Guillaume grumbled.

"Because," Poppy said sensibly, "everyone knows you're here."

"So?"

"So," Poppy said impatiently, "the only way to deal with this is to act like it was one giant mistake on the part of the guy who brought you room service. There was nothing unseemly going on in your room at any time."

"I don't follow your logic," Guillaume muttered.

"Of course you don't," she shot back irritably. "You're completely mad."

I stared straight ahead, pretending to myself that I wasn't trapped in an elevator with two people who sounded very much like they were involved in some sort of lovers' spat.

"I have no idea what to say to the press," Poppy had

confided in me desperately five minutes earlier while we stood outside Guillaume's door, waiting for him to put his shirt back on and make himself look as presentable and presumably sober as possible. "I'm so bad at this. I can write the press releases and spin all these stupid situations the next day, but I'm terrible at knowing what to say on the spot. That was what Marie was good at!"

"So why don't we take some time to think about it?" I had suggested.

"Because we need to go down *now* to distract attention from the girls leaving," she said. "Because if we wait, someone's bound to spot them, and they'll tell the real story."

"What story will *we* be telling?" I asked.

"I haven't a clue." Poppy's face had clouded over, and she'd looked like she was about to cry.

"Okay," I'd said slowly. I put a hand on her arm. "Don't worry. We'll figure something out."

So while Poppy and Guillaume bickered during the seemingly interminable elevator ride, I tried very hard to stop finding Guillaume attractive and instead formulate a plan.

"Let me handle the talking, okay?" I said, glancing past Guillaume to an exhausted-looking Poppy as the elevator finally touched down on the ground floor. "Poppy, can you just take care of translating whatever I say into French?"

She stared at me with concern. "Emma, are you sure?"

"Yes," I said firmly, although of course I wasn't sure at all.

"I mean, because you don't have to—"

"I know," I said. "Don't worry."

Fortunately, we had time to have this entire conversation, because the elevator was clearly designed to open as slowly as humanly possible. First it landed, then it locked shakily into place, then the door gradually eked open, and finally we had to push ourselves out of what appeared to be a rusty, gold-chipped cage of some sort, which, in turn, was heavy, unwieldy, and badly in need of WD-40.

By the time we had emerged from the gilding, with flashbulbs exploding frantically all around us, I was ready. Well, as ready as I was going to be, anyhow.

The media interest in Guillaume was far more intense than I had expected. It was like nothing I'd experienced back home with Boy Bandz, even when the 407 boys were at the height of their popularity. Poppy had always told me that European journalists were relentless, especially when it came to celebrity coverage, but I hadn't expected anything to this degree. There were dozens of clamoring reporters and scores of photographers shouting Guillaume's name.

I am in control, I told myself. Realizing that in this situation, at least, I could take charge of something made me feel a little more like myself again.

Filled with this false confidence, I strode out of the elevator, with Poppy following me, herding a sheepish Guillaume between us.

"Mesdames et messieurs," Poppy said quickly as we approached a makeshift podium off to the side of the lobby. She raised her hands until the crowd of journalists had fallen into an expectant hush. A few flashes went off, and

Guillaume grinned for the cameras as if oblivious to the fact that anyone here could wish him ill. "*Puis-je avoir vôtre attention, s'il vous plaît?* May I have your attention please?"

The crowd shushed further and waited expectantly. Poppy stared at them for a moment, like a deer caught in headlights—or at least flashbulb lights. Then she cleared her throat and glanced at me. Guillaume elbowed me gently in the ribs; when I looked at him, he grinned charmingly and batted his thick eyelashes at me. I rolled my eyes and tried not to blush.

"May I present my new colleague, Emma Sullivan," Poppy said. She glanced nervously at me again and then looked back out at the quieted press corps. "Emma will be making a short announcement in English. I will be translating to French. Thank you. *Merci beaucoup.*"

She nodded, raised her eyebrows at me, and took a step back. I cleared my throat, took a step forward, and forced a smile at the twenty or so journalists who were clustered in front of me, looking hungry, tired, and eager.

"Good evening," I said formally, stepping forward.

"*Bonsoir,*" Poppy translated behind me. I drew a deep breath and continued.

"It has come to our attention that there have been some rumors this evening about Guillaume Riche's behavior," I began. Behind me, Poppy translated, and as she finished speaking, several hands shot up in the air. I held up a hand, indicating that I wasn't finished.

"Sometimes, people tell stories for personal gain or call the press for reasons of their own making," I continued. I debated for a moment whether I should feel badly about calling the busboy's honesty into question, but after all he *had* been the source of this madness. And wasn't a hotel guest's private business supposed to remain private? "I cannot guess at the motives of the individual who called you," I said, pausing so that Poppy could translate after each sentence. "Or perhaps it was just an innocent mistake. But I assure you, there was nothing unseemly going on in Guillaume Riche's hotel suite this evening."

Poppy translated in a voice that was growing more confident by the moment, and again, half a dozen hands shot up, reporters clamoring. I glanced at them and, without meaning to, locked eyes with a dark-haired thirtysomething guy with glasses in the front row who was staring at me with a creased forehead.

He was cute. Very cute. He had classic French good looks: green eyes, thick lashes, darkly tanned skin, and a square jaw darkened by stubble. Unfortunately, he was also wearing an expression of deep skepticism, which made him exponentially less attractive at the moment. I could almost hear the words *I don't believe you* emanating from him. I cleared my throat and glanced away before I accidentally looked guilty.

"This evening, my colleague, Poppy Millar, and I met Guillaume Riche in his hotel suite to go over plans for the highly anticipated launch of his album in Britain and the United States in three weeks," I continued, with Poppy hurriedly turning my words into French. I glanced again at the journalist with the glasses, who hadn't looked away, and my resolve faltered a bit. Why was his gaze making me so nervous? "We've been at it for hours," I said, "and

I think you'll be very pleased with the result at our big launch party in London three weeks from now."

Poppy translated while I paused to give myself a mental pat on the back for sneaking in a promotion for the upcoming launch—twice. So far, so good.

"The three of us have simply been brainstorming for the past several hours, and I assure you, there hasn't been anyone else in the room," I concluded. The lie came out easily, but I didn't see any other way around the issue. This seemed to be the only way Guillaume could escape from this situation.

More hands shot up, and I took a deep breath and pointed to a sleek, dark-haired woman who looked about fifty.

She asked something in French, her voice tense and clipped.

"She wants to know if you deny the reports that there were four women in the room," Poppy translated softly.

"Yes, it was just the three of us," I lied.

"And ze reports that all of you, were, er, without your clothing?" the reporter pressed on in thickly accented English.

"Well," I said slowly, making sure to appear perplexed by the question. "The suite *was* rather warm, and we'd been working for hours. I do admit that Poppy and I took off our jackets and that Guillaume was in a T-shirt."

"Reports say you were in your underclothes," the reporter persisted, glaring at me. "And that there was some sort of card game going on."

Crap, I thought. I forced a smile.

"Um, well, I actually had a camisole underneath my jacket, so it may have looked like I was in underclothes," I said, keeping my voice slow and patient. "And as for the cards, yes, you've got us there." I smiled sheepishly and shrugged. "We took a break and played . . . er . . . Go Fish."

The moment the words were out of my mouth, I wanted to smack myself in the forehead. Go Fish? Why had I said that? Who plays Go Fish?

"Go Fish?" asked the man in the front row, the one with the glasses, the dimples, and the suspicious expression.

"Yes, it's a card game where—" I began.

"I know what it is," the man said in English, sounding surprisingly American for someone who seemed to fit in so well with the European press corps. "I'm just surprised. I didn't realize Guillaume knew how to play. Guillaume, have you learned Go Fish?"

Guillaume started to respond, and Poppy elbowed him in the ribs.

"Please direct all questions to Emma or me," Poppy said, fixing the reporter with a stern look.

"I'm sorry," he replied, not sounding sorry in the slightest. "The whole thing just sounds a little suspicious. In fact, it sounds sort of like Guillaume was probably up there with several girls playing drunken strip poker, and things got out of hand."

I gulped and glared at the reporter, who was staring evenly back at me with a small smile on his face.

"I'm sorry if that's the impression you've gotten," I said through gritted teeth, refusing to break eye contact for fear it would make me look like I had something to hide. Which, of course, I did. "But I'm afraid tonight was simply a rather boring evening of organization and planning on our part. Nothing to get excited about."

I looked deliberately away from the reporter and scanned the room. "Are there any more questions?" I called on a few more reporters, whose queries Poppy translated into English for me, and gave several more safe answers. Yes, Guillaume had been fully clothed the whole time, except for when he had spilled a glass of water and needed to change his shirt. No, we didn't expect this evening to ruin his appeal to younger listeners, because of course nothing had happened. Yes, he was excited to make his English-language debut. No, he wasn't ashamed to be standing here, because of course nothing had happened.

I glanced nervously at the dimpled guy a few times. As he gazed evenly back, I had the uncomfortable feeling that he could see right through me.

"You were great in there!" Poppy whispered to me twenty minutes later as the crowd of reporters reluctantly dissipated and we hustled a subdued Guillaume into a stretch Hummer that Edgar had summoned during our impromptu press conference. Véronique had called Poppy to tell her that she'd gotten Guillaume a room at the Four Seasons George V Hotel for the night so that he could stay there in seclusion, with Edgar and Richard guarding his room, until the interest in this story had died down.

"I didn't *feel* great," I grumbled as the Hummer made its

way down the darkened, tree-lined Avenue des Champs-Élysées toward the Arc de Triomphe. "I felt like a liar."

"You *did* lie," Guillaume pointed out helpfully. I glared at him.

"I'm aware of that," I said. "Which I wouldn't have had to do if you hadn't been such an idiot."

There was a moment of silence, and I could see Poppy's face tense up. I knew I had crossed a line. I immediately regretted it. You simply didn't talk to the talent that way. I held my breath, waiting for Guillaume to freak out and demand that I be fired.

But instead, he started laughing.

"I like you, Emma!" he said, grinning at me. "You have spunk!"

I could hear Poppy exhale beside me, and even the impassive Richard smiled slightly.

"I shouldn't have said that," I muttered, glancing at Guillaume. "I'm sorry."

"No, you're right," Guillaume said, still smiling at me. "I *am* an idiot, as you say. But, Emma, it's what keeps things fun!"

"Fun?" I asked.

"After all, if I was some boring guy who didn't know how to have a good time," he said with a wink, "you'd be out of a job!"

Chapter Seven

"So who was that reporter guy last night?" I asked the next morning after Poppy and I arrived at the office. I'd finally put up a few photographs in my cubicle—one of my nephew, Odysseus, one of me with my mother, and one with me and Poppy from a decade ago.

"Which one?" Poppy asked absently.

"The dark-haired guy with glasses who was staring at me like I was lying?"

"You *were* lying," Poppy reminded me.

"Yes, but *he* wasn't supposed to realize that," I said.

Poppy shrugged. "He always seems to suspect something," she said. "Frankly, he's rather a pain. He's a reporter for the UPP wire service. His name is Gabriel Francoeur." She pronounced it *fran-KOOR*.

"Is that the service that provides stories to newspapers around the world?"

"Right," Poppy said. "Like the Associated Press. But with better international distribution. Especially in Europe. In other words, Gabriel Francoeur can single-handedly make or break Guillaume Riche. Which means that for the next few weeks, he's your new best friend."

"He was kind of cute," I said, glancing away.

Poppy looked at me sharply. "Yeah, but he's a pain in the arse."

I ignored her. "He barely had an accent. Is he American?"

Poppy shook her head. "No, French, I think. He must have lived in America for a while, though. He does have your Yankee accent, doesn't he?"

Just then, there was a loud buzzing sound from overhead. I jumped, startled.

"What was that?" I asked.

Poppy sighed. "It's our front door. I keep asking the building to get that bloody buzzer fixed. It sounds like an air raid siren."

"I didn't even know we *had* a buzzer," I said. After all, this was my fifth day here, and not once had anyone appeared at our front door.

"I'm sure it's a delivery," Poppy said. "I'm expecting a shipment of eight-by-ten glossies of Guillaume. Can you answer it? I'll get my checkbook. The copy shop always sends the photos COD."

I crossed the tiny room and pulled open the front door. I blinked a couple of times at the tall dark-haired figure with glasses in the hallway before I registered who he was.

"Well, speak of the devil," Poppy said somewhere behind me.

"You two were talking about me, were you?" Gabriel Francoeur said with an innocent grin, glancing past me and into the office. "I'm sure you were saying only wonderful things."

"Ah, you know me too well," Poppy said drily.

Gabriel refocused his attention on me. "So," he said. "You're Emma. Guillaume's new publicist."

"You're quite observant," I said, feeling suddenly uncomfortable. I couldn't shake the feeling of transparency I'd had last night with his eyes boring into me.

Gabriel studied me for a moment and then smiled slowly. "I pride myself on my powers of perception," he said.

"Do you?" I asked, trying to affect boredom. I couldn't help but notice his evergreen eyes and the way they sparkled behind his glasses when he looked at me.

"I do," Gabriel confirmed with a nod. He raised an eyebrow. "In fact, one of the things I happened to notice last night was that your little story about Guillaume didn't completely add up."

I struggled not to blush. "I don't know what you're talking about," I responded stiffly.

"I'm sure you don't," Gabriel said, looking amused. We stood there staring at each other for a moment until I began to notice the little waves in his thick hair, and the way I could already see a dark shadow beneath the surface of his strong-looking jaw, although he had clearly shaved this morning. I could feel heat creeping up the back of my neck. I shook my head and glanced away.

"So," Gabriel finally said, breaking the uncomfortable silence. "Are you going to invite me in?"

I opened my mouth to say no, but somewhere behind me Poppy preempted me.

"Of course," she said smoothly. She elbowed me in the back. "Come in, Gabriel, of course."

He nodded, glanced down at me with a smile, and walked into the office, brushing against me a bit as he did. I felt a little uninvited shiver run down my spine. Geez, I was *attracted* to him. How was that possible?

"I don't know why we need to invite him in," I muttered to Poppy as Gabriel settled himself into *my* seat at *my* desk, without even asking.

"*Because*," Poppy whispered, leaning close into my ear, "he basically holds Guillaume's career in his hands. We have to be very, very nice to him."

"Even if he's a jerk?" I whispered back, eyeing him warily. He ignored us and leaned in to look more closely at the photos on my desk.

"Even if he's a jerk," Poppy confirmed.

"Good to know," I said. "Because he is."

"Is what?"

"A jerk."

Poppy looked at me closely. "Methinks thou doth protest too much," she said with some amusement.

I made a face and took a few steps closer to Gabriel.

"You're in my chair," I said bluntly, pointing to the seat he had made himself comfortable in.

"Oh," Gabriel said. He smiled at me for a moment and then stood up. "I'm sorry. I didn't realize. I didn't see anywhere else to sit."

"I didn't realize you'd be staying that long," I said.

"What Emma is trying to say," Poppy interrupted smoothly, stepping in front of me, "is that we would be pleased to help you with whatever you need so that you can be on your way."

She elbowed me in the ribs, and I shrugged. Gabriel, with all his dark-haired, green-eyed good looks, was starting to make me uncomfortable.

"Ah, I see," Gabriel said. He glanced at Poppy then returned his gaze to me, where it lingered a moment longer than it had to. "Well, ladies, I was just stopping in as a favor, actually."

"A favor?" Poppy and I said in unison. We stared at him incredulously.

He looked a bit taken aback by our reaction. "Hey, I can't be a nice guy?" he asked.

"There's a first time for everything," Poppy muttered.

Gabriel looked wounded. "Now that's not fair, Poppy," he said. "I'm just doing my job."

"And we're just doing ours," I said.

Gabriel glanced at me and nodded. "I know," he said. He hesitated a moment and then locked eyes with me. "That's why I thought you'd appreciate knowing that Guillaume has a big night planned Sunday at Buddha Bar. You may want to, er, keep an eye on him. He always gets himself into trouble there."

"He's *never* gotten into trouble there," Poppy corrected quickly.

"Ah, so the fire in the men's room there last month?" Gabriel asked.

"Not his fault," Poppy said, too quickly.

"And the sexual harassment charges from the waitress?"

"A mistake, obviously."

"Hmm," Gabriel said. He stroked his chin thoughtfully.

"That's interesting. How about the drug dealer who was arrested there and told the police he'd sold to Guillaume just the night before?"

"He doesn't do drugs," Poppy said, her voice tight. Oddly, Gabriel still looked amused.

"How is it," I interrupted, "that you somehow know that Guillaume is going to Buddha Bar Sunday night?"

"I have my sources," Gabriel said, fixing me with an even stare.

I cleared my throat. "And you're just here out of the goodness of your heart?"

He laughed. "Not entirely," he said. "I was sort of hoping that you two might remember this next time around. And that you might consider being a bit more honest with me in the future."

"That's it?" Poppy asked.

"Well, that and an exclusive first listen to his album," he said. I could tell he was trying to sound nonchalant. "So that the UPP gets first dibs on reviewing it."

Poppy shook her head. "You're a real piece of work, Gabriel," she said.

He shrugged. "I'm just doing my job."

"To be honest," Poppy said, "I don't actually believe that you have a source that says Guillaume will be at Buddha Bar. I think you're making it up."

Gabriel looked a little troubled. "Okay," he said. "Suit yourself. Don't say I didn't warn you."

He glanced at Poppy and then turned his attention back to me.

"Emma," he said. "It was a pleasure to meet you. Officially, anyhow."

He extended his hand. I reluctantly slipped my hand into his, noticing immediately how warm and big it was. I expected a handshake, but instead, he raised my hand to his lips and kissed the back of it.

"Ladies," he said, nodding at us as he lowered my hand slowly. He hadn't broken eye contact, and I was startled to feel my heart beating more rapidly. My hand still tingled where he had kissed it. "I'm sure I will be seeing you again soon. *Au revoir.*"

With that, he backed out of the office, pulling the door closed behind him.

"Jerk," Poppy muttered once the door was shut.

"Yeah," I said, absently holding my hand up to examine the spot where it had just been kissed. "What a jerk."

Poppy took me to dinner after work that night to celebrate the fact that I had saved her from getting fired the night before—at least temporarily. After first courses of escargots and green salads with a Dijon dressing, I had coq au vin and noodles while Poppy had a steaming bowl of cassoulet—a French stew of beans, sausages, chicken, duck, and tomatoes. We split a bottle of house red and shared a crème brûlée for dessert.

"That's the best chicken I've ever had," I said in awe, patting my full stomach as we left.

Poppy grinned at me. "This isn't even a particularly

good restaurant," she said. "I suspect you're going to like France very much, dear Emma."

I was tired after dinner, but Poppy insisted that we go out again.

"You're never really going to get over Brett, are you, if we sit around the flat moping?" she asked, linking her arm through mine and pulling me along the street. "Besides, it's a Friday night! The perfect night to go meet guys!"

"How do you figure?" I was almost afraid to ask.

"According to *Take Control of Your Lover's Soul*, Fridays are *the* night that men are most psychologically primed to meet women," Poppy said. "It's something about the negative endorphins in their bodies after a long day of work as well as the positive endorphins in their bodies because they know they have two days of relaxation coming up."

I rolled my eyes. She had a theory for everything.

Against my dwindling protests, we wound up at another English-language pub, the Frog & Princess, a microbrewery tucked away in a back alley in the sixth arrondissement near Saint-Germain-des-Prés.

"So what's the deal with Guillaume?" I asked as we settled into seats at the bar, each of us clutching a glass of Maison Blanche, one of the Frog & Princess's house brews. Around us, a Justin Timberlake song blared from the speakers, and a handful of college-age blond girls in jeans gyrated on the dance floor, which was ringed with nervous-looking guys clutching beers like lifelines. Again, except for the smoke and plethora of smoking Frenchmen, it felt suspiciously like I was back at a bar in the United States.

"You've been dying to ask me that all day, haven't you?" Poppy said.

I nodded and smiled. "Maybe. So what's the story? Why does KMG put up with stunts like last night?"

"Because he's really something special," Poppy said. Her face softened a bit. "You haven't seen him perform yet. But don't worry. You'll understand when you do."

"I don't know about that," I said. Although I had to admit that hearing the "City of Light" single had blown me away.

Poppy shook her head. "No, believe me. You think you hate him now. I know; I felt that way, too. But as soon as you see him perform, trust me, you'll fall just a little bit in love with him. That's his charm. That's why he's going to sell millions of records all over the world. That's why he's going to be a bigger star than David Beckham."

"You're comparing him to a soccer player?"

Poppy feigned horror. "A soccer player? First of all, it's called *football*. Second, my dear, David Beckham is so much *more* than a football star. Just as Guillaume Riche is so much more than simply a singer. He will be a household name. Little girls everywhere will have his poster on the wall."

"Or post offices will have his wanted poster," I grumbled.

"Oh, he's harmless," Poppy said dismissively. She laughed, but I could detect a hint of nervousness behind her smile. "He just keeps us on our toes."

"Yeah, about that," I said slowly. "What about what Gabriel Francoeur said? About Buddha Bar?"

"He was just trying to get under our skin," Poppy said quickly.

I hesitated. "Are you sure? I mean, he seemed pretty confident."

"That's Gabriel for you," Poppy said. "He's just messing with our heads. He doesn't have any inside source. That's nonsense."

"He *did* seem to know an awful lot about things in the past that never made the papers," I said carefully.

Poppy shrugged. "So he's a good reporter. Fine. But we cover all our bases so that even when he's right, his editors won't risk going with the story because we make him sound wrong. I know it drives him crazy. This is probably just his attempt to get even."

"Probably," I agreed after a moment. But I wasn't entirely convinced.

"You're moping," Poppy accused me an hour later as she returned from the bar, where she'd been flirting with a tall blond guy. She was holding two beers, one of which she handed to me.

"I'm just tired," I said.

"No," Poppy said. "You're moping. About Brett. Who is a complete tosser."

I couldn't help but laugh. Poppy was so matter-of-fact.

"He's not a tosser," I protested weakly. "We just weren't right for each other."

"Oh, come on," she said, rolling her eyes. "If he didn't want to be with you, he's a wanker. Plain and simple.

You're fabulous. And anyone who can't see that is completely useless."

"Well"—I mustered a smile—"I'll drink to that."

"That's the spirit!" Poppy exclaimed. "Cheers!" We both took a long sip, then Poppy spoke again. "Look, I'll make you a deal," she said. "If I can get you a date within the next thirty minutes, you have to give this thing a try. You have to start dating again. Not to fall for some smooth-talking French guy, but because it's fun and they know how to say all the right things, and believe me, they know how to kiss. And right now you need that."

"Poppy—" I started.

"Didn't you have fun last night?"

"Before or after Guillaume?" I muttered.

She made a face at me. *Before,*" she said. "Obviously."

"Seriously, Poppy," I said after a moment. "I don't think this is going to work. I'm about the most unglamorous person in Paris right now. Even if I wanted to date, I doubt I'd have much luck."

"We'll just see about that," Poppy said with a smile. "Let me work my magic."

Unglamorous or not, I somehow had a date twenty minutes later.

"Told you so!" Poppy singsonged triumphantly as my new Monsieur Right excused himself to go buy us a round of drinks. "I told you I could get you a date!"

"What did you say to him?" I demanded. Poppy had disappeared into the crowd and returned ten minutes later with Thibault (which sounded like *T-bone* when he said it), a thirtysomething architect who lived nearby. He spoke good English, had deep brown eyes rimmed with thick, dark lashes, and was the stereotypical tall, dark, and handsome Frenchman. In short, he seemed perfect. And he'd had the charm turned on full-force since arriving at our table and asking if I'd like to meet him at noon tomorrow at Notre Dame for a little tour of Paris.

"I just said that my very beautiful American friend was new in town and hadn't met anyone yet," Poppy said with a nonchalant shrug. "He wanted to meet you right away."

I looked at her skeptically. "You're kidding me. *That* gorgeous guy wanted to meet *me*?"

Poppy sighed. "I'm getting a little tired of you selling yourself short. You're a doll, and any man would be lucky to have you."

I shrugged and looked away. I didn't believe her.

The next morning, after a quick breakfast of cappuccino and *pains au chocolat* at Café de l'Alma, a little café near our apartment, Poppy and I were standing outside the Galeries Lafayette, the biggest and most famous department store in Paris, when the doors opened at nine thirty. Despite my exhaustion and reluctance to be dragged around what I figured would be an oversize Macy's, I couldn't help but be dazzled when we walked in.

My jaw must have literally dropped, because Poppy started laughing. "I had the same expression on my face the first time I came here," she said. "It's nine floors of pure fashion heaven. If I ever win the lottery, I'm coming here straightaway."

"Oh, my," was all I could manage in reply.

From where we were standing, I could see only the ground floor, but it was breathtaking. There were colorful clothes, beautiful salespeople, and seemingly endless rows of accessories and cosmetics as far as the eye could see, all in dazzlingly bright colors and patterns. I felt like a kid in a candy store. A very big, very beautiful candy store.

But it was the ceiling that really blew me away. Rising above us, nine floors off the ground, was an enormous dome of stained glass and wrought iron, through which the morning light was pouring, illuminating the center arcade. It reminded me of something you might find in an exquisitely decorated old church, except that here we were worshipping at the altar of fashion. Each level of the enormous department store overlooked the ground floor in a beautiful tiered arrangement that made me feel like I was inside a wedding cake. It was like nothing I had ever seen.

"Okay, Wide Eyes," Poppy said after a moment. "Stop gawking. Let's get going."

We had a mission today. Poppy had vowed to help me pick out an outfit for my tour of Paris with Thibault, and we had only two hours before I had to meet him.

"Spending the day with someone creates the perfect opportunity for romance," Poppy informed me solemnly as we wove our way through endless accessories. "It's what *Date for the Day* is all about. It's one of my favorite dating advice books."

I tried not to feel uneasy, thinking of the fact that I was about to go on my first date since Brett.

Poppy took me by the arm and led me past row upon row of jewelry counters, gorgeous handbags, silky hosiery, ornate watches, and facial care displays that promised to restore youthful skin to all buyers. I gaped the whole way. I felt sure this was what my heaven would look like. In fact, I even pinched myself once to make sure I hadn't fallen back asleep on Poppy's floor and dreamed it all.

"Ouch!" I exclaimed when the pinch did, in fact, hurt. Okay, so I was awake.

Poppy glanced at me. "No offense, but you should probably stop staring and start acting nonchalant. You'll fit in a lot better. You look very American at the moment, you know."

I snapped my mouth closed and tried to look casual. Poppy was right. All around me, bored-looking French-women, who looked far too put together for nine thirty on a Saturday morning, browsed among the endless accessories, looking like they weren't impressed at all to be here. It had to be an act! How could they not feel like dancing gleefully through the aisles, touching scarves and bags and belts in all sorts of rich fabrics and beautiful shapes?

"*Bonjour,*" Poppy said to the woman at the Clinique counter as we walked up. The woman's makeup and hair were impeccable, and her black wrap dress looked perfect. I felt even frumpier than usual next to her. "My friend here needs to have her colors done. Do you speak English?"

The woman beamed at me.

"*Oui*, I do speak English, a little," she said. "I would love to do your makeup. Have a seat."

I smiled, feeling suddenly shy as I sat down in the makeup chair.

"I'll leave you here for a bit," Poppy said. "Good luck! I love this counter. They always do such a great job."

Thirty minutes later, when she returned to retrieve me, I was a whole new person.

The makeup artist, whose name was Ana, chattered pleasantly in broken English while plucking foundations, blushes, shadows, and lipsticks from the enormous counter beside us as if it was second nature. She wouldn't let me look in the mirror until she was done.

"*Voilà!*" she said finally. Poppy grinned at me. "What do you think?"

Ana handed me a mirror. I hardly recognized the woman reflected in it.

Gone were the constant dark circles beneath my eyes and the reddish shade of my chin, something I'd never been able to correct on my own. My skin looked silky smooth and completely even, yet natural at the same time. My cheeks had a healthy, dewy flush to them, and my lips were a perfect shade of pale pink.

"Emma, you're lovely!" Poppy exclaimed.

"I can't believe it," I replied. I looked at Ana in astonishment. "How did you do that?"

She laughed. "Nothing complicated. I used a little more foundation, a different color *rouge*, and better moisturizer. You're really quite pretty."

I bought all the makeup on the spot (despite the fact that I hadn't received my first paycheck—but really, how could I not?) and, with a final thank-you, followed Poppy upstairs to the women's clothing department.

An hour later, after paying for a sheer pink blouse and a cream-colored tulip skirt that fit just as perfectly, I went back to the dressing room to change into my new clothes and then let Poppy help me pick out a pair of shoes to match. We settled on a silky pair of ballet flats in the same color as the new shirt, as I figured I'd need something easy to walk in if I was going to be accompanying my new Frenchman around Paris all day.

Poppy walked me to Notre Dame by eleven forty-five, and as we parted ways, she gave me a peck on the cheek.

"Your date is going to be fabulous," she reassured me. "You look beautiful. Thibault will fall for you in an instant. Trust me, you're going to love your new city. And Paris is going to love you right back."

Chapter Eight

Poppy had actually succeeded in getting me excited about my date.

I hadn't expected to feel that way. After all, the Brett wound was still wide open. Being dismissed nonchalantly by the man I'd been with for three years, the man I'd planned to *marry* in September, wasn't exactly confidence inspiring.

And while I still felt vaguely like I was betraying Brett in some way (although I knew that was utterly illogical), there was also a part of me that was looking forward to spending the day with someone new. After all, as Poppy had said, it wasn't like I was going to spend my life with this guy. It was just a few hours. And maybe there *was* something to be said for being with someone who made me feel attractive and interesting. I hadn't felt that way around Brett in quite a while.

Despite myself, I had to admit that there was something to Poppy's theory. Or at least to the magic of this city. I couldn't help but feel a bit overwhelmed by the romance of it all as I sat in a little park in front of Notre Dame, gazing up at the seven-hundred-year-old Gothic church with its stately towers and soaring stained-glass windows.

As I waited, I let my imagination wander. Perhaps Thibault would arrive with red roses. Don't Frenchmen always go around giving red roses to their dates in movies? I felt sure he'd give me a peck on each cheek and perhaps gallantly take my small hand in his strong one as he led me into the church, where he had promised we would begin our Parisian tour by climbing the steps to one of Notre Dame's towers. Perhaps afterward we'd take a little boat ride on the Seine, followed by a trip to the top of the Eiffel Tower, then dinner in some yummy French restaurant.

I felt a little shiver of anticipation. And then, just as quickly, I felt a little pang of guilt. I knew it was ridiculous, but waiting for a romantic date in this romantic city so soon after my breakup made me feel a little like I was cheating on Brett.

"Stop thinking about him. He left you," I said aloud, prompting an odd look from the woman on the other end of the bench. She stared at me for a moment. Then she closed the book she was reading, stood up, and hurried away.

Okay, so perhaps I should avoid talking to myself in public. Duly noted.

I *hated* that I missed Brett. Poppy would have killed me for saying so, but I would have given anything in that moment to be waiting for Brett to turn the corner of the cathedral to sweep me off my feet, declare how wrong he had been, and take me on a whirlwind tour of the City of Love.

But no, I shouldn't think like that. Brett was in the past. Thibault was in the future.

My French knight in shining armor would be here at any moment.

Except Thibault never showed up.

I waited until twelve fifteen before I called Poppy from the cell phone she'd given me yesterday (presumably to be reachable twenty-four hours a day, so that I could come running whenever Guillaume got himself into a scrape).

"You're kidding," she said flatly when I announced that my date was a no-show.

"Nope."

She hesitated for a moment. "Maybe he's just late. Give him another fifteen minutes."

So I did. I sat back down on the bench and tried to distract myself by trying to guess the nationality of the tourists who streamed by my perch.

Fifteen minutes came and went. Still no Thibault. I'd been stood up.

So much for my confidence-inspiring leap back into the dating pool.

I pulled out my phone to call Poppy back. Then I stopped. What was she going to say that would make me feel better? I didn't want to go back to her tiny apartment and mope about my bad luck with guys. I'd done quite enough of that on my own, thank you. And wasn't it Poppy who had gotten me into this mess in the first place? I felt pathetic.

I sighed and stood up from the bench. I didn't need a

guy to see Paris with, did I? I'd take myself to lunch and go on my own tour of the city.

Trying not to think about the fact that I'd just been dumped *before* the first date (a new record for me), I walked west on the Île de la Cité, then I crossed to the Right Bank over the Pont Neuf, feeling my heart leap a bit as I looked off to the left and saw the tip of the Eiffel Tower soaring above the gleaming water. I should have known better than to spoil my time here by letting Poppy talk me into trying out some dating game.

I found a little café across the street from the water on the Right Bank, just to the left of the bridge. As I ducked inside the dimly lit café, which had burgundy walls and neatly spaced little round tables of dark wood, the waiter at the door said something to me in French, but of course I didn't understand.

I shook my head. *"Je ne parle pas français,"* I mumbled, feeling like an idiot.

He smirked a bit at me. "Ah, *une americaine,*" he said, as if it were a bad word. "Sit anywhere."

"Merci." I nodded and walked to a table for two by the window, overlooking the sidewalk outside, which filled with Parisians and tourists hurrying to and fro. Off to the left, I knew, was the Hôtel de Ville, Paris's ornate city hall. Off to the right was the enormous Louvre. Perhaps I'd join the crowds and see it after lunch today.

I glanced around and noticed several clusters of people close to the bar. One group, obviously American, judging from their baseball caps, sneakers, and loudly familiar accents, were chugging beer.

The waiter came and plunked down a menu in front of me without a word. I glanced at it and realized immediately it was all in French.

"Um, excuse me!" I said. The waiter stopped in his tracks and turned. "Do you have a menu in English?"

He smirked at me some more. "No. Only French."

"Oh." I was temporarily deflated. I reached into my bag, where I kept *Just Enough French*, a little French travel dictionary I'd picked up at the airport before I left the States. I flipped to the "In a Restaurant" section and began to try to decipher the menu. I hadn't thought I'd need it today, I thought glumly. I'd thought I'd have a handsome Frenchman with me to serve as a translator. But no such luck.

"You would like a large Coca-Cola?" the waiter asked a moment later, reappearing at my elbow.

I looked up in confusion. "No. I'll have a café au lait and a glass of water, please."

"What? No Coca-Cola?" He smirked some more. "I cannot believe it."

"No," I repeated, puzzled.

"All Americans want Coca-Cola," he said. He laughed. "A large Coca-Cola for all Americans!"

Then he pranced away, leaving me staring after him.

"Just ignore him," said a voice from behind me. I turned and saw a sandy-haired guy with thin-rimmed glasses sitting a few tables away, by himself, with a tattered paperback open in front of him. He looked like he was about my age, and he spoke with a thick French accent. "There is a certain stereotype of some Americans. It's silly, really."

I attempted a smile. "Do we all really order large Coca-Colas?"

"Most of you do, yes." He grinned. "You are new in the city?"

I nodded. "I just got here a week ago."

"You are dining alone?" he asked. He closed his book and peered closely at me.

I hesitated then nodded. "Yes. I was supposed to meet someone, but . . . Well, it doesn't matter, does it?"

"May I join you?" he asked. It should have sounded presumptuous, but somehow it didn't. He didn't make a move to stand up, as if waiting for my approval before his next step.

I hesitated. After all, I didn't know this guy. And hadn't I just made a self-aware promise to be independent and experience Paris alone for the day?

"I'll help you translate the menu," the guy prompted with a smile.

I hesitated. I *did* need help. "Well . . . okay."

He picked up his book and his mug of coffee and made his way over to my table.

"I'm Sébastien," he said. He smiled and sat down in the chair beside mine.

Over a deliciously heavy lunch of *magret de canard à l'orange*, incredibly tender duck breast in a Grand Marnier sauce, and a bottle of red Burgundy, Sébastien and I chatted, and as the wine warmed me up, I found myself beginning to enjoy talking with him.

He said that he was thirty-one and a computer programmer who lived in a tiny apartment in the Latin Quarter, the neighborhood directly across the river, which was rife with students and nightlife. Every Saturday, he said, he took a stroll around Paris and chose a different restaurant to try. Today, he had chosen this one, Café Margot. He was three-quarters of the way through a Gérard de Nerval novel and had been looking forward to finishing it over lunch.

"Then why did you let me interrupt you?" I asked.

"You looked like you needed some help with the waiter." He grinned. "Once he said *Coca-Cola*, I knew there was a problem. Plus, I love to practice my English."

He winked at me, and I could feel myself blushing.

"So," he said after a moment, "you have had a tour of Paris, *non*?"

I shook my head. "No," I admitted sheepishly. "I was going to do that today."

I neglected to mention that I hadn't thought to bring a guidebook along, as I'd assumed I'd be meeting a Frenchman for a romantic tour of the city. So much for that idea.

Sébastien looked at me for a long moment. "I know the perfect place to show you. If you will allow me?"

I studied his face for a moment. He was, after all, a total stranger. But he had translated the menu for me and seemed pleasant enough. And hadn't I promised Poppy that I'd give this dating thing a try? Not that Sébastien's proposal necessarily constituted a date.

Besides, I'd been ready to spend a day with Thibault, whom I really didn't know at all either, right? At least Sébastien was right here and wasn't likely to stand me up.

"Okay," I agreed. "Where do you want to go?"

"To the most magical *quartier* in Paris," He leaned forward and smiled at me. "Montmartre. It is the neighborhood of *les artistes* and the bohemians. It is Paris as it is meant to be. Plus, from the steps of Sacré-Coeur, you can see all the city. *C'est très impressionnant.* It is magic."

My only experience with Montmartre so far had been at the Hôtel Jeremie on Thursday night with an insane rock star. That hadn't exactly been so magical.

"Please? May I show you my Paris today?" Sébastien's eyes sparkled as he looked at me imploringly. I hesitated a moment. What did I have to lose?

"Yes," I said slowly. "That sounds wonderful."

And it was.

After lunch—which Sébastien insisted on paying for, despite my protests—we took a long walk up the Rue du Louvre, passing the famous museum, which I couldn't take my eyes off. It was absolutely massive; it seemed to go on forever.

"It's the largest art museum in the world," said Sébastien, who was evidently taking his job as tour guide seriously. He led me up through the second and the ninth arrondissements, pointing out sights along the way, and at the foot of a big hill he pointed upward.

"That's Sacré-Coeur," he said. "Do you know it?"

I looked up at the glistening white Byzantine-looking dome and shook my head. I'd heard of it, of course, and seen it in photographs. I knew it was one of Paris's most famous landmarks. But I was ashamed to admit I didn't know a thing about it.

"It was begun in the late 1800s after the war with Prussia and was *consacré* after *la Premiere Guerre Mondiale*, the First World War," Sébastien said as we walked. "It is built of stone from Château-Landon. The most amazing thing about the church is that the stone constantly releases *le calcium*—I believe it is the same in your language—which means that it stays forever white."

The afternoon was amazing. Sébastien took my hand as we rode a funicular up the hill to the top of Montmartre, and I didn't pull away. His palms were soft and his fingers just a little rough as they threaded through mine. We saw the inside of the church, ate sugared crêpes on the church steps as we gazed out over the hazy city, visited the Musée de Montmartre and the Salvador Dalí museum, and even had a street artist sketch a portrait of us in the Place du Tertre, a square that Sébastien called the tourist center of the *quartier*.

When darkness fell, Sébastien took me to dinner at a tiny place called Le Refuge des Fondues that was like nothing I'd ever seen. The narrow dining room had space for only two very long tables, so everyone in the packed restaurant ate together. After waiting for a spot for twenty minutes, Sébastien and I were shown to the back of the room, where a gruff French waiter had to help me climb on top of the table to cross to the other side. I had to basically straddle the table, hovering over other laughing diners, to the bench on the other side. The second we sat down, we were handed small glasses of kir royale, and the moment we finished those, we were offered red wine—in baby bottles!

"Baby bottles?" I'd asked Sébastien incredulously, inspecting the bottle that had been handed to me. It even had a nipple!

"This place is a favorite of Americans!" he shouted back over the din.

We talked and laughed over a little feast of olives, cheese cubes, spicy potatoes, and *saucisson* sausage, several wine refills, and the most enormous fondue meal I'd ever had. The huge yellow pot of silky white cheese between us never ran dry, and our waiter seemed to be constantly refilling our bread basket. Just when I thought I couldn't eat any more, the waiter brought over dessert—lemon sorbet frozen into hollowed-out lemon halves—and two small glasses of Alsatian sweet white wine, which Sébastien had ordered for us.

"What a perfect day!" I exclaimed as we left the restaurant and walked out onto the winding, cobbled Rue des Trois Frères to make our way toward a main street to find a taxi stand.

"I'm glad you had a nice time," Sébastien replied. He reached up and touched my cheek gently. My world was spinning a bit, maybe from his touch, maybe from the wine. Either way, when he leaned down to kiss me, it felt amazing.

Is this what I'd been missing in all those years of kissing

Brett? *No wonder French kissing was named after these guys*, I thought. His lips were soft, and as his tongue gently parted my lips and probed my mouth, I could feel my toes curl up in pleasure.

"You taste like lemon," Sébastien said as he pulled away.

"You taste like wine," I said with a smile, blinking at him a few times and trying to regain my balance.

"You are so beautiful," he said, his voice soft.

I could feel myself blush. "Thank you." I couldn't remember the last time anyone had said that to me. "May I ask you something?"

"Anything," Sébastien replied with a charming smile. He ran a finger slowly down the bridge of my nose, ending at the bow of my lips. I could feel my whole body come alive with goose bumps.

"What made you talk to me at the café today?" I asked. "What made you want to stop reading your book and spend the day with me?"

Sébastien studied my face for a moment. "You seemed lost," he said. "And," he hastened to add, "very beautiful. I would have been foolish not to suggest us spending the day together."

Although the words sounded vaguely rehearsed, they did something to me. I couldn't seem to stop smiling. No one had said anything that romantic to me in a long time.

Thirty minutes later, we stood outside Poppy's building, with Sébastien gazing into my eyes.

"May I come inside?" he asked, brushing the hair back from my face.

"My roommate is there," I said, my voice full of apology. "It's a really small place."

"I cannot spend the night?" Sébastien asked. The question startled me. He'd been a perfect gentleman all day, and the only moves he'd made had been to hold my hand as we strolled and to kiss me after dinner.

"Um, no," I stammered. "I mean, there's really not room."

"But you are American," he said, looking baffled.

I'm sure my expression was equally confused. I had no idea what he was getting at. "What does that matter?"

"American girls are usually happy to spend the night," he said.

I frowned. "What are you implying?"

He backed off. "Nothing, nothing," he said hastily. "Maybe another day, then? When your roommate is out?" He moved closer and ran his thumb lightly along my bottom lip.

I didn't know what to say. "Um, maybe." After all, the kiss had been amazing, even if he was being a little pushy now.

"You will give me your phone number, then?" he asked.

I almost gave it to him. But then I paused. After all, what did I expect would happen with Sébastien? We'd had a nice day, but I wasn't looking for a relationship, was I? I tried to keep Poppy's words in mind. It was *okay* to go out with someone without turning him instantly into the man of my dreams.

"Why don't you give me yours instead?" I asked. He looked taken aback, but he acquiesced, scribbling his mobile number on a piece of paper.

"You will call?" he asked uncertainly. "I hope you will call."

"Maybe," I said. I felt a bit mean. But at the same time, the noncommittal answer filled me with a little rush of power. Perhaps it was nice to know that I could go to bed tonight without a stomach full of butterflies, without wondering if the man would call *me*.

"It has been a pleasure spending the day with you, Emma," Sébastien said formally. He leaned in and kissed me again, a long, lingering, probing kiss this time. I knew it was supposed to make me change my mind. I knew I was supposed to grow weak in the knees and invite Sébastien in despite my earlier refusal. And I very nearly did.

After all, it was the perfect French kiss.

But perhaps that didn't mean anything at all.

Chapter Nine

"Ah, so you met Sébastien?" Poppy said, eyeing me in amusement the next morning.

I was confused at Poppy's reaction. She'd been in bed by the time I arrived home, and I'd been eager to get up the next morning to tell her about my unexpected date the day before. Perhaps, I thought, she'd been right about the potential of these French guys after all.

"What?" I asked. "You know him? That's impossible." How could she know a person I'd randomly encountered in a city of millions?

"Let me guess," she said drily. "He was tall with glasses. Sitting alone. Reading a novel. Told you he goes to a different café each week?"

I stared. Was she clairvoyant? "Yes," I said. "But how . . . ?"

"I met him my second week in Paris," she said, the left corner of her mouth curling upward into a smile she was clearly trying to fight. "I'd been taking a walk near Notre Dame, and it started to rain, so I ducked into Café Margot. He was there, reading a Gérard de Nerval book. The moment he realized I was British, he came right over."

"What?" My mouth felt dry.

"I didn't realize until I was telling my American friend Lauren about it that it's apparently his routine," Poppy said. "He did the exact same thing to her. Wined her, dined her, took her on a tour of Montmartre, got her drunk at that great fondue place up there. Is that what happened to you?"

"Yes," I said, flabbergasted.

"Right. Me, too. And then he walks you home and asks if he can come in?" Poppy finished the story for me.

I gaped at her and nodded silently.

"Well, at least you were smart enough to say no," she said. "I wasn't as smart. He wound up spending the night."

"You're kidding," I said flatly.

"Not at all." Poppy grinned. "Nothing happened. But imagine how foolish I felt when I told Lauren the story and found out the same thing had happened to her."

"Probably just about as foolish as I feel right now," I muttered.

"Don't feel that way," Poppy said brightly. "That's the game they play. They know exactly how to woo you. But as soon as they get what they want, they're on to the next conquest. It just proves my point. You have to jump ship before you get too attached."

I was feeling a little ill. "Are all French guys like this?" I asked in horror.

Poppy laughed. "No. I believe Sébastien is a rare case. But he's a great example of why you can't believe a word they say. Never. Men just want to tell you lies, whether they're French or American or British. It's universal. At least according to Janice Clark-Meyers, the author of *Different Language, Same Men*."

I looked at her for a moment. "You sound awfully bitter," I said carefully. "Darren must have really hurt you."

Poppy looked away. "No. I'm just a realist."

Poppy went out Sunday evening to meet some guy for drinks, and I spent the time finally unpacking my two massive suitcases, hanging clothes in my tiny wardrobe chest and putting away T-shirts, lingerie, and nightgowns in the little drawers under my bed.

I was lost in trying to decide whether to put my shoes under my bed or buy an over-the-door shoe rack somewhere when the phone rang, startling me.

"Emma, I've missed you," said Brett's familiar voice on the other end when I picked up. I froze, stunned. It had been nearly five weeks since I'd last seen him, and already his voice sounded unfamiliar to me. "Your sister gave me your number," he added. "It hasn't been the same here without you."

I breathed into the phone. I didn't know what to say. Had he, by some sixth sense, realized that for the first time last night, I'd fallen asleep without thinking about him? I'd just been getting used to a life without him.

"Emma? Are you there?"

"Brett," I said finally, trying to keep the wobble out of my voice. "Why are you calling?"

"Because I miss you," he said, sounding wounded. "Don't you miss me?"

"No," I said. There was silence on the other end, and I felt guilty—not just for hurting his feelings but because it was a lie. I *did* miss him. But that was pathetic, wasn't it?

"I shouldn't have said the things I did," he said after a moment. "I was stupid, and I'm so sorry. It was all a mistake."

I was silent. I didn't know what to say.

"What about Amanda?" I asked finally.

There was silence and then heavy breathing on the other end of the line.

"You know about that?" he asked in a small voice.

I didn't bother answering. "You're such an asshole," I said instead.

"Oh, Emma, I'm so, so sorry," he said quickly, his words tumbling out on top of each other. "Emma. Please. Can you hear me? I'm sorry. More sorry than you know. It was just a mistake. A huge mistake. I was trying to get over you."

"That's an interesting technique," I muttered. "If it doesn't work out with your fiancée, screw her best friend?"

Brett sighed and continued. "Emma. Please. I don't know how to tell you how sorry I am. But I love you. I still want to marry you. I just got cold feet, that's all."

It was exactly what I'd wanted to hear five weeks ago. But now his words just made me feel empty and confused.

"Emma, will you come home?" Brett asked. "Please? Give me another chance?"

I walked into the living room and sat down on the sofa, facing the window. Outside, mere yards away, the Eiffel

Tower loomed like a reminder of all I had yet to discover in this city.

"No," I said finally, trying to sound far more confident than I felt. "I think this is where I belong now."

I hung up before he had a chance to protest.

"Well, it was what he deserved," Poppy said at work the next morning as she leaned over me to grab a permanent marker from the other side of the conference table. We had arrived early to work on the layout for the cover of the press folder for Guillaume's London launch. We couldn't agree on the perfect photo to use; I wanted to use one where Guillaume was holding his guitar and smiling, while Poppy wanted to find one where he had on his signature sexy sulk.

"Are you sure?" I asked as I took a sip of coffee and studied the display of photos we had laid out in front of us. "I mean, maybe it just took him a little while to realize what a huge mistake he'd made. Maybe he *did* just get cold feet."

"You were with the guy for three years," Poppy recapped. She picked up two of the photos and put them in our discard pile. "You've been engaged for almost a year. And then suddenly he dumps you and tells you to move out? I don't care whether he's changed his mind or not. Is that really the kind of guy you'd want to be with?"

"I guess not," I muttered. We worked in silence for a few minutes.

I tried hard to concentrate on the task at hand. Guillaume's single was due to hit airwaves around the world that night, so it was a big day for us. *Focus on Guillaume*, I told myself. *Not on Brett.*

"So," I said lightly, trying to change the subject. "I guess Gabriel *was* wrong about Guillaume getting into trouble at Buddha Bar last night."

"I told you he was full of it," Poppy said.

"You were right," I said. "How stupid of me to have believed him."

"Not stupid," Poppy said. "Just naive. You can't trust these reporters, though."

"I'm sure they're saying the same thing about us," I said.

Poppy grinned. "Yes, and they're absolutely right."

We finally agreed on a photo of Guillaume in a Cuban-looking military jacket with sliced-up sleeves that showed off his incredible arm muscles. In the picture, he was holding his custom-made red Les Paul guitar, which he had nicknamed Lucie, after his little sister, and he was giving the camera one of his signature smoldering looks that was practically enough to make any red-blooded woman melt on the spot.

"Okay, I've got to run to that lunch meeting in London," Poppy said after we'd called the printer and added the photo to the layout we'd already given them for the press pack, which they'd have printed and ready for us by the end of the week. "Will you be okay on your own for the afternoon? You have plenty to keep you busy, right?"

Poppy had a one fifteen meeting in London with the president of the British Music Press Association that she'd spent the past few days preparing for. She'd catch the eleven thirteen Eurostar out of Gare du Nord in time to make it to a restaurant just outside the train station in London for lunch. She'd leave just after three to make it home in time for dinner. It was amazing how quickly you could hop between the two national capitals.

"Of course," I said brightly. I'd been here a week now, and thanks to eight years of working in the industry, I certainly knew how to handle myself around a PR office. On top of that, I was getting excited about Guillaume's London launch. It would be one of the biggest projects I'd ever been involved in, and I was proud of the work Poppy and I had already done. I had dozens of calls to make to American music journalists that afternoon, and I needed to verify some things with the London hotel where we'd be holding the event in less than three weeks.

"Okay, sweetie," Poppy said, getting up to grab her handbag, which was a perfect-looking Kelly knockoff. "Wish me luck. I'll have my mobile on if you need me."

Thirty minutes later, I had made five media calls, all of which went well. I was particularly happy with the chat I'd had with a London-based writer from *Rolling Stone*, who had promised she'd be at the junket.

"Guillaume Riche looks just yummy!" she had exclaimed. "And the advance copy of the 'City of Light' single you sent me sounds amazing. You really have a star on your hands!"

The call had left me with a warm glow, which is exactly

what I was basking in when my phone rang again. Assuming it was one of the British journalists I'd left a message for calling me back, I cheerfully answered the phone, "Emma Sullivan, Millar PR!"

A deep voice on the other end of the line blurted out several sentences in French.

"I'm sorry," I said quickly, interrupting the flood of words. Even if I couldn't understand the language, I knew he was upset. *"Je ne parle pas français."*

I was getting awfully tired of saying that.

"Who eez thees?" the voice asked in thickly accented English. "Where eez Poppy?"

"Poppy is away at a meeting," I said. "This is her new colleague, Emma. I'm also working on Guillaume Riche's English-language launch. Is there something I can help you with?"

There was dead silence on the other end.

"Yes," the man said finally. "Emma, you must hurry. This eez Guillaume's manager, Raf. I'm een Dijon, so you are going to have to help me."

"Help you with what?"

"Guillaume just called me," Raf said rapidly. "Emma, he somehow fell asleep een a storage room near ze lifts on ze second floor of ze Eiffel Tower last night."

I gasped. "What?"

"I'm afraid eet eez true," Raf said. "The morning cleaning crew discovered heem, and as you can imagine, he eez een a lot of trouble."

I groaned. "Could it get any worse?" I asked rhetorically. Only it turned out the question wasn't so rhetorical after all.

Raf paused for another moment.

"Well, yes, eet could," he said with a sigh. "There eez one more thing I may have forgotten to mention. The young lady he was with clearly thought eet would be amusing to steal heez clothes while he slept. So eet seems he was een ze lift with just heez briefs when ze crew found him."

"What?"

"Mais oui."

"Where is he now?" I asked, starting to panic.

"He's een ze Eiffel Tower security office being interrogated," Raf said, his voice sounding weary. "But there eez a lot of press outside—ze same journalists who have been bothering heem for a week, mostly. You are going to need to get down there and do some damage control."

Raf read me Guillaume's mobile number and told me that the tower's security manager had already okayed a press rep being allowed in to speak to him. I was to call him as soon as I got to the tower, and I'd be escorted up.

"Emma, there eez one piece of good news een all of thees," Raf added at the end. "The security guards have not called ze police. They know who Guillaume is and prefer to handle this privately. So there may be some opportunity there for you to sort things out."

"Okay," I said. "Thanks."

I hung up and pounded my head on the desk for a moment. This couldn't be happening.

I dialed Poppy's mobile number, but there was no answer. I tried again. Still nothing. I left her a panicked message explaining the situation. Then I dialed Véronique's number. I was sure that she—or one of the company's in-house PR reps—would know how to handle things.

"Well, you obviously need to take care of this," she said calmly when I was done recapping my conversation with Raf. Why was it that the French never seemed to panic?

"Me?" I tried to stop myself from freaking out. "But I can't reach Poppy!"

"Unless I'm mistaken," Véronique said, her voice cold, "you are being paid as part of Guillaume's PR team. So if you and Poppy want to keep your jobs, I suggest you hurry down to the Eiffel Tower to solve this little problem before word gets out. Or should I hire another PR firm that is more reliable?"

I sat there in shock for a moment before mumbling a reply, slamming down the phone, and hurrying out of the office.

"Oh, dear, Emma, I am so sorry I can't be there," Poppy whispered into the phone when she called me back fifteen minutes later. I was en route to the Eiffel Tower, and I'd broken out in a cold sweat in the back of the cab. "I'm already on the train. We've left the station."

"I understand," I said through gritted teeth. "But what am I supposed to do?"

"I don't know," Poppy whispered back. "Lie?"

"Yeah." I shook my head. "I'm going to get lots of practice with that here, aren't I?"

"Look, I'll call you as soon as I'm done," Poppy said. "I'm so sorry to make you handle this on your own."

I asked the cabbie to swing by the Celio store on the Rue de Rivoli on the way. He waited while I dashed inside to buy Guillaume a shirt, cargo pants, and flip-flops. I guessed on his size, assuming that even if the clothes weren't exactly right, he'd appreciate wearing something other than his underwear when he was escorted outside.

Ten minutes later, the cab drew to a halt in front of the Eiffel Tower.

"You will love it!" the driver said, turning around to me with a smile. Obviously he'd mistaken me for a care-free tourist. "It eez ze best tourist sight in Paris. You must go up to ze top."

"Uh-huh," I said, counting out his fare with trembling hands. I could feel sweat beading at my brow.

"Oh, no, do not be nervous!" he exclaimed. "I see you are transpiring." I guessed he meant *perspiring*. "But do not worry," he went on encouragingly. "There are guardrails. It eez completely safe."

"Merci beaucoup," I mumbled, pressing a handful of bills into his hand. "Keep the change."

"Just take ze deep breaths and you will be fine, *ma-demoiselle!*" the cabdriver shouted behind me as I slammed the door and began my dash across the courtyard to the entrance. "It eez nothing to panic about!"

Unfortunately, before I reached the tower, I had to pass a horde of journalists clustered near the base of its west pillar. Gabriel was the only one who spotted me as I tried to sneak by.

"Emma!" he shouted out. The other reporters, snapped

to attention by his voice, spun to face me, too. Suddenly I was in the center of a storm of questions that were being hurled toward me far faster than I could respond to them.

"Is it true that Guillaume Riche is in custody inside the Eiffel Tower?"

"Was he drunk?"

"Has he been taken to jail?"

"Will this delay his album launch?"

"Does KMG have an official statement?"

"No," I muttered, trying to make my way past them.

"What about the allegation that he was trapped in the tower overnight?" Gabriel's oddly American-sounding voice rose above the others. "Are you denying it?"

"I don't know what you're talking about." There was hardly room to move as I elbowed through the crowd. I quickly explained who I was to one of the guards, who thankfully spoke enough English to understand. He radioed someone, and in a moment he reluctantly ushered me through and pointed me toward the south pillar.

"What about the allegation that he's naked?" Gabriel yelled after me as I began to stride away, trying to stop myself from panicking.

"Not true." I stopped and glared at Gabriel. Who did he think he was anyhow?

"Then what are you doing here if there's nothing going on?" Gabriel asked smugly. His deep green eyes sparkled triumphantly behind his thin-rimmed glasses. He grinned at me, and I was disappointed to realize that his dimples were just as charming, even when he was annoying the heck out of me. Which was unfortunate, because I really wanted to dislike Gabriel Francoeur.

"Er . . . we're doing a promotional thing for his new album, *Riche*, which will have its launch party two weeks from Saturday," I said, thinking quickly. I glanced at Gabriel and then at the other journalists. "I'm sorry you all appear to have been misinformed again. But I hope you're looking forward to the album release as much as I am."

With that, I began striding toward the entrance.

"If there's nothing wrong," I could hear Gabriel shouting behind me, "then bring Guillaume out to talk to us when you're done inside!"

I ignored him and tried to swallow the lump in my throat. I clutched the Celio bag tighter. How could I bring him out past the media horde if he was in custody? I was in serious trouble here. I had no idea how I would talk the security guards out of having Guillaume arrested.

After a quick consultation with a security manager outside the tower, I was escorted sixty yards up to the first level by elevator. I hardly had time to marvel at the fact that, for the first time in years, I was once again inside one of my favorite buildings in the world. I barely noticed the intricate, crisscrossing geometric ironwork of the tower as we were whisked quickly up toward what I suspected would be a much crazier scene than the Hôtel Jeremie last week.

My escort led me down a series of hallways on the first floor and into a small office behind the Eiffel Tower's post office, where I was introduced to two of the security guards who had Guillaume in custody.

"Where is he?" I asked wearily. Smirking, one of the guards gestured toward a closed door in the back.

"Bonne chance, mademoiselle," he said. Good luck, miss.

The guard opened the door for me, and for a moment I just stood there, staring.

Inside the small, mostly bare room, Guillaume was sitting in a plastic chair, naked but for a pair of faded Hanes briefs, which were red with a thick white band around the waist. He had one leg crossed casually over the other and was reading a tattered copy of *Fear and Loathing in Las Vegas*. And as if things couldn't get any stranger, he was wearing a black top hat. A black cane with a white tip was propped against the chair.

"Allons-y," the officer urged. Let's go. I gulped and stepped inside. The officer slammed the door behind me with a definitive bang, and Guillaume looked up. He stared at me for a moment as if trying to place me, then blinked a few times and grinned.

"Ah, *bonjour*, Emma!" he said brightly, as if I had just dropped in on him in his penthouse as opposed to a security cell in the Eiffel Tower. He snapped his book shut and set it down. "You are looking lovely this morning."

I tried to control my impulse to blush—and also my impulse to stare at his mostly naked body. "Guillaume, what on earth are you doing?"

"It's not my fault, Emma," he said with a casual shrug. He tipped his top hat to me and stood up lazily. I blinked a few times and looked away. After all, it was irrelevant that his was the nicest body I'd ever laid eyes on, right?

"I'm sure you're totally innocent, once again," I said

drily. I thrust the Celio bag at him. "Please get dressed, Guillaume," I said, still trying not to look too closely.

He looked at me for a moment then took the bag from me. He peered inside and his face lit up. "Emma!" he exclaimed. "You brought me clothes! How nice! And I didn't get you anything! How rude of me!"

I glanced back at him. He was smiling happily, as if there were nothing in the world wrong with the present situation.

"Yeah, I'm a real angel," I muttered. I looked him up and down. "What exactly were you doing, anyhow?"

Guillaume regarded me blankly. "I was doing a dance number, Emma," he said.

"A *dance* number?"

He nodded. "Want to see?"

"Not particularly," I said.

Guillaume smiled and shook his head. "Oh, Emma, where is your sense of adventure?"

"I don't know," I muttered. "Where are your clothes?"

He ignored me. "I was just seeing what it was like to be Fred Astaire. You're American. You should appreciate that, right?"

With that, he stood, dropped the bagful of clothing on the ground, and picked up the cane.

"Guillaume—"

He held up a hand. "Do not interrupt the artistic process, Emma."

He closed his eyes, breathed in and out, and whispered, "Zen." Then, wearing just his red briefs and top hat, he began to do a little barefoot tap dance.

"*Have you seen the well-to-do,*" Guillaume began to sing loudly in a booming voice, waving his cane grandly around.

I stared in horrified awe as he pranced back and forth in the little cell, swinging his cane, tipping his hat, kicking his legs up and dancing around me until he concluded with, *"Puttin' on the Ritz!"*

There was a moment of silence after Guillaume finished the song, on his knees, the top hat in one hand and the cane in the other. He looked at me hopefully, and I sensed that I was supposed to applaud.

Instead, I shook my head slowly. "You are seriously insane," I said.

Guillaume pouted, dropping his hat and cane dejectedly to the floor. "Aw, Emma, I'm just having a little fun."

I closed my eyes for a moment and took a deep breath. "Okay, Guillaume, wonderful," I said. "Seriously, would you put some clothes on and let me deal with this? Otherwise you're going to be performing your next dance routine at the local jail."

"I was going to suggest you join me," Guillaume sulked. "You'd be great dancing with me to 'Cheek to Cheek.' It's my favorite Astaire number, you know."

"Maybe some other time," I said. "Now please? Get dressed!"

Guillaume looked a bit disappointed, but he picked up the Celio bag, pulled out the shirt, and shrugged. "Whatever you say, Emma," he said sadly as he began to pull the shirt over his head. I lingered a second longer than I needed to (hey, it's not every day you get to see the world's most handsome man in his underwear, okay?), then made my way back out to the main office, where I asked who was in charge. The Eiffel Tower security chief offered me a seat and called over the two other guards who were standing in the room.

"I'm so sorry about this," I said after introducing myself and apologizing for my lack of French proficiency. "What happened?"

In broken English, the security manager described how a guard who'd just started his morning shift had found the nearly naked Guillaume fast asleep in a room near the tower's south pillar. They couldn't imagine how he had snuck in, as security at the tower had been tight since 2001. It had taken the guard several minutes to wake the snoring Guillaume; he had then alerted his superior and escorted the singer to the security office. That's when Guillaume began doing his little tap-dance routine.

"He continued to say he was Fred Astaire," said one of the guards, scratching his head. "And he began to sing a song about tomatoes, tomahtoes, potatoes, and potahtoes."

"That is when I realized that it wasn't just some bum," the security manager interrupted, leaning forward conspiratorially. "It was Guillaume Riche! One of the most famous celebrities in France!"

I sighed. "Yes. That's why an incident like this could really be a problem for his image, you understand."

The manager exchanged glances with his two deputies.

"I thought so," he said with a nod, looking back at me. He lowered his voice. "That's why we're prepared to . . . negotiate."

I looked at him blankly. "Negotiate?"

His eyes darted from side to side then settled on me. *"Oui,"* he said. "We can do a little, how you say, exchange? And we can forget that this happened. We have not called the police yet."

"Okay," I said slowly, not quite understanding what he meant by an *exchange.* "But the police obviously know there's something going on, right? I mean, there are dozens of reporters outside."

"Oui," the security chief said. "But we are willing to say that this was all a misunderstanding. We can say that Guillaume Riche had our permission to be here."

"You would do that?" I asked.

"Oui," he said. "If we can reach an agreement." He rubbed his hands together and winked at me.

"And if he promises to put his pants on," one of the guards muttered.

"And not to dance anymore," said the other. All three men nodded vigorously.

Suddenly I understood.

"Are you talking about a bribe?" I asked incredulously.

The three men exchanged looks.

"A bribe?" the security chief asked. "What does this mean? I do not know this word."

Okay, so obviously he was going to play dumb. I took a deep breath and nodded. "Let me see what I can do," I said. "I need to talk to Guillaume, okay? I'm sure we can work this out."

"Oui, mademoiselle," the manager said, still looking confused.

I asked them to hold on for a moment. I knocked on Guillaume's door. "Are you dressed?"

"Do you want me naked?" he shouted back. I rolled my eyes and opened the door. Thankfully, he had managed to find his way into the T-shirt and pants. He had one of the flip-flops on his feet; he was holding the other one in his hands, examining it as if it were the key to the universe. "It's amazing how they put these things together," he said, gazing at the flip-flop in awe. Inexplicably, he was also still wearing the top hat.

I shook my head. There was seriously something wrong with the guy. "Guillaume, I think the security guards are asking for a bribe to let you out of this," I said. I felt a little ill; I couldn't believe that I was about to resort to bribery to extract my insane client from a potentially disastrous situation. I wondered vaguely what the penalties were in France for such an offense. I sighed. "Do you have any money on you?"

I realized as soon as the words were out of my mouth what a ridiculous question it was. Of course he didn't. He didn't have any clothes on until I'd brought him the Celio garb. Where would he keep his money?

But clearly I had underestimated Guillaume Riche.

"Of course," he responded with a shrug. "I always keep some cash in my underwear."

"You . . . you do?" I had no idea whether he was kidding.

"Of course," Guillaume said. He reached down the front of his pants, felt around for a moment, and pulled out a thick fold of bills. "Do you want to borrow some?"

he asked pleasantly, holding up the bills. I stared. "To buy a souvenir or something?"

"Um, no, not a souvenir."

Guillaume shrugged and tossed the fold to me. I caught it reluctantly, trying not to think about the fact that it had spent the night down his briefs. I tried to remember that desperate times called for desperate measures, and if being responsible for a naked, top-hatted rock star trapped in a major monument wasn't a desperate time, I didn't know what was.

"I don't know how much is there." He shrugged. "Take what you want. I don't care."

While he returned his attention to his apparently intriguing flip-flop, I looked down at the bills in my hands. My eyes widened when I realized that the bill on top was a hundred. I quickly counted the rest.

"Guillaume, you keep twenty-eight hundred euros in your underwear?" I asked after a moment, looking up at him in confusion.

He shrugged. "So what?" he asked. "You never know what you might need a little cash for."

He smiled at me like nothing was wrong.

I shook my head. "Um, okay." I didn't know what to make of this guy.

"Night and day, you are the one!" Guillaume suddenly broke into song again and began to dance around.

"Guillaume!" I said sharply.

He abruptly stopped. "What, you do not like Fred Astaire? That was 'Night and Day,' one of his greatest hits."

"No, Fred Astaire is fine," I said through gritted teeth. "I just need to handle this situation. So can you stop dancing for a moment and talk to me?"

Guillaume shrugged. "Okay."

"Great." I took a deep breath. "I can have this money?" I asked, holding up the bills.

"That's fine." He nodded and smiled at me. "Whatever you want, Emma. You should buy a souvenir, too. To remember this day."

"I think I'll pass on that," I said drily.

I knocked on the door to the security office and slipped inside, holding the roll of bills in my hand. The eyes of all three guards widened as I held it up.

"Okay, I have twenty-eight hundred euros here," I said.

"*Mademoiselle*, where did you get that?" asked one of the guards.

"You don't want to know," I said.

"*Mademoiselle*," the security chief said slowly. "I think you misunderstand. You are trying to make a *pot-de-vin*?"

"What?" I asked. I rapidly translated the words in my head. "A pot of wine?"

"No, no," he said, looking troubled. "It is an expression. It means to, eh, to try to get somebody to do something by giving them the money?"

"A bribe?" I asked. We seemed to be talking in circles.

"I do not know that word," the guard said. "But in France, *mademoiselle*, it is *illegal* to trade money for a favor."

"Oh," I said, reddening. "I thought that's what you were asking for."

"No, no, *mademoiselle!*" the security manager said, shaking his head violently. I glanced at the other two, who were staring at the money rather more lustily than their boss. "I meant that perhaps we could trade a favor for a favor, so to speak."

"A favor?" I asked hesitantly. I jammed the wad of bills into my pocket, feeling like an idiot.

"Oui." The chief glanced at the other guards and then back at me. "Could it be arranged to have Guillaume Riche play a private concert for my daughter and her friends? I would be the best father in the Île-de-France."

"And my daughter, too," said one of the guards. "She would also like to go to the private concert."

"I do not have a daughter," the youngest guard said. "But my girlfriend, she would like to see Guillaume Riche."

I stared at the three of them for a moment.

"You just want Guillaume to perform a private concert?" I asked.

"At my house," the security chief said boldly. "My wife will even cook him dinner."

I sighed and closed my eyes. "I think that can be arranged."

Twenty minutes later, after extracting a promise from a reluctant Guillaume that he would put on a private show for the security guards' loved ones, I was on my way downstairs in an elevator, my Celio-clad rock star in tow.

"Here," I said, thrusting a piece of paper at him. I'd spent five minutes jotting out some notes while he signed autographs for the starstruck security staff. "This is what you're going to say to the media."

"I have to make a statement?" he whined. "C'mon, Emma! I just want to go home and go to bed."

"You should have thought of that before you wound up naked in the Eiffel Tower," I said.

"I wasn't naked," he pointed out with a grin. "I had my briefs on. *And*," he added pointedly, "a top hat."

"You are the strangest person I've ever met," I muttered. "Anyhow, unless you want me to go out there and tell the truth, you're going to have to read this."

"You're very tough, Emma," he said sullenly. "You know that?"

I sighed. "Can we lose the top hat, too, Guillaume?"

He shook his head sadly, removed the hat from his head, and handed it over, along with the cane.

I led Guillaume outside to the wall of reporters. The moment they spotted us, they started shouting. I tried to avoid locking eyes with Gabriel, who was in the front of the crowd, staring at us in disbelief.

"Guillaume and I have a statement to make, and then we won't be taking any questions," I said firmly. The crowd quieted down a bit. "This has all been a mistake. Guillaume will be filming scenes for his 'City of Light' music video here, and he was simply scouting out locations. There was a miscommunication, which is why I wasn't here with him. 'City of Light,'" I added, throwing in a promotional plug, "is the first single off Guillaume's debut album. I have no doubt you'll be blown away. It's the story of a man meeting the woman of his dreams in Paris, which is why this location makes so much sense for the video shoot. Of course the song will hit radio stations across the world this evening, for the first time.

"Now," I concluded, "Guillaume has a few words to say to you."

Guillaume looked at me for a moment, then shook his head, looked down at the piece of paper I had given him, and began to speak.

"I regret that I was locked accidentally into the Eiffel Tower last night while scouting locations for the 'City of Lights' video," he read slowly and stiffly. It was obvious his words were scripted. I cringed and snuck a look at the media. Some of the reporters looked skeptical (especially Mr. Skepticism himself in the front row), but all appeared to be listening and jotting down notes. "I feel terrible that all of you have come here to report on what isn't really a story. It was an unfortunate incident, and I'm sure you'll understand when you see the video next month. Thank you for your concern."

"Thank you very much," I added quickly. "Please direct all questions to my office."

The reporters started shouting out questions, but I ignored them and hustled Guillaume toward the dark-windowed limo idling at the curb. I'd called Poppy before coming down and asked her to order one for us. It was the least she could do from her cushy seat on the Eurostar.

"Nice job, Emma!" Guillaume said admiringly once the car pulled away from the curb and the Eiffel Tower began to disappear behind us. He had put his top hat back on his head and was fiddling with his cane.

I rolled my eyes and shook my head. "Guillaume, what were you doing in the Eiffel Tower without your clothes anyhow?"

He looked puzzled. "You know, I haven't the faintest idea," he said slowly. "One minute I was drinking *manzana* with a girl I met at Buddha Bar. The next thing I knew, I was waking up without my clothes with some security guard staring at me. Rather embarrassing, you know."

"You were at Buddha Bar?" I asked, startled. I thought back to Gabriel's warning.

"Oui," Guillaume said. "Although it's all a blur, really."

"You are unbelievable," I muttered.

"Thank you!" Guillaume said brightly.

I shot him a look. "That wasn't a compliment," I said.

He grinned and tipped his hat to me. "I know."

Chapter Ten

I filled Poppy in on everything when she returned from London late that afternoon, and she apologized about a thousand times for not being there to help out.

"It's fine, Poppy," I said. "Really." And I meant it. Knowing that I could handle a situation like that changed something inside me. Perhaps I hadn't been giving myself enough credit—for anything.

That night, all the news stations in Paris ran reports on Guillaume's Eiffel Tower incident, and they showed clips of him addressing the media. He looked even more handsome on TV, and I knew that girls all across the world, wherever this was being aired, were probably swooning and saving up their money to buy his album. Poppy translated what the anchors were saying, and it was all good. Guillaume's debut album, which would be mostly in English, was one of the most highly anticipated releases of the year, one anchor said. His good looks already had girls around the globe plastering his poster on their walls, said another. A third network's anchor interviewed the president of the Club d'Admirateurs de Guillaume Riche—the Paris-based Guillaume Riche Fan Club.

"He has a *fan club*?" I asked incredulously.

"He has three hundred forty-one fan clubs around the world, at last count," Poppy said mildly. "Including one in a remote village in Siberia where they don't even get TV reception. It's mind-boggling."

That night, for the first time, Poppy and I heard "City of Light" on the radio while we were eating the premade meals from French supermarket chain Champion that we'd heated up. We both squealed and leapt from our seats.

"He's really on the radio!" Poppy exclaimed, jumping up and down.

"He sounds fantastic!"

We went out that night to celebrate at the Long Hop, and thanks to my ebullience over the quick save at the Eiffel Tower, I didn't even protest when Poppy brought two cute guys back from the bar along with our cocktails. She quickly disappeared into another corner of the bar to flirt with Alain, the sandy-haired, slightly freckled one she'd evidently chosen. That left me with Christian, who was tall with bushy dark brown hair, glasses, and a slightly crooked nose. He was cute, nice, and spoke great English. By the time we went home that night, Poppy had persuaded me to go on a double date with her and the guys later that week.

The next morning, the e-clipping service Poppy subscribed to had found 219 new hits for the name "Guillaume Riche" in the past twenty-four hours, and even the *New York Times* had dedicated five paragraphs to describing the "misunderstanding" that had ensued when a false tip led the press to believe "rising rock star and international playboy Guillaume Riche" was trapped inside the Eiffel Tower without his clothes.

"That report was false," the security chief was quoted as saying. "We opened the tower so Guillaume and his production company could have a tour for their new video."

The article went on to mention that Guillaume's just-released single was already heating up airwaves across the United States and Europe and that his "Coldplay-meets-Jack-Johnson style" (a quote from my press release!) was expected to catch on.

"He's the next big thing," the paper quoted Ryan Seacrest as saying.

I was still riding high from all the success when Gabriel Francoeur called to rain on my parade.

"Hi, Emma, I'm glad I caught you," he said when I answered. "It's Gabe Francoeur from the UPP."

The smile fell from my face. "What can I help you with?"

"Nothing big," he said. "I just want to see if I can schedule an interview with Guillaume about some of his, um, odd behavior lately."

"There's nothing odd about his behavior," I said right away, hating how stiff my voice sounded. "I'm not sure what you're referring to."

"Ah." Gabriel sounded amused. "Right. I'm sure you're not. But in any case, I'd just need a few minutes of his time. And yours, of course, if you'd like to sit in and comment."

"I'm afraid that will be impossible," I said. "His schedule is really quite busy right now."

"Really?" Gabriel asked. "That's funny, because I

happen to know that right now, he's sitting on the sofa in his apartment, watching cartoons. He doesn't *seem* busy."

"How would you know that?" Panic prickled at the back of my neck. "Are you *spying* on him?"

Gabriel laughed. "No, Emma! Of course not. But a good reporter never reveals his sources. So how about it? An interview?"

"No, really, we're not doing interviews right now."

He sighed dramatically. "Okay then," he said casually. "I'll just have to go with the story I'm working on about how he keeps getting into unsavory scrapes that his publicity team manages to get him out of."

"Mr. Francoeur, I assure you that's not true!"

"Call me Gabe," he said. "All my American friends do. And, Emma, I won't really have another option if I can't get that interview, will I?"

"Is that blackmail?" I demanded.

"Call it creative negotiating," he said. He paused and added, "I'm sure *you* know all about creative negotiating."

"What?"

"I'm sure you know what I mean." Gabriel sounded smug, and I felt suddenly uneasy. Did he know about the Eiffel Tower bribes? How would he know? But I couldn't take any chances.

I cleared my throat. "I'll get back to you about your interview request later this week," I said stiffly.

"I'll look forward to hearing from you, Emma."

I hung up feeling like I'd just been outmaneuvered. And I didn't like it one bit.

★   ★   ★

The rest of the workweek was spent studiously avoiding Gabe's calls. He called every morning and every afternoon, like clockwork, and I always made sure to wait until at least 8 p.m. to call him back and leave an apologetic gosh-I'm-sorry-I-missed-you-again-but-maybe-we-can-connect-tomorrow message. So far, the avoidance seemed to be working, although I was slightly concerned that all this call dodging was just going to make him more annoyed at me.

Meanwhile, Poppy and I were working overtime to prepare for the press junket in London. We had a confirmed list of journalists, we'd ironed out all the reception details, and I was beginning to believe that everything would go off without a hitch. On top of that, Guillaume hadn't gotten himself locked half naked in any major monuments lately.

On Friday, Poppy and I went out on our double date with Alain and Christian. They took us to dinner at Thomieux, a restaurant in our neighborhood specializing in southwestern French cuisine. Afterward, we went to Bar Dix, which Poppy said was one of her favorite hangouts. It was like no place I'd ever seen; it was small and had two levels that looked as if they'd been carved into the side of a cave. We wound up wedged into a tiny booth in the basement, sharing three pitchers of the best sangria I'd ever had. Poppy and I told stories, and Alain and Christian, both of whom had their arms thrown protectively over our shoulders, laughed and leaned in to give us pecks on our respective cheeks.

As our taxi pulled away from the curb at the end of the evening, leaving the two Frenchmen staring wistfully after us, I turned to Poppy, who was smiling.

"See?" Poppy asked. "Doesn't it feel good to leave them in the dust?"

"I guess . . . ," I responded, my voice trailing off. But actually, it didn't feel that great at all. They seemed like nice enough guys. There was really no reason to reject them.

"Oh, stop worrying," Poppy said. "They'd eventually do the same to you anyhow. You're just beating them to the punch. You know what the author of *How to Date Like a Dude* says!"

That weekend, Poppy and I went out a few times, to a disco near the Place de la République and to a Latin American bar near Bar Dix. Both nights, she flirted with guys like crazy in fluid, rapid French, while I blushed and tried hard to make myself understood in English.

On Monday night, Poppy had a date and I was planning to stay home alone and watch *Amélie*, a French movie Poppy had insisted I needed to see. So, figuring that there was no rush, I decided to work late at the office to finish the following week's junket interview schedule. Hours after Poppy had flitted out the door in a cloud of perfume, I was still hunched over a list of TV reporters who had requested interviews with Guillaume. Suddenly a deep voice above me startled me so much that I nearly fell off the edge of my chair.

"I figured you'd still be here."

I looked up in shock and saw Gabe Francoeur smiling down at me. I was so shaken that I stood up too quickly and knocked over a box full of ballpoint pens in the process.

"Sorry," he said, bending down to help pick up the pens that littered the floor. "I didn't mean to startle you."

"Uh, no," I said. "You didn't startle me. I just, uh, wasn't expecting anyone. How did you get in?"

"The door was ajar," he said. I rolled my eyes; Poppy must not have pulled it closed behind her when she left, starry-eyed, for her date. "Still," Gabe added, "I should have knocked. I'm sorry."

"Yeah, well, whatever," I grumbled.

Gabe straightened up and handed me the pens he'd retrieved. I righted the box, put them back inside, and tried to give him my best impassive expression.

"So I see you've been ignoring me?" he said, arching an eyebrow at me.

I cleared my throat. "Um, no," I said. "What would give you that idea?"

"I don't know," he said. "Maybe the fact that you're never available, no matter how many times I call?"

"I've been busy," I said defensively. "Besides, I've called you back."

"Yes, this may surprise you, but I'm not generally in the office after eight in the evening," he said, looking almost amused. "But then again, you know that, don't you?"

I ignored him and sat back down in my seat. I gestured halfheartedly to Poppy's chair, which he dragged over so that it was facing me. He settled into the seat. "So, what is it you want?" I asked, trying to sound mean. "Clearly it's something important, since you've called twenty times."

"I just wanted to tell you that I don't believe a word of what you've said," he said pleasantly.

My eyes widened and I stared at him. "What?"

"About Guillaume. I don't believe you. I know you're covering for him."

"Well, it's not really my concern what you do or don't believe," I sputtered, feeling my temper rise. I hoped it wasn't too obvious that he was making me nervous.

Gabe smiled. "I realize that," he said. "But I'm working on a profile of Guillaume for the UPP. I think he's going to be big in the United States. Really big. And don't get me wrong. I think he deserves to be. He's quite talented. I just wanted to let you know that I'm not buying the things you and Poppy are saying. I know you're lying."

I felt a little sick. I stared at him for a moment. "So that's it? You don't have a question for me or anything?"

Gabe shrugged. "Nope. Just wanted to let you know." He stood up and added nonchalantly, "Oh, and I'll be needing that interview with Guillaume, too."

"What, I'm supposed to give you an interview now despite everything you've just said?"

He grinned. "No. You're supposed to give me an interview now *because* of everything I've just said."

I glared at him.

"And even if I'm right about all his insanity, certainly a rock star like him should be able to charmingly explain it all, right?" Gabe continued, that same amused look on his face.

"Well, I—" I started to retort, but then I stopped and clamped my mouth shut. I thought about it for a moment. I hated to admit it, but he was right. Obviously, Gabe wasn't going to stop until he had some kind of story. "He's not insane," I finally said in a weak attempt to defend my completely nutty client.

"Oh, I know." Gabe nodded. "He adores the attention, though. And lately, he's been going too far. So about that interview?"

"Fine," I said through gritted teeth. "I'll try to schedule something for this coming week."

Gabe seemed to consider this for a moment. "Okay," he said finally.

"Okay," I echoed. I swiveled back around in my chair to face my computer, hoping the man would disappear.

Unfortunately, he didn't seem to get the hint.

Finally, I rolled my eyes, shut down my computer, and said loudly, "Okay, well, I have to be going now, Gabe. Thanks so much for stopping by!"

"My pleasure," he said cheerfully. "I'll give you a ride home."

I just looked at him. "What? No, I'll take the Métro."

"Oh, c'mon, Emma," he said. "It's like a hundred degrees outside. And I'm talking Celsius. The Métro will be miserable."

I shrugged. What was he, Jekyll and Hyde? He was ready to destroy my career one second, and the next he wanted to drive me home? "I'll be fine," I mumbled.

"My car is air-conditioned," he said, raising an eyebrow.

"I'm sure I'm out of your way."

"Where do you live?"

"Rue du Général-Camou," I said, knowing that he wouldn't have heard of the tiny side street between Avenue Rapp and Avenue de la Bourdonnais.

Wrong again.

"Oh, fantastic!" he exclaimed. "I live in the seventh, too! What a coincidence. You're just a few blocks from me."

I gaped at him. I was out of excuses.

"So? Are you coming?" Jingling his car keys, he started toward the door.

In the passenger's seat of Gabe's immaculately clean Peugeot, I braced myself for an onslaught of questions about Guillaume, but instead he made pleasant conversation, asking me where I was from, why I'd come to Paris, and where I'd gone to school.

"You went to the University of Florida?" he exclaimed as soon as the words were out of my mouth. "I can't believe it!"

I looked at him, startled. "Why?" I asked defensively. How on earth had he even heard of the school? Sure, it was well known in the States thanks to its dominance in football and basketball. But how could some guy in France have such strong feelings about my alma mater?

"Because I went there, too."

I was sure I'd heard him wrong. "What? But you're French!"

"Emma, French people *are* allowed to go to school in the United States, you know," he deadpanned.

I blushed, feeling stupid. "I know that."

"Besides," Gabe added, "I have dual citizenship. My father is French. My mother is American. They divorced when I was a baby. I spent summers here with my dad and the rest of the year in Tampa with my mom."

"You lived in Tampa?" I stared in disbelief. "I grew up in Orlando." The cities were only an hour apart. Gabe laughed.

"That's unbelievable," he said. "What a small world."

"You really went to UF?"

Gabe nodded. "Yes. I got a journalism degree there ten years ago and then got my master's at the Sorbonne, here in Paris. That's when I decided to move here to work for the UPP. Being bilingual really helps."

"You graduated from UF ten years ago?" I asked. "I graduated seven years ago. Also from the journalism school."

"Wow, we overlapped a year," Gabe said. "That's unbelievable. How come I never saw you?"

I shrugged. "I don't know. Maybe we crossed paths and didn't even know it."

"No," Gabe said, staring straight ahead. He made the left turn onto Avenue Rapp. "I think I would have remembered you."

My heart fluttered bizarrely for a moment, and I shot a quick glance at him. Maybe he wasn't as bad as he'd initially seemed.

A moment later, Gabe turned right down my street, and I pointed out my building.

"You're right next to the American Library," he said. "That's so weird. I come here all the time."

"You do?"

He nodded. "Yeah. I'm a big reader. Well, maybe some weekend when I'm over here, we can grab a cup of coffee."

"Um, maybe," I said slowly, thinking that, although he seemed nicer than I had expected, I would probably have to wear my ice skates to such a meeting, because it would be a cold day in hell before I voluntarily subjected myself to coffee with Gabe Francouer. He would no doubt spend the entire time we were together pumping me for information about Guillaume. No thanks. "Well, thank you for the ride," I said awkwardly.

"It was great to talk with you, Emma," he said. "I'm afraid I have to get going, though. I have dinner plans."

I felt myself blushing again. "Oh, of course," I said. Wait. *I* was supposed to blow *him* off. Why had he just made me feel like he was eager to get rid of me?

I opened the car door and stepped out. "Well," I said awkwardly. "Thanks again." I slammed the door behind me.

"No problem!" Gabe said through the open window. "Cheers!" He gave me a little wave and then sped off without looking back.

Chapter Eleven

That night, Poppy came across the gum wrapper Edouard had scribbled his name and number on the first night I'd been to the Long Hop.

"Who's this guy?" she asked, holding the wrapper in the air.

"That chain-smoker I met the first night we went out."

"You should call him," Poppy had said. "He seemed nice!"

"You didn't even talk to him," I said. "And he smoked like a chimney."

"Nonsense," she said firmly. "He liked you. And I guarantee, he'll be great for your confidence."

Against my protests, Poppy dialed for me and handed the phone to me. "Try to sound sexy," she said. I rolled my eyes.

Edouard sounded surprised to hear from me, but he said that of course he remembered "ze pretty blond American girl" and would still love to take me on a romantic picnic in Paris. We agreed to meet on Wednesday night.

"Let's go buy you something to wear!" Poppy said on Wednesday afternoon. We left the office early, and I let her talk me into a black strapless dress from Zara on the Rue de Rivoli and a new pair of way-too-expensive strappy black heels from Galeries Lafayette.

"See?" Poppy asked on the Métro on the way home. "Don't you feel sexier now?"

I had to admit, she had a point. I spent longer than usual that evening blow-drying my hair, applying my makeup, and slipping into my dress. By the time I was done, I saw a completely different person in the mirror.

Perhaps the more different I felt, the easier it would be to forget about the life I'd left behind in the States.

"So you said you are new to our beautiful city?" Edouard asked as we walked to his car, his hand resting lightly on the small of my back.

"I'm getting to know it," I answered.

"And I hope you are loving it so far?"

"I am."

After a brief drive along the Seine in his little Renault, Edouard parked near the Musée d'Orsay and, with an enormous picnic basket in hand, led me toward the Pont des Arts, the beautiful pedestrian bridge that spanned the river between the Louvre on the Right Bank and the Quai Malaquais on the Left. When we found a spot on the bridge, he pulled out a perfectly folded white-and-red-checkered picnic blanket.

"My lady," he said, gesturing to it after he'd spread it neatly, aligning the corners with the planks of the bridge.

"Can I help?" I asked, watching him in awe.

He smiled at me. "Just relax and enjoy." He pulled out an iPod and mini speakers, then turned it on. "I've organized some selections from Serge Gainsbourg, to intro-

duce you to one of our country's legends," he said. Soft
jazz music began to waft from the speakers as Edouard
lit a cigarette and busied himself pulling perfectly pack-
aged foods from the basket and setting them up in front of
us. I stared as the picnic materialized; he seemed to have
brought at least a dozen dishes, some of which I'd never
even seen before.

"You did all this for me?" I asked as he uncorked a bottle of red wine and began to fill two glasses. "You barely
even know me!"

He shrugged and stubbed out his cigarette on the bridge.
He exhaled a mouthful of smoke and smiled. "You said
you hadn't had a proper Parisian picnic yet," he said. "I
knew no better place to start than here."

His chain-smoking aside, it felt like something out of a
dream. To the west, the Eiffel Tower rose gracefully over
the Seine, and to the east, I could see the twin towers of
Notre Dame. To the north, the palatial Louvre seemed
to go on forever; southward, the beautifully antiquated
buildings of Paris dotted the Left Bank. As the sun began
to dip low in the sky over the Eiffel Tower, the bright blue
of early evening gave way to muted pinks and oranges
on the horizon. It was breathtaking, the kind of scene
that made me wish fervently I could paint or even take
good photographs. It was the kind of evening mere words
couldn't describe.

While I looked on in awe, Edouard patiently explained
some of the dishes he had brought to share with me. "This
is goose *rillette*," he said of the first item. It looked like a
grayish, brownish box of mush, but when he spread it on a

slice of baguette and I took a bite, my taste buds did a little happy dance on my tongue.

"This is amazing!" I said, my mouth still full. It was salty and sweet all at the same time, and it tasted entirely unfamiliar.

He grinned at me in amusement. "It's a French specialty," he said. "You can't get it in your country."

Next up were several fresh cheeses, including an herbed chèvre and a strong blue cheese, then a jar of tiny sour pickles called cornichons and a series of little salads, including a shredded carrot one that I couldn't seem to get enough of. There were two kinds of meat pâté, both of which were amazing, and a strange-looking dish that appeared to be hard-boiled eggs wrapped in ham and encased in gelatin but turned out to be surprisingly delicious.

By the time we were finished with our meal—which ended in espresso from a Thermos and fruit tarts that looked almost too beautiful to eat—the stars were starting to come out, and a crescent moon was rising above Notre Dame. Thoroughly stuffed, I lay back on the picnic blanket beside Edouard and looked up at the night sky.

"It is beautiful, no?" Edouard said after a moment, puffing on a cigarette.

"It's amazing," I breathed. I felt like we were in our own little world, although there were passersby walking to and fro and another couple on a blanket a few yards away making out like hormonal teenagers. The vague, sweet smell of marijuana wafted over from a trio of snickering teenage boys clustered on the other side of the bridge. I turned my head to the side to look at Edouard. "I think this is one of the most wonderful evenings I've ever had."

"We are just getting started," he said. He put his cigarette out and took a sip of water. Then, inching closer to me, he pressed his lips to mine. Even though I could still taste tobacco on his breath, I kissed him back, spurred on by the food, the wine, the starry night, and the romance of it all. He pulled me closer and parted my lips with his tongue, threading one hand tenderly through my hair and stroking the side of my face with the other. It was perfect. I didn't want the moment to end.

I cracked my eyes open as he kissed me and looked up at the night sky with the Eiffel Tower glowing ethereally white in the background. It was a quintessential moment of French romance—exactly what I needed. As I kissed back, I thought about Brett and all I'd left behind in Florida. These last few days, I'd been missing him—and my old life—a lot less. Somehow, Swanson frozen meals eaten in front of the TV while Brett watched Fox News didn't compare to picnicking on a bridge over the Seine while a handsome Frenchman gazed into my eyes and made me feel like the only woman in the world.

I was just falling into the kiss when a ringing sound jolted me out of the moment.

"Is that yours?" Edouard asked after a moment, between hungry kisses.

"Is that my what?" I whispered back, wondering who could have been rude enough to leave their cell phone volume up on a bridge meant for picnickers and lovers.

"Is that your *phone*?" Edouard asked, kissing me again and biting my lower lip gently. I shuddered.

"My phone?" I asked vaguely. Then I sat straight up. "Oh, no, it *is* my phone!"

I'd forgotten that I'd left it on. I could feel heat rising to my cheeks.

Just then, the ringing stopped. I breathed a sigh of relief.

"Do you need to see who was calling?" Edouard asked.

"No," I whispered back. "I'm sure it's not important." All I wanted was for him to kiss me again. Fortunately, he acquiesced. Unfortunately, whoever was calling me apparently had different plans for the evening.

"Do you think you'd better answer?" Edouard asked on the fifth series of rings. People around us were starting to stare.

I heaved a sigh and pulled myself reluctantly away from him. I groped in my purse until I found my phone, then flipped it open. Poppy's name was on my caller ID. I gritted my teeth. "This had better be important," I said as I answered.

"I am *so* sorry to interrupt your date," she said hurriedly. "But I need your help, Emma. Guillaume has done it again!"

My heart sank. I glanced at Edouard, who was still lying on his side on the picnic blanket, gazing at me hopefully. "Done what?" I asked.

Poppy sighed. "All I know is he's hanging from a rope between two apartment buildings in the seventeenth."

I swore under my breath. "You're kidding. Right?" I asked hopefully. Maybe this was her idea of a joke.

Poppy was silent for a moment. "I wish I was," she said. "Seriously, Emma, could he make our lives any more difficult? His launch is barely a week away!"

I glanced at Edouard again. "Poppy," I whispered, turning away from him a bit. "I'm on a date with Edouard!"

"I'm sure he'll understand," she said quickly. "Just explain it to him. Tell him you have to go for work."

"Fine," I said through gritted teeth. I jotted down the address and promised to meet her there as soon as I could.

"Everything okay?" Edouard asked as I hung up.

I took a deep breath. "No," I said. "I'm sorry, but I have to go. There's a work emergency I have to help take care of."

Edouard just stared at me.

"You are leaving?" he asked.

"I'm so sorry." I glanced around at the remnants of the perfect picnic. "Really," I said. "You have no idea how disappointed I am."

He stared at me for another moment then shook his head. He stood up without another word and started grabbing empty dishes and tossing them back into the picnic basket, muttering under his breath.

"Edouard?" He was obviously upset, and I couldn't blame him, especially after all the effort he had gone to.

"It's just not natural," he grumbled as he tossed the last of the dishes back into the basket.

"What's not natural?" I asked, confused.

"This," he said, shaking his head. "In our country, women do not leave dates early to go to work. Perhaps things are different in America, but here the women are women and the men are men."

"What?" I couldn't imagine what he was talking about. What did being women and men have to do with anything?

He studied me for another moment then shook his head. "It's too late. We shall go. Let's go to the car."

"I can find a taxi . . ."

"Nonsense." His voice was stiff. "I will drive you."

He gathered up the blanket, threw out the empty wine bottle, and began striding quickly, picnic supplies in hand, back toward the Left Bank, away from our perfect little spot on the perfect little bridge. With Edouard puffing aggressively away on a series of cigarettes, we drove in uncomfortable silence to the seventeenth, where he found his way to the address on a side street off Avenue Niel that Poppy had given me.

"The avenue is blocked," Edouard said stiffly as we pulled up. There were several Paris police officers motioning for drivers to keep going. I groaned. I had no doubt that they were there because of whatever Guillaume had done. Edouard pulled down the next side street and looped around to the top of Rue Banville. "This is as close as the police will let me get."

"Thank you," I muttered. "And again, I'm sorry."

"You know," Edouard said, his face stony as he watched me exit the car. "You will never find a boyfriend if you continue putting your career first."

I stared at him. "But I'm not looking for a boyfriend."

"I'm just giving you some advice," he said. *"Bonne nuit."* And with that, he nodded at me and sped away. I stared after him for a moment.

"Hot date?" came a voice from behind me. I spun around to see Gabe standing there on the curb, watching me with a look of amusement on his face.

"None of your business." I narrowed my eyes at him.

"Seemed like a nice guy," Gabe said, raising an eyebrow.

"He was," I said curtly, feeling foolish, wondering how much of the conversation he'd heard.

I brushed past him and into the throng waiting outside. I could feel Gabe following me, but I didn't turn around. When I rounded the corner onto Rue Banville, I stopped dead in my tracks.

"He doesn't look too comfortable up there, does he?" Gabe asked from behind me, his voice far too cheerful for the situation at hand.

"Oh, no," I breathed. High above the street, which was blocked off by police barricades, Guillaume was dangling by his ankles from a thick rope suspended between two buildings, at least twelve or thirteen floors off the ground. He was belting out a slurred version of "City of Light," complete with grandiose arm gestures.

Mon amie, mon coeur et mon amour
Won't you show me what our love is for?

His words rang out, deep and melodic, between the buildings.

"He sounds good," Gabe said, as nonchalantly as if we were listening to his song on the radio. I turned to glare at him.

Beneath Guillaume were four Parisian fire trucks, one with its ladder extended up a few stories, and several fire-fighters gazing up at him. But no one seemed to be making a move to get him down.

"Someone has to do something!" I exclaimed, more to myself than anyone else.

"This is France," Gabe replied cheerfully. "The *pompiers* will stand around all night and gaze up at him, waiting for someone to tell them what to do."

"But . . . what if he falls?" I asked.

"Then I guess you'll get your big publicity push," he said.

I turned around and glared. "What's *wrong* with you? He could get hurt up there!"

Gabe looked slightly abashed. "Emma." He reached out and put his hand on my arm. "I'm just sure he'll be fine. He always is. He's always getting himself into scrapes like this. He loves them. Relax."

I glared at him and shook my arm away. "Go back and wait with the other media," I muttered. I focused my attention away from him and turned to the police officer standing at the top of the street, keeping the crowds away.

"Hello," I began politely. He looked down at me, his forehead creasing. "I'm Guillaume's publicist. May I please get through?"

"Comment?" he asked sharply. Darn it. He didn't understand me.

"Um, I'm the publicist. For Guillaume Riche." I spoke slowly, firmly, keeping eye contact with the officer, who still looked confused.

"*Comment?*" he asked again. *"Je ne parle pas anglais."*

Great. I'd found the only Parisian who didn't speak even basic English. Just my luck.

"Um, okay," I said, trying to seize on whatever French I'd picked up. "Um, *je* . . . um, *amie* of Guillaume."

"*Vous êtes une amie de ce fou?*" the police officer asked slowly. I gathered that he was confirming that I was Guillaume's friend. I wished I knew how to say "publicist" in French, as I was certainly no friend of the wacky rock star.

"*Oui,*" I confirmed confidently.

The police officer started to laugh. He shook his head and said something in rapid French that I didn't understand. Then he said in clear English. "You no come. Too many girl."

"No, no, I'm not actually a friend," I started to protest. "I'm his publicist." I couldn't for the life of me think how to say the word, so I said the closest thing I could think of. "Um, *journaliste.*"

Clearly that was the wrong thing to say, because the moment the word was out of my mouth, the police officer began pushing me away and muttering in French.

"No, no wait!" I protested, realizing too late that I was being pushed back to where the press was kept waiting. But the officer ignored me.

"Well, hello again," said a voice behind me as the officer guided me forcefully around the corner. I glanced up and saw Gabe, along with several other members of the press pool. Great. The officer had brought me back to the media horde, thinking I was one of them. "Do you need some help?" Gabe asked, arching an eyebrow at me and glancing between me and the policeman.

I sighed. "Yes," I muttered.

He smiled at me—a triumphant smile, if I wasn't mistaken—and turned to the officer. He said something in rapid, confident French, and the police officer responded in a low, grumbling voice. Gabe spoke again, and finally the officer shrugged, took my arm, and began guiding me away from the media horde.

"I told him you were Guillaume's publicist and to bring you inside to find Poppy," Gabe said as the officer pulled me away.

"Thank you," I said through gritted teeth.

"Anytime!" Gabe gave me a cheerful little wave. "And hey, be careful in there."

The officer guided me through the crowd and into the lobby of one of the buildings Guillaume was dangling between. He said something to one of the other officers inside, and in a moment yet another policeman appeared to escort me farther into the building. I found Poppy around the corner, waiting for me.

"What on earth is going on?" I asked.

Poppy sighed and glanced toward the ceiling. "Well, the good news is that he's not violating any laws, so for once we don't have to worry about him being arrested. Apparently in this city, you can hang upside down by your ankles thirteen stories above ground and no one minds."

"Of course you can," I muttered.

She nodded tersely. "The bad news is that he's not being

particularly responsive to the *pompiers*, and they can't get him down without his help," she said.

"Oh, no."

"It gets worse," Poppy said grimly. "He and some friends tied the ropes themselves. The police have secured the ends, but who knows how well he's knotted on to the rope? Or how long it can hold his weight?"

"This is awful," I said. I thought about it for a moment. "Have you tried to talk him down?"

Poppy nodded. "He won't listen. He just keeps on singing."

I hesitated. "Let me give it a shot," I said.

"You think he'll listen to you?"

"I think we sort of, um, bonded during that whole Eiffel Tower thing," I said. "It's worth a try."

Poppy shrugged and led me to the elevator, which we took up to the thirteenth floor. When the doors opened, we stepped into a hall filled with police officers, firemen, and paramedics, all of whom appeared to be standing around, doing nothing but sipping coffee and smoking cigarettes. Had I not known that a man was dangling above the pavement outside the window, I would have mistaken this for a friendly hall party.

I shook my head, and Poppy led me past them and into a room at the end of the hall. Inside, several officers were gathered around the window, looking just as casual as the people in the hallway. It was as if they dealt with dangling rock stars every day. After a quick glance around the room, I could see the end of a thick length of rope tied to a bed pushed against the wall. I followed the rope to the window and looked outside. Suspended in midair, Guillaume was cheerfully belting out the lyrics to "City of Light." I shook my head. This was insane.

I checked the rope and made sure it looked like it was securely tied. While Poppy conferred with one of the police officers, I leaned out the window, trying not to think about how dangerous this was for the man we were responsible for.

"Guillaume!" I called. I couldn't resist looking down, and when I did, I felt sick to my stomach. Thirteen floors was a long way. Definitely far enough to worry about a splattered rock star on the pavement. In a city where most of the residential buildings topped out below ten floors, how had Guillaume managed to find two buildings beside each other whose height made this stunt so potentially deadly?

Guillaume turned his head slowly toward me. It seemed to take him a moment to focus, but when he realized who I was, a broad grin spread across his face. "Emma!" he exclaimed, as if I had simply surprised him in the recording studio as opposed to suspended in midair. "Hi! You're here! Welcome! Join the fun!"

Below us, a murmur ran through the crowd as it became obvious that Guillaume had stopped singing and was now conversing with someone inside. For a moment I wondered what Gabe was thinking on the ground below, but just as quickly I banished the thought from my mind. Who *cared* what he was thinking? Why had that been the thought that popped into my panicked brain?

Guillaume kept grinning. I stared for a moment and sighed. "Guillaume," I began wearily. "What on earth are you doing?"

He looked puzzled for a moment—or at least he appeared to (it was rather hard to tell considering that he was hanging upside down by his ankles). "Well," he began. "I was drinking with a few of the guys from the band. This is Jean-Marc's apartment, you know. He's my drummer. So his girlfriend, her name's Rosine, well, Rosine says wouldn't it be fun if we string a rope between her apartment and his and see if we can get across? That's Rosine's apartment over there."

He paused and pointed to the window across the street where the rope disappeared into another apartment building. "So we did that, and then no one else wanted to go first, so I said I would," Guillaume continued cheerfully. "So they tied this cord to my foot just in case I fell or something. I guess it's good that they did, because, Emma, this rope is slippery. I started across, but about halfway I just couldn't hold on anymore. I let go, and, well, here I am. Hanging upside down. By my ankles.

"By the way, where did Jean-Marc go?" Guillaume asked, looking suddenly around in confusion. "Where are the other guys?"

I shook my head at him in disbelief. "They're gone, Guillaume," I said wearily. I took a deep breath and exhaled slowly, trying to calm myself down. "Look, we have to get you down from there before you get hurt."

He shrugged absently. "I don't know. I kind of like it here. I can see the Eiffel Tower, you know!"

That was the cue, in Guillaume's mind at least, to begin singing again.

"Night has fallen on this City of Light!" He belted out the opening line of his single enthusiastically, his baritone still sounding surprisingly perfect, considering that his throat had to be swelling up thanks to all the blood rushing to his head.

The crowd below, which had grown even larger as word had apparently gotten out that there was a bona fide rock star hanging between buildings, started clapping, cheering, and whistling. Guillaume grinned and started singing even more loudly.

"I think of you and tears fill my eyes," he continued. The crowd below cheered wildly.

"I dream of you when you're not here with me. You're all I've ever wanted and you set my soul free!"

Down below, unbelievably, people started singing along the third time he reached the chorus. By the time he was done, he had a whole group of amateur backup singers below.

"They love me, Emma!" he shouted to me when he was done. Below us, the whistles, cheers, and catcalls continued.

"Guillaume—" I began wearily. But I didn't know what else to say. This guy was clearly a lunatic. And somehow, my PR education hadn't included lessons on how to talk singers with a screw loose down from ropes dangling between buildings in foreign cities. I'd have to get in touch with my college's dean about that; there'd clearly been a gap in the curriculum. "Guillaume," I tried again, keeping my voice firm. "You need to come in now."

Guillaume studied me for a moment. "I have a better idea. Why don't you come out and get me?"

"What?"

"Come out here with me, Emma!"

"Are you crazy?"

"Probably!" Guillaume seemed to be gathering steam. "But it will be fun! We will sing a duet!"

"There is no way I am going out there with you!" I shot back.

"Then I am not coming in!" Guillaume said. He stuck out his bottom lip stubbornly and crossed his arms over his chest. "And if something happens to me, it will be your fault."

I stared at him. "You can't be serious!"

"I am completely serious, Emma," Guillaume said. "I am not coming down until you come out and sing with me."

I slowly turned around to see a roomful of people staring at me. I locked eyes with Poppy.

"What are you going to do?" she asked softly.

"I don't particularly want to die from falling out a thirteenth-story window while singing a duet with a lunatic," I said.

"We can guarantee your safety," one of the police officers piped up. Poppy and I turned to look at him. He was young with flushed cheeks and bright blue eyes. "I mean, the rope itself is secure, and it's thick enough to hold your weight. If you let us hook you on, you will not fall."

I stared at him. "You really think I should do this?"

The young officer shrugged uncomfortably. "It is not

for me to say, *mademoiselle*. I am only saying that we can keep you safe if you choose to go out there."

I turned back to Poppy. She looked at me for a long moment. "It's up to you," she said finally.

I glanced out the window.

"Are you coming?" Guillaume yelled. "The view is amazing, Emma! You must come see!"

I thought about it for a moment, then turned back to the young officer.

"You promise you can keep me safe?" I asked.

He nodded solemly. *"Oui,"* he said. "I can almost guarantee it."

I pretended I didn't hear the word *almost*.

I walked back over to the windowsill. "Hang on, Guillaume," I yelled halfheartedly. "I'm coming!"

Fifteen minutes later, after borrowing a spare pair of police pants from the back of a police car so that no one would see up my dress as I dangled above the street, I was trying not to panic. Secured with several ropes and attached to the main rope with a pulley contraption, I inched my way out the window, praying that I wouldn't die.

"Your face looks a little green, Emma!" Guillaume said as I started down the rope toward him.

"I'm afraid of heights," I said stiffly as I inched closer and closer. The young officer had given me a pair of gloves and showed me how to walk my hands down the rope to get closer to Guillaume. He had promised that even if I lost my grip, I'd be fine; I was attached to both the rope and the window, so allegedly I wouldn't fall. I might, on the other hand, slide down the rope and smash into the side of the building. I tried not to think about it.

"Afraid of heights?" Guillaume asked. "That's impossible! Look around! It's so beautiful here!"

I glanced up for a second and realized that he was right. I could see all the way to the Eiffel Tower. But I could *also* see the Eiffel Tower from my living room, which is where I would have greatly preferred to be at the moment.

Below us, the crowd was murmuring and pointing. I wondered momentarily what Gabe was thinking. He was probably having a field day. This would make one great UPP story.

"Okay, Guillaume," I said as I made my way to his side. "Let's just get this over with quickly."

"You're no fun!" he said. I looked down at him and shook my head. Not only was I dangling beside a rock star on a rope strung over the streets of Paris, but I was head-to-toe with him, as he had secured himself to the rope by his ankles.

"Your feet smell," I retorted.

"That's not very nice." Guillaume sounded wounded.

"Neither is making me risk my life for you. Now, are we going to sing or what?"

"Fine, fine." He sighed. "What would you like to sing?"

I rolled my eyes. "Whatever, Guillaume! Can you just choose something so we can get down from here?"

I was starting to get more and more nervous. The rope was swaying, and I felt sick to my stomach. I glanced toward the window. Poppy and the young officer were leaning out.

"Are you okay?" Poppy shouted. The officer slipped a comforting arm around her shoulder, and Poppy glanced up to bat her eyes at him. Great. Even in the midst of my death-defying tragedy, she was flirting.

"I'm fine!" I shouted back.

"How about 'Cheek to Cheek'?" Guillaume asked. I turned my attention back to him. He smiled up at me and patted his cheek, which appeared very red thanks to all the blood rushing to his head. "Fred Astaire debuted it in 1935, long before Sinatra got his hands on it!"

"No more Fred Astaire!" I groaned.

"Good point," Guillaume said thoughtfully. "I don't even have my top hat with me. I couldn't do it justice." He thought for a moment. "Do you know 'Jackson'? By Johnny Cash and June Carter?"

"No."

"How about 'Islands in the Stream'? Kenny Rogers and Dolly Parton?"

"No!" I exclaimed in frustration. How on earth did he know so many country songs?

Guillaume thought for a moment.

"How about 'You're the One That I Want'?'" he asked. "From *Grease*?"

"You've *got* to be kidding me," I muttered.

"You know it?"

"Yes, I know it," I said. I just didn't want to sing it.

"Okay, I'll start! This will be beautiful! You are just like Olivia Newton-John!"

I groaned. Guillaume shouted to the crowd. "For my finale tonight, I will be performing a hit song from the musical *Grease* with my lovely publicist, Emma!" He repeated the same sentence again in French.

The crowd below applauded, hooting and hollering like they were at a real concert.

"They love us already!" Guillaume said. "Doesn't this feel good, Emma?"

"Yeah, it feels just fantastic." I was still trying not to throw up.

Guillaume cleared his throat and began to sing. *"I got chills! They're multiplying! And I'm loooosing control!"*

"You can say that again," I muttered. Guillaume made a face at me and sang the remainder of his verse.

"Your turn!" he urged.

I began singing Olivia Newton-John's words unenthusiastically.

"Louder, Emma!" Guillaume grinned at me. "They can't hear you!"

I took a deep breath and continued with the rest of the verse, feeling like a complete idiot.

Below, the crowd applauded wildly. Miraculously, we managed to make it through all the verses and several renditions of the chorus, ending with a drawn-out *"Ooh, ooh, ooh"* that we sang together as the crowd went wild. Dozens of flashbulbs went off, and I closed my eyes. I just wanted this night to be over.

"Emma?" Guillaume said after a moment, after the screams had finally receded a bit. "You know, I'm getting a bit of a headache."

"Yes, Guillaume," I said stiffly. "It's probably because you've been hanging upside down for two hours."

He appeared to think about this for a moment. Then he shrugged, which unfortunately made us both swing wildly from side to side. I *really* wanted to vomit.

"Maybe you're right, Emma," he said slowly after the swinging had slowed. "It's probably time to come in then, right?"

"Yes, Guillaume," I agreed. "I think it's time to come in."

"Really?" he asked. He seemed to consider this. "Okay then. Thanks!"

As the young officer had instructed, I asked Guillaume to grab my ankles. He acquiesced, and I shouted inside to let the officers know we were ready. Slowly, three officers pulled on the rope attached to my back so that Guillaume and I, locked in a strange head-to-toe position, were slowly dragged along the length of the rope, via the pulley I'd been connected to. Five agonizing minutes later, Poppy's young officer and two others pulled Guillaume and me to safety.

"That was fun!" Guillaume exclaimed, grinning at me as the police untied his ankles and unhooked him from the rope. There was some yelling outside as the officers in the building across the way discussed how to detach the rope. As soon as Guillaume was free, he reached out and pulled me into a hug. "You saved me!" he declared in a deep, theatrical voice.

I rolled my eyes and gritted my teeth. "You're insane." I didn't mean it facetiously.

"Emma, you were worried about me!" Guillaume said, pulling back and studying my face.

I avoided his glance. "I was worried about the *album*," I mumbled.

"No, you were worried about *me*!" Guillaume insisted triumphantly. He turned to Poppy and gave her a hug, too. "Poppy! Emma loves me!" he announced.

Poppy frowned. "Then she's even crazier than you are."

After Guillaume had been ushered out a back entrance by Richard and Edgar, who had arrived during my dangling duet, Poppy and I walked outside to where the police were keeping the waiting journalists at bay. I'd taken the police pants off.

"Do you want to do the talking?" Poppy whispered as we walked.

I just looked at her. "Are you kidding? I just dangled thirteen stories above Paris singing a duet from a John Travolta musical. I think it's your turn to handle this."

"Fine." We arrived at the bank of microphones and tape recorders that the reporters had thrown together, and Poppy raised a hand to silence the crowd.

"I'm pleased to announce that Guillaume Riche is perfectly fine and is on his way home with his bodyguards," Poppy began. "Thank you all for your concern."

She repeated the words in French. As she went on to explain that Guillaume's stunt certainly wasn't illegal and certainly wasn't the result of drunken stupidity, I gazed around at the journalists, trying to gauge their reactions. Most were listening and nodding as if Poppy's words were entirely sensible. Were they crazy? There were a few skeptical faces in the crowd. Oddly, Gabe didn't appear to be watching Poppy, although once in a while he scribbled something on his pad. Instead he appeared to be staring hard at me.

Every time I caught his eye, I glanced quickly away, but he kept right on looking, as if he could see right through me. It was making me feel uneasy.

"This was simply an impromptu demonstration on Guillaume's part," Poppy concluded, "to show you how much he enjoys singing with regular women. Like my colleague, Emma."

I smiled weakly. After a round of questions, each of which Poppy answered quickly and crisply, she finally called on Gabe. I braced myself for something sarcastic.

Instead, looking straight at me, he spoke softly. "That was really brave, Emma," he said in English. "Are you okay?"

I gulped and nodded. "Yes, I'm fine," I said.

Once the press conference had ended and the reporters began to go their separate ways, Poppy returned to me, looking exhausted.

"Feel like going out for an Our-Rock-Star-Isn't-Splattered-on-the-Pavement celebratory drink?" she asked. She leaned in. "That cute officer asked me out!" she whispered.

I smiled weakly and shook my head. "No," I said. "I'm sorry. I'm just worn out. I think I'm going to go home and go to bed."

Poppy nodded. "I understand."

I smiled. "Have fun with Officer McDreamy, though. See you at home."

We hugged good-bye, and I began walking toward the Porte Maillot Métro stop, which was several blocks away, according to the little "Plan de Paris" map Poppy had loaned me.

There was a chill in the air, and with the uneven cobblestones of some of the sidewalks I was beginning to doubt the logic of wearing high heels in a city like this. How did Frenchwomen do it, anyhow? I glanced around, hoping I'd see the gleaming light of a taxi somewhere, but the streets were empty. As I walked through the puddles of light cast from the street lamps, my feet ached more and more with each step.

I'd walked four blocks and was just beginning to contemplate whether it would be worse to keep my heels on (I was already getting massive blisters), or walk barefoot on the grimy streets, when I heard a car horn honk beside me. I turned my head wearily to the right, gritting my teeth against the pain, and was somehow unsurprised to see Gabe sitting there in his little Peugeot, smiling at me.

I stopped walking, and he rolled down his window. "Need a ride home?"

"No," I said grumpily. I regretted it the moment the words were out of my mouth. It was another few blocks to the Métro, then, after I got off the train at the closest stop to our apartment, I'd still have to walk all the way home, which meant crossing the Pont de'lAlma and walking halfway up Avenue Bosquet—a good half mile. I'd surely have to have my feet amputated. But I was in no mood to need anyone—particularly Gabe—so I started walking again, pretending to ignore him. Better to go through the rest of my life without sensation in my feet, right?

"Okay," Gabe said cheerfully. I expected him to speed up and drive off, leaving me and my aching feet in the dust, but instead, as I walked and stared straight ahead, I could sense his car beside me, creeping slowly along, keeping pace.

Ignore him, I told myself. *It's like he's not even there. Don't look.*

That worked for a block. But when I turned left onto Boulevard Péreire and Gabe turned with me and continued inching along beside me, I'd finally had enough.

"Stop following me!" I snapped, halting in my tracks and turning to face him.

"Oh, you're still there?" Gabe feigned surprise. He stopped his car. "I hadn't noticed."

I glared at him.

"Oh, come on, Emma," Gabe said after a moment of smiling at me. His face looked serious now. "Just get in the car, already. I know your feet hurt in those shoes."

"I'm fine," I said through gritted teeth.

"No, you're not," Gabe said simply. "Stop being proud and just get in. I'm going to your neighborhood anyhow."

I opened my mouth to say something sarcastic in reply, but what was the point? My feet *were* killing me.

"Fine," I grumbled. I marched over to his car like *I* was doing *him* a favor, yanked the door open, and slammed it behind me after I'd flopped into his passenger's seat.

"Um, you appear to have shut your dress in the door, Emma," Gabe said. I glanced at him and was perturbed to see that he appeared to be hiding a smile.

I looked down and realized that in all my righteous indignation, I had, in fact, managed to shut the hem of my dress into the car door. "Thanks," I mumbled. I opened the door, pulled in my dress, and slammed the door again, fervently hoping that my cheeks hadn't turned too red.

Gabe pulled away from the curb, and I looked out the window, trying to ignore him—admittedly difficult when I was sitting two feet away from him. We drove in silence for a few moments.

"So really, Emma, are you okay?" Gabe asked finally.

I glanced at him and nodded. "Yeah."

"I meant what I said back there," he said. "That was really brave."

"Thanks," I said, surprised.

"And really foolish," he continued.

I made a face. I should have known his apparent kindness was too good to be true.

"I didn't exactly have a choice," I snapped.

"Guillaume would have come down eventually on his own," Gabe said softly.

"You don't know that," I protested. "Maybe I saved his life."

Gabe was quiet for a moment. "You know, he's not as crazy as he looks," he said finally. "He just enjoys the attention."

I ignored him and looked out the window. What was he, Guillaume's psychiatrist?

"So, how was that date of yours tonight?" Gabe asked casually as we entered the roundabout that circled the Arc de Triomphe.

I could feel the heat rising in my cheeks again. I blinked a few times. "None of your business," I muttered. After all, what was I going to do, admit to him that it had been a horrible failure? That I had thought Edouard was perfect until his chauvinistic resentment came pouring out? I glanced up at the Arc, which loomed, big, glowing, and impressive, over the street, casting its pools of light every which way. I tried to ignore Gabe.

"No, I suppose it's *not* my business." Gabe paused and glanced at me as we pulled out of the roundabout and up to a stop sign. "But you *do* look really pretty in that dress."

I looked at him in surprise. Of course he was being sarcastic, right? "Um, thanks," I mumbled, feeling like I was on the outside of some inside joke.

"I mean it," he said softly.

"Oh," I said awkwardly, not quite knowing what to make of him.

We drove in silence down the crowded Champs-Élysées, and Gabe didn't talk again until he was on Avenue Franklin Roosevelt, heading toward the Seine.

"So how about that interview with Guillaume, Emma?" he asked just as the Eiffel Tower came into view on the horizon, off to the right. "Can you help me out?"

Ah. So *that* was it. That was why he was giving me a ride and pretending he thought I was pretty. Typical.

As if I'd be stupid enough to eat up his compliments and respond by giving him carte blanche to harass my client.

Then again, if I was smart enough to realize what his ulterior motives were, why was I feeling disappointed?

"I've told you that I'll book an interview for you," I said wearily, staring out the window. We were passing the entrance to the tunnel where Princess Diana had died, and as always I felt a little twinge of sadness.

"I know," Gabe persisted. "But we're all leaving for London next Saturday for the press junket. Why don't you set it up for Tuesday? We can meet for coffee. I don't think Guillaume has any plans."

I turned to look at him. "How would *you* know if Guillaume has any plans?"

Gabe had the decency to look a bit embarrassed. "Well, I wouldn't, exactly. I just meant that no public appearances have been announced or anything. So how about it? I need only half an hour for a UPP write-up. I promise I'll go easy on him."

I studied his profile for a moment, noting for the first time that there was a small, nearly imperceptible bump on the bridge of his angular nose, probably from a break at some point in his life, as well as a small scar just above his right eyebrow.

"Do you promise the write-up will be positive?" I asked, trying to ignore the fact that I had also just noticed for the first time how long his dark eyelashes were. We were on the Left Bank now, a few blocks from my apartment. I had to admit, this had been much easier than walking and taking the Métro, even with Gabe's constant questions.

Gabe smiled. "You know I can't promise that," he said. "But I *can* promise you that I'm not going into this with any bad intentions. I just want to ask Guillaume about all these crazy antics lately. I'll also ask him about the new album, and his much-anticipated launch, and everything. You can't ask for better publicity than this, Emma. My story goes out to hundreds of papers around the world."

"I know," I grumbled. I tried to weigh in my mind how much harm Gabe could do versus how much extra publicity he could bring us. In the end, I knew I had to grant him the interview, if for no other reason than that I had already given him my word. "Fine," I said finally. "I'll call you tomorrow with a time and place."

Gabe turned left onto my street and came to a stop along the curb.

"Wonderful," he said. "Thanks, Emma. Will you be there?"

"Will I be where?"

"At the interview."

"Oh," I said. I unbuckled my seat belt. What, did Gabe think I was as crazy as Guillaume? I wasn't going to leave my client alone with some muckraking journalist! "Of course I'll be there."

"Great," Gabe said again. "I'll look forward to it, then."

I sighed. What was I supposed to say? "Um, thanks for the ride."

"No problem," Gabe said. "You're on my way home anyhow."

I gritted my teeth and stepped out of the car.

"Talk to you tomorrow, Emma!" Gabe said cheerfully as I shut the door behind me. I stood and watched him as he pulled away from the curb and disappeared down Avenue Rapp without looking back.

Chapter Twelve

After a few more days of working long hours to prepare for the junket and to do more preemptive damage control by sending out releases about all of Guillaume's great charity work, Poppy and I spent the weekend shopping, eating out, and, of course, flirting with strangers Poppy had picked out at bars, although Poppy abandoned me briefly for a Saturday night date. Despite myself, I was starting to enjoy feeling attractive to Frenchmen. It *was* good for my confidence, in a way I had never expected.

On Tuesday, Guillaume and I arrived by taxi at Café le Petit Pont, the same place Poppy had taken me on my first night in Paris, for the interview I'd reluctantly promised to Gabe.

"I promise we'll keep this short," I said to Guillaume as we sat down at a table in the outside courtyard, facing the river. "We just have to appease this Gabriel Francoeur guy, and maybe he'll leave us alone."

"I've heard he's terrible," Guillaume said with what appeared to be an expression of amusement on his face.

"The worst," I muttered. I glanced around and saw that most of the people near us were staring at Guillaume, who seemed oblivious. Several tourists were surreptitiously snapping photos, and others were holding up cell phones to capture his image. No matter how many times I'd been responsible for my Boy Bandz clients in public, I'd never quite gotten used to the attention that fame brought with it.

"What's wrong?" Guillaume asked me after a moment, leaning across the table.

"Nothing." I shook my head. "It doesn't bother you? All these people staring and taking your picture?"

Guillaume glanced around, as if noticing for the first time that we weren't entirely alone in the restaurant.

"Oh," he said. "I guess I don't even think about it anymore." He smiled broadly and waved a few times to excited fans. Then he turned his dazzling smile back to me.

When our waiter arrived with a basket of French bread, we both ordered café au lait, which arrived within seconds. Amazing the kind of service you got when you lunched with a superstar.

"Okay," I said once we'd each taken a sip. "Gabriel will be here in twenty minutes. We need to go over some things first."

"Whatever you say, beautiful Emma," Guillaume said, flashing me a winning smile. "Then perhaps we can make sweet music together again, you and me?"

I rolled my eyes. He was so strange sometimes. "No, Guillaume."

He pouted. I ignored him.

"So I think it goes without saying that you can't admit to Gabe that you were drunk on any of the occasions he'll be asking you about," I began.

Guillaume recoiled in mock horror. "Drunk? Me? Never!"

"Riiiiiiight."

"Really, Emma, excessive alcohol consumption is wrong," Guillaume said. He batted his lashes sweetly. "Drug use is wrong."

"Oh, yeah, I'm sure Gabe will be won over by your puppy-dog eyes."

Guillaume looked confused. "Puppy-dog eyes?"

I realized the expression didn't translate. "I mean, innocent expression."

"I am innocent," Guillaume said. "I've never hurt anyone."

I thought about this for a moment. I supposed it was true. All of Guillaume's antics seemed only to harm himself—and of course the PR people who had to clean up the messes he made.

"You know, Emma, your eyes look very blue when you smile," Guillaume said softly, gazing at me so intently that I started to squirm. "They are beautiful. Like little pools of sparkling Mediterranean water."

I could feel my cheeks heating up. "Okay, Guillaume," I muttered. "Let's just stick to preparing for this interview."

He leaned over closer. "But you are so lovely, Emma," he said, still staring into my eyes. I felt my heart hammering in my chest. Sure, he was insane. But he was also gorgeous. And there was something about being gazed at by the most handsome man you'd ever seen that made your heart go pitter-patter, even if he was completely nuts.

"Guillaume, cut it out," I said, hating that he could certainly see that my cheeks were on fire.

"Cut it out?" He looked confused. It was another expression that didn't cross the language barrier.

"I mean, stop it," I clarified. "We're here to talk business. I don't know why you're saying these things all of a sudden."

"I just say what's in my heart, beautiful Emma." He smiled softly at me, and I tried to tear my eyes away.

I cleared my throat loudly and took a big sip of my café au lait, burning my tongue in the process. I coughed and tried to recover quickly. "Okay," I said, all business again. I avoided Guillaume's eyes. He was still staring at me in that unnerving way. "Here's what you need to say: You need to mention how excited you are to be reaching such a broad English-speaking audience. You need to say how wonderful it is to be helping to bridge a cultural gap with music. You need to talk about how 'City of Light' is about finding love in Paris and how you haven't found your own special woman yet."

"But *you're* very special, Emma," Guillaume interjected.

"Please stop."

"I can't stop my heart from beating for you, can I, Emma?" Guillaume said, reaching out to fold his hand over mine. I yanked my hand away as if his touch had burned me. He grinned.

"Be serious, Guillaume," I mumbled.

"Okay, I am totally serious now," he said, furrowing his brow.

"If Gabe asks you about any of the recent incidents you've had—the hotel room, the Eiffel Tower, or the whole rope thing the other day—just laugh and explain that it was all a misunderstanding," I continued, trying to sound as businesslike as possible.

"It *was* all a misunderstanding," Guillaume said.

"Right." I nodded. "Good start. Just explain that the hotel was nothing—simply me and Poppy working with you, with our clothes on. The Eiffel Tower was research for your video shoot. And the rope thing was a joke gone wrong. Okay?"

"Whatever you say, beautiful lady," Guillaume said.

"Oh, and one more thing. I know you and Gabe are both French. But can you speak in English, please? So I can make sure to stop Gabe if he's asking anything inappropriate?"

"Anything for you, my dear," Guillaume said, bowing his head. "I can never refuse the requests of a beautiful lady."

Before I had time to respond, I spotted Gabe striding confidently through the front door of Café le Petit Pont. He was scanning the room for us, and I had to admit he looked really good. He was dressed in a pair of dark jeans and a pale green button-down shirt that made his green eyes stand out sharply behind his glasses, even from across the room. I felt a little shiver run through me, and I pinched myself to get rid of it.

Guillaume waved. Gabe spotted us and came over.

"I'm sorry I'm a few minutes early," he said as he reached the table. He shook hands with Guillaume and then with me. "I hope I'm not interrupting anything, like, for instance, the two of you plotting what you're going to say to me."

I glared at him. Guillaume laughed.

"You've always been so skeptical, Gabe," he said, raising a finger and moving it side-to-side in a *tsk-tsk* motion. I glanced between the two of them.

"You already know each other?" I asked. Somehow I had expected that Gabe knew Guillaume only from afar, or perhaps from a few brief interviews during the past year. But they were behaving as if they had met many times in the past.

"Let's just say we go way back," Gabe said drily, shaking his head. He sat down in the chair between Guillaume and me and ordered a kir royale from the waiter.

"Ah, drinking in the afternoon, are we?" Guillaume said, leaning back in his chair and inspecting his café au lait with disdain. He grinned at Gabe. "A man after my own heart."

"Says the alcoholic," Gabe muttered.

"He is not an alcoholic," I said quickly, "and I would appreciate you not joking about such a serious matter." I was already getting a headache. I shot him a withering look.

"Right," Guillaume said stiffly. I could tell he was fighting back a grin. "I am not an alcoholic. Everything that has happened has been a—what did you call it, Emma?— a misunderstanding."

I glared at him. "It *was* a misunderstanding," I said through gritted teeth.

Gabe stared at me for a long moment. Then, thankfully, he switched gears. "So, Guillaume," he began, looking away from me and focusing on Guillaume, his pen poised over a pad of paper. "Tell me about your debut single, 'City of Light,' and why it's the ideal record to cross over to English-speaking listeners."

I breathed a sigh of relief as Guillaume started rattling off the perfect answer, describing how love is the universal language and how the song is, at its core, about falling in love, no matter where it takes place, or in what language. His answer was so perfect, in fact, that I was a bit transfixed myself, even though I knew Poppy and I had practically spoon-fed him the words.

Gabe took Guillaume through several questions about the album, his appeal to English-speaking audiences, and his music career.

The questions were surprisingly innocuous, and I was just starting to get comfortable when Gabe rapidly switched tracks.

"So these three recent incidents—the Hôtel Jeremie, the Eiffel Tower, your little high-wire act over Rue Banville—you claim they were all innocent mistakes?" Gabe asked, leaning forward. I cleared my throat loudly in an attempt to remind him not to press too hard.

"Yes, yes, of course," Guillaume said, shooting me a look. "You journalists are always getting it wrong."

Gabe, clearly sensing a challenge, arched an eyebrow and went in for the kill.

"Oh, so *we're* the ones getting it wrong?" he asked, looking half amused, half pissed off. Uh-oh. "So I suppose it's relatively commonplace to get locked in the Eiffel Tower without your clothes. Or to get caught in a hotel room with a bunch of naked girls. Or to get drunk or high or whatever and convince yourself that it's just a fantastic idea to hang upside down over a city street fifteen stories up."

"It was thirteen stories," Guillaume said, waving a hand dismissively. "And things aren't always what they appear." I looked back and forth between them nervously. So far, Guillaume seemed to be doing fine. His answers were nonchalant, nondefensive. Perfect. Then he glanced at me. "Besides," he added. "I have the beautiful Emma here to always come to my rescue." He smirked at Gabe.

I turned toward Guillaume and fixed him with a glare. What was he doing?

"Yeah, well, maybe if you could control yourself, she wouldn't have to keep disrupting her life to help you," Gabe snapped immediately.

"Who says it's a disruption?" Guillaume shot back.

"Guillame—" I started.

"Well, I'd say that making a woman risk her life to come get you down from a stupid high-wire act is a disruption," Gabe said.

"Gabe!" I interrupted hastily. Guillaume was still smirking, and Gabe looked peeved. "That's my job. Don't worry about it."

"Yeah, Gabe. We were singing a duet!" Guillaume said. "Emma loved it! Why are you so uptight? Is it because you haven't had a girl to sing a duet with in years? Are you jealous?"

Gabe's eyes flashed angrily, and he said something to Guillaume in rapid French. Guillaume laughed and answered. Whatever he said made Gabe look even angrier, and he barked another few unintelligible phrases at my annoying pop star.

"Guys?" I interjected. "Could we switch back to English?"

"Sorry, Emma," Guillaume said. "I was just telling Gabe here that I *do* respect you."

"And I was telling him that he obviously doesn't," Gabe retorted, his face stormy. "Because if he did, he wouldn't be making your life so difficult."

"Now, Gabe," Guillaume responded slowly. "Aren't *you* the one who's making Emma's life difficult? By hounding her so much for an interview with me?" He had a point. I glanced at Gabe, but Guillaume wasn't done. "In fact," he continued with a little grin, "just a few minutes before you got here, Emma was telling me you were, how did you say it? *The worst*, I think she said."

Gabe flinched and glanced at me. I felt the blood drain from my face.

"Guillaume!" I chided. He was smirking at Gabe now, pleased to have elicited a reaction. "I didn't mean it that way, Gabe," I tried to explain. "Just that you were hard to deal with sometimes."

"I wasn't aware I was such a problem, Emma," Gabe said stiffly. "I certainly apologize."

Guillaume hooted with laughter.

"Oh, I'm so sorry, Emma!" he mocked. *"I'll never bother you again!"*

"Guillaume!" I exclaimed.

"Don't worry, Emma, it's fine," Gabe said stiffly. "He's just being *un imbecile*." He pronounced the word the French way, but it wasn't difficult to guess at the meaning.

"Gabe!" I exclaimed. I'd never had a reporter talk to a client that way before—particularly not a client who was already such a big star.

"Don't worry, babe," Guillaume said, patting me on the arm and glowering at Gabe. "I can handle this."

Gabe retorted with something in French that I didn't understand, and Guillaume responded in French, too. The two men went back and forth for a moment with Guillaume smirking, Gabe glaring, and me trying desperately to interject, when finally Guillaume interrupted Gabe in English.

"That's it. Interview's over," he said abruptly, glancing at me. "I'm tired. Time to go home."

Gabe checked his watch. "But I have five more minutes," he protested.

"No," Guillaume said. "I believe your watch must be slow. Right, Emma?"

I sighed and looked back and forth between the two men, both of whom were gazing at me expectantly. I felt exhausted.

"Look, Gabe, if Guillaume says he's done, he's done," I said finally. "I'm sorry."

Gabe started to protest, but I held up a hand. "Guillaume," I said. "Since you did guarantee Gabe thirty minutes, and we're only at twenty-five now, would you answer one more question for him please?"

Guillaume tilted his head to the side, closed his eyes as if in deep thought, then nodded. "Yes. Okay. One more question." He opened his eyes and looked at Gabe.

"Thanks," Gabe said drily. "You're too kind." He looked back at his notes, and I began visualizing the worst. Perhaps he would ask something about Guillaume's reputation for frequenting strip clubs (something we had, thus far, kept out of the press). Or rumors that he had to go to rehab for a coke addiction before KMG would sign him (something no one, including Poppy and me, had ever been able to verify). But instead, Gabe's face settled into a look of calm. "So, Guillaume, do you talk to all women with the same disrespect you talk to Emma with?" he asked pleasantly.

I choked on the sip of coffee I had just taken. I looked at Gabe, my eyes wide, then I turned to Guillaume, who didn't look offended at all.

Guillaume grinned. "Just the ones who like it," he said, winking at me. My jaw dropped.

"Wonderful," Gabe said tightly. He stood up. "Nice to see both of you. You can expect an article about Guillaume on tomorrow's UPP wires. Thanks for setting up the interview, Emma. And thank you for your time, both of you."

My stomach was tying itself into hard knots. "Gabe, you're not going to write anything bad, are you?" I asked, trying to keep the desperation out of my voice. I didn't know how things had spiraled to such an extent.

"I'll only write what's fair, Emma," Gabe said, looking hard at me. I gulped. That wasn't good. I knew as well as Gabe probably did that *fair* would mean skewering the crazy rocker.

Gabe reached out and shook my hand briskly, then Guillaume's. "Until next time," he said, turning to Guillaume and putting a hand to his forehead in a little salute. Guillaume cheerfully and grandly saluted back. I waved weakly, feeling shell-shocked. "Have a nice day," Gabe added. Then he stood up and strode toward the door without looking back.

I waited until he was gone, then turned slowly to Guillaume. "What was that all about?" I demanded. "You acted like a jerk!"

Guillaume looked a bit offended. "Emma! Relax!"

"Relax? You want me to relax? You just ruined an interview with a guy whose story will literally be picked up all over the world! Seriously, Véronique will fire Poppy and me!"

"No one's getting fired," Guillaume said calmly. He smiled and reached across the table to put a hand on my arm. "Just relax, Emma. Gabe's article will be fine."

"You don't know that," I grumbled. "What was that all about, anyhow?"

"Ah, I was just having a bit of fun," Guillaume said, shrugging grandly.

"A bit of *fun*?" I repeated.

Guillaume nodded. "He obviously likes you," he said, as if it was the plainest thing in the world. I stared at him. "I just thought I'd see if I could get under his skin a little," he added. "I guess it worked! Good for me!"

Chapter Thirteen

I tossed and turned all night worrying about what horrible things Gabe would write in the UPP article. Would my career be ruined? Would Guillaume's? Exactly how far would Gabe go? Poppy had tried to calm me down by serving a slightly overdone baked chicken for dinner and filling me up with wine, but I only wound up feeling more nervous. I was at work the next day by 7 a.m., and I quickly logged on to my computer to see what KMG's in-house electronic clipping service had pulled up for the day. I was anticipating the worst from Gabe. After all, Guillaume—and I—probably deserved it.

As the results came in, I saw that Guillaume had been mentioned in 123 publications in the past twenty-four hours; that 119 of them were different versions of the same article (undoubtedly Gabe's, sent over the UPP wires and picked up in entertainment sections worldwide). There would certainly be more additions popping up over the course of the day as papers in the States began to add us. It was only 1 a.m. in New York and 10 p.m. in LA, and many papers hadn't closed yet.

Gulping and steeling myself for the worst, I clicked on READ TEXT and waited for the first article, from the *Sydney*

Morning Herald in Australia, to load. When it came up, it was indeed from the UPP wire service, with Gabriel Francoeur's byline. The headline screamed at me from the page.

CONTROVERSIAL CROSSOVER ROCKER OPENS UP ON EVE OF DEBUT ALBUM!

I gulped. I wasn't ready for this. Not yet. Not now. I loved my new job. I was falling in love with Paris. I was even learning to consider that there might be life after Brett. Now Gabe would probably bring it all to a close. I braced myself and began to read.

Celeb bachelor Guillaume Riche's debut album hits stores worldwide next Tuesday, and his first single, "City of Light," is already burning up the charts across Europe as well as in the United States and Australia. But although the buzz about Riche's album is strong and he's already being hailed as "the greatest European export since the Beatles" by *Rolling Stone* magazine, the eccentric star is perhaps currently better known for his many mishaps than for his music.

From getting trapped in the Eiffel Tower— reportedly without his clothing, although publicists for Riche deny it—to getting trapped in midair between two high-rise apartment buildings earlier this week, Riche is anything but your typical rock star.

"Sure, Ozzy Osborne can eat bats and Pete Wentz

can wear eyeliner," Riche said in an exclusive interview yesterday. "But no one can be Guillaume Riche."

Antics aside, though, Riche has the musical muscle
to back up his record label's claims that he'll be the
next big worldwide sensation. Not only do his vocals
span the range from early Paul McCartney to Coldplay's Chris Martin to John Mayer, but he has a writing credit on all the songs on his much-anticipated
album, called simply *Riche*.

"Music just speaks to me," Riche says. "And if I
can channel that into something that touches other
people, then that's a gift, isn't it?"

Riche is, of course, a French television star better
known for his status as one of Europe's most eligible
bachelors. The actor-turned-playboy has been widely
linked to women including Dionne DeVrie, Jennifer
Aniston and Kylie Dane.

Born in Brittany, France, to Pierre, an accountant,
and Marie, a stay-at-home mom, Riche began taking piano lessons at the age of four and was proficient
on piano, guitar, trumpet, saxophone and percussion
by the age of seven. He wrote his first song when
he was nine, and after spending two months in the
hospital following a serious car accident that claimed
the life of a schoolmate, he was performing in pubs
by 15. A short stint in jail after a public disturbance
charge just before his 17th birthday exposed him to
famed producer Nicolas Ducellier, imprisoned in the
same jail on a drug charge, and Riche's musical for-
mation was complete after working with this mentor

for 30 days. His informal recordings lit up northern France's airwaves around the time he turned 18, and he had earned a cult following by 20. Now, 10 years later, he's finally about to make his musical debut on the world stage.

"I'm excited," Riche says. "This is quite an opportunity. I think that music is the universal language, so if I can bridge the gap between English speakers and French speakers through my songs, then perhaps that's one step closer to global harmony."

The article went on to talk about Guillaume's tour plans and to quote several record execs talking about how wonderful "City of Light" was and how eager the world was to hear the whole CD. It concluded with a mention that the upcoming press junket would be Guillaume's official launch to the music world.

I sat in stunned silence for a moment after reading the article. I couldn't believe it. Not only had Gabe not blasted Guillaume (despite the few early mentions of his antics), but he had actually sounded *positive* about the singer and his music. How could that be after the debacle yesterday?

I reread the piece. It was wonderful, but I was puzzled about something. Where had Gabe gotten the information about Guillaume's past in Brittany? Sure, it wasn't a secret where Guillaume was from; a few profiles in the past had mentioned it. But how had Gabe known about Guillaume's parents? Or about his proficiency on so many instruments at such a young age? Or about his thirty days in jail at the age of seventeen? None of that had ever been printed, and I knew that Guillaume's parents, sister, and half brother had never agreed to an interview before; Poppy had said they were an extremely private family.

Had Guillaume told Gabe about his background during our interview yesterday, while he was speaking in rapid French? I didn't think there had been enough time for a conversation like that, but perhaps I'd just missed it.

In any case, there was no point in worrying, was there? Gabe had gone easy on Guillaume. We were out of the woods. I breathed a giant sigh of relief.

Poppy took me to lunch that day to thank me for somehow preventing whatever damage Gabe had intended to do, and when we got back to the office, there was an enormous bouquet of white lilies—my favorite flower—sitting in a vase in front of the door.

"I wonder who these are from?" Poppy asked, beaming as she picked them up and unlocked the door. Inside, she set them down on the corner of her desk and opened the attached envelope. "You know what? I bet they're from Paul, the guy I went out with on Saturday. He seemed like quite the romantic!"

Still smiling, she pulled out the card and scanned it quickly. She blinked a few times, and her smile faltered for a second.

"My mistake, Emma," she said, handing the envelope over to me. "The flowers are for you."

Surprised, I took the card from her.

To Emma: Beautiful flowers for a beautiful woman, it read.

There was no signature. I could feel my cheeks burning.

"So?" Poppy asked eagerly. "Who are they from?"

She picked up the vase from her desk and carried it over to mine. I stared at the flowers in confusion for a moment.

"I have no idea," I said. But even as I spoke, I realized that I was harboring a small hope that they were from Gabe, perhaps to thank me for the interview. But that was ridiculous, wasn't it? Reporters didn't send publicists flowers. And reporters like Gabe probably made it a general rule never to do anything nice at all, except when they were trying to get something out of you.

"Oh, come on," Poppy said, smiling at me. "You must have *some* idea."

"Really, I don't," I said. "I don't think many people even know I work here." I certainly hadn't given my work address to any of the random dates I'd had. As far as I knew, Gabe, Guillaume, the KMG staff, Poppy, and my family were the only people who knew where to find me.

"Ooh, a mystery man!" Poppy squealed. "See? The whole French-kissing thing is working already!"

My phone rang a few times that afternoon, and each time I picked it up, I half expected to hear Gabe's voice on the other end, admitting to sending me flowers and apologizing for the blowup during the Guillaume interview. Maybe he'd even ask me out—not that I would necessarily say yes. But he never phoned; the calls were all junket-related questions about catering, room accommodations, and journalists' flight information.

I was still confused when the phone on my desk jingled again at five that evening. I dove for it.

"Hello?"

"Emma? It's Brett."

My heart stopped for a second. It had been two weeks since I'd heard his voice. The familiar depth of it sent a jolt through me. My mouth suddenly felt dry.

"Emma?" he asked tentatively after a moment. "Are you there?"

"I'm here," I said shakily. "How did you get my work number?"

"Your sister," he responded promptly. I made a face. I wished Jeannie would just mind her own business. But then again, she never had; why would I expect her to start now?

"Oh," I managed.

"So," Brett began slowly, "did you get the flowers?"

I felt an unexpected twinge of disappointment. "Those were from *you*?" I asked.

"Of course, Emma." Brett sounded surprised. "Who else would send you flowers?" He paused, and a thought seemed to occur to him. "Wait, you're not dating someone over there, are you?"

"So what if I am?" I responded stubbornly.

He was silent for a moment. "I'm sure you're just being facetious, Emma," Brett said dismissively. "And I guess I deserve that, don't I?"

Why was he so sure that I couldn't be serious? I felt insulted.

"Look, Emma," he went on before I could respond. "We really need to talk. You need to know something."

"What?" In the silence, I could feel my palms beginning to sweat.

Brett spoke slowly and carefully. "I love you, Emma," he said. "I always have. I always will. I just got scared."

I didn't know what to say. I drew a deep breath.

"Brett, you threw me out," I said after a moment. "You slept with one of my best friends." I looked up and saw Poppy staring at me.

Are you okay? She mouthed the words at me. I nodded and looked down.

On the other end of the line, Brett sighed. "I know," he said. "And I can never tell you how profoundly sorry I am, Emma. It was incredibly stupid and wrong."

"No kidding," I muttered.

"Please, Emma, let me make it up to you," Brett pleaded. "Come home. This is where you belong. Let me show you how sorry I am. I love you."

I paused. It was everything I'd thought I wanted. But I was fairly certain that it was too little, too late.

"I'll have to call you back," I said. I broke the connection before Brett could respond.

As soon as I hung up, Poppy announced we were going straight to Bar Dix for pitchers of sangrias and a conversation about Brett.

"Maybe he deserves another chance," I mumbled once we'd ordered a pitcher and begun drinking. I was half hoping that Poppy wouldn't hear me. I drowned my response—and apparently my self-respect—with a swig of sangria, wishing that the buzz would start to set in. No such luck.

"Another chance?" Poppy repeated carefully. She took a sip of her sangria, never taking her eyes off me. "Haven't we been over this, Emma?"

I looked down at the table and thought about it for a moment. I knew I sounded crazy. And I knew that Poppy—in all her one-date-and-leave-'em wisdom—would be the last person in the world who would understand where I was coming from. I supposed she was right. But sometimes, unfortunately, there's a difference between what your brain tells you and what your heart feels.

I sighed. "I know you think I'm crazy," I said finally. I took a big sip. "It's just that it's hard to throw away three years without looking back."

"You didn't throw them away," Poppy said slowly.

I fumbled with my words, trying to explain. "I know. But can I just walk away from him, just like that? He says he made a mistake. Do I refuse to give him a chance just because he screwed up once?"

Poppy shook her head. "He didn't just screw up, Emma. He slept with *your best friend* after unceremoniously chucking you."

I could feel tears prickling at the backs of my eyes. "I *know*. But he left her. It only lasted a few weeks. Maybe he was just confused. Maybe I pushed him into getting engaged. Maybe he wasn't ready and he freaked out."

"Freaking out makes guys do a lot of things," Poppy said firmly. "It doesn't make them move into the beds of your friends. Not if they're decent guys, anyhow."

As Poppy studied my face, I could read pity in her big green eyes.

It made me sad. I didn't want her to feel sorry for me. But on some level, I knew she was right. I was acting pathetic. Still, I couldn't stop myself from feeling like maybe it was *my* fault that Brett had gotten scared away, had gone looking for something else with Amanda. After all, obviously there was something he wasn't getting from me if he was so quick to move on to her. Obviously there was something lacking in me. Or had I simply been too obsessed with work? Or too concerned with dragging him down the aisle?

"Look," Poppy said after a moment. "Are you happy? Here, I mean?"

I only had to think about it for a second. "Yes. I am."

"Happier than you were in Orlando?"

I stopped for a moment. Was I? It was hard to compare. My life here was so different than it had been back home. My job in Paris was stimulating and exciting but at times infuriating and nerve-racking. But wasn't that better than a nine-to-five job that was the same thing day in and day out? My social life in Orlando had been stable and secure; I was with Brett constantly, and I had my three-peas-in-a-pod girlfriends. Here, with Poppy as my social planner, I was going on interesting dates and spending my free nights sitting in cavelike bars sipping sangria. I had to admit, I was having fun.

"Yes," I said slowly, realizing it for the first time as I said it. "I guess I *am* happier here."

"Has he even taken a few days off to come over and apologize to you in person?" Poppy asked. "To try to win you back?"

"No," I answered in a small voice.

"And you want to leave this life you love behind to give a second chance to someone who hasn't exerted any more effort than picking up the phone?"

I stared hard into my glass of sangria as if it were a wishing well that would give me the answers, if only I looked hard enough. But the fact was, I already knew the answers I needed, didn't I?

"No," I said again. Maybe I just needed to look inside myself and stop placing blame where it didn't belong. Maybe I needed to be a little more like Poppy and learn to take control of my own life instead of letting myself be a doormat. After all, I could do it at work—and I *had* been doing it since I got here. Why was I so seemingly unsure that I deserved to be respected in my personal life?

"But I'm going home in a few weeks anyhow, right?" I asked softly. Maybe all this Paris-driven self-discovery was for naught.

Poppy paused. "Well, I was going to wait to tell you this," she said slowly. "But I've talked to Véronique. And based on all your good work these last few weeks with Guillaume, we'd really like you to stay."

"What?"

Poppy smiled. "KMG would like to offer you a longer assignment," Poppy said. "That is, if you can stand Guillaume Riche for the next year."

"A year?" I asked.

"A year," Poppy confirmed. "So will you do it? Will you stay?"

★ ★ ★

After Poppy went to bed that night, I sat in the living room for a long time, staring out the window at the Eiffel Tower until the lights went out and the tower faded into the shadows, making me feel all alone again. I looked at my watch. It would only be 8 p.m. back in Florida. I took a deep breath and picked up the phone to call Brett.

"I'm going to stay in Paris for a while," I said when he answered.

There was silence for a long moment on the other end of the phone. "Is this some kind of joke?" he asked.

"No," I said. I tried to put into words how I felt. "I'm really happy here. I'm finally part of something important. I finally feel needed."

Brett was silent for a moment. "So I guess it doesn't matter if *I* need you," he said. "I guess that's just not important?"

"I didn't say that," I said. I took a deep breath and thought about Poppy's words tonight. "Besides, if I'm so important to you, why don't you come over here for a while? I'm really happy here. Maybe we could give it a try in Paris."

"Are you crazy?" Brett asked. "I don't even speak French."

"Neither do I," I said. "But maybe you could just take some vacation time from work. Take the time you were going to use for our honeymoon, even. Come stay with me for a few weeks and see how you like it."

I was testing him, and I knew it. I was holding out my hand, and if he took it, I was willing to give things a try and admit that Poppy may have been wrong.

"Haven't I been clear with you about the fact that I intend to stay in Florida?" Brett said after a moment, "If I wouldn't move to New York, why would you think I'd come to France?"

"Because *I'm* here," I said right away. There was silence on the other end of the line. I struggled to fill it, because that's what the insecure side of me did—rushed to fill in words when the silence between them felt too heavy. "Besides, you wouldn't have to *move* here. Just come for a little while to see where I'm living. This is my life now, Brett. And I still want you to be a part of it, if you want to."

I wasn't sure if I meant that last part or not. I felt terribly torn. But I owed him at least that, didn't I? I owed him a chance. It was more than he had given me, but I was trying to live by my rules, not his. At the end of the day, there was comfort in that.

"Emma," Brett said slowly, as if talking to a child or someone whose mental comprehension was in question. "I thought you told me you were coming home."

I looked out at the darkened silhouette of the Eiffel Tower and felt a sense of calm settle over me. "I know," I said. "I think I *am* home."

Chapter Fourteen

The thing about Paris is that it's seductive. It's not the men or the dates or even the perfect kisses that have the power to seduce you, as Poppy would have me believe. No, it's the city itself—the quaint alleyways, the picturesque bridges, the perfectly manicured gardens, the rainbow of flowers that bloom everywhere in graceful harmony in the springtime. It's the way the sparkling lights illuminate everything at night, the way the stars dangle over the city like someone placed them there by hand, the way the Seine ripples softly like a supple blanket stretched between the banks. It's the hidden cafés, the tiny, self-righteous dogs, and the cobblestone streets where you least expect them. It's the bright green of the grass, the deep blue of the sky, the blinding white of the Sacré-Coeur.

It is perfection. And in perfection, there is seduction. Because maybe if you stay long enough in a city that's so perfect, you'll find perfection in your own life, too.

The night before I was scheduled to leave for the junket in London, I worked late and walked home alone, looking forward to a night by myself, for once. Poppy had left for London a day early to visit some friends and work out some last-minute details at the hotel. As I turned down my street and started walking the several yards to my building's front door, I stared up at the Eiffel Tower, which loomed over me from two blocks away. For the hundredth time, I marveled at how lucky I was to live here. How could I honestly live in the shadow of that and consider, even for a moment, leaving to go back to my old life?

I was so focused on the Eiffel Tower that I didn't notice the door to the American Library swing open in front of me. Nor did I notice a man walk out, balancing a tall stack of books that swayed uncertainly to and fro as he looked in the opposite direction. In fact, I didn't notice anything but the Eiffel Tower until I ran smack-dab into the man, sending the books flying everywhere.

"Oh!" I exclaimed in horror. "I'm so sorry! Um, *je suis désolée!* Is there anything I can do to . . ."

My voice trailed off in midsentence as the man stood up and grinned at me.

"Well hello, Emma," he said. "Imagine running into you here. Literally."

My jaw dropped.

"Gabe," I said stiffly. "It's you."

"Indeed it is," Gabe agreed cheerfully. He looked down at the books lying around us like a pile of rubble. "I suppose this was your revenge for the little incident in your office with the box of pens?"

"What? No!" I said sharply. "It was an accident. I didn't mean to run into you!"

"Mmm, so you say," Gabe said, arching an eyebrow at me.

I stared at him for a moment before I realized that he was kidding. I smiled reluctantly. "Hey, I wasn't the only one not looking where I was going, you know."

"Duly noted," he said with a mock-solemn nod. "Now, don't you think we'd better clean up this mess?"

I bent to help Gabe pick up all the books. "Big weekend of reading?" I asked as I stacked the final one—a James Patterson novel—on the sidewalk beside him.

"I don't know about you, but I have a junket to go to," Gabe said with a little grin. "This is just some light reading for the train ride over."

I smiled. "Good plan." I paused and looked down. "Hey, I meant to thank you for the nice article the other day," I said softly.

"Oh, that?" Gabe waved a dismissive hand. "No need to thank me."

"Yeah, but—" I paused. "The interview was a little weird. I know Guillaume was not exactly . . . nice to you. You could have been a little harsher on him in the article. I appreciate you going easy on him."

Gabe sighed. "Look," he said. "This isn't easy for me to say. The guy's a nutcase. But Guillaume is very talented, Emma, even if he's an obnoxious *bricon*. I didn't say anything that wasn't the truth."

I just looked at him. After a moment, he rolled his eyes and smiled.

"Fine, fine," he said. "Also, my editors make sure I stay nice."

"Oh," I said awkwardly. I didn't know why I was suddenly feeling tongue-tied. I realized it was the first time I'd seen Gabe out of work attire. He was dressed casually in dark jeans, a gray T-shirt, and maroon Pumas, and I had to admit, he didn't quite look like the annoying journalistic foe I usually thought of him as. He looked great.

"So, Emma, I'm glad I ran into you," Gabe said. "There's something I've been meaning to ask."

"Oh." Inwardly, I groaned. It was just my luck that I'd be cornered on the street by the very journalist who seemed to be a master at getting his way. "What is it?" I braced myself for him to ask me about Guillaume's mental state. Or his alleged alcohol addiction. Or something equally horrifying.

"Do you skate?" he asked. I blinked at him a few times in confusion. Was that code for something embarrassing? Was it some sort of French slang?

"What?" I asked.

"Do you skate?" Gabe repeated.

"Like . . . with roller skates?" I asked tentatively.

He nodded enthusiastically. "Yes, yes! Do you?"

I stared at him for a moment. With his bright eyes and his big smile, I swore he looked just as crazy as Guillaume for a moment. I blinked a few times.

"Um, yes," I said after a moment. "I mean, I used to sometimes in Florida. But . . . why?"

"Excellent!" Gabe exclaimed. He beamed at me. "You must come skating with me tonight!"

I furrowed my brow at him. "What?"

"The Pari Roller!" he said excitedly, as if I would know

exactly what he was talking about. Of course I hadn't a
clue.

"The what?"

"The Pari Roller," he repeated. "Every Friday night,
twenty thousand people meet in the fourteenth arrondissement and skate all over Paris!"

I stared at him. "Twenty thousand?" I repeated. "That
sounds insane!"

"It is," he replied with delight. "It's the most insane
thing ever! It's the biggest group skate in the world.
There are dozens of police along to block off the roads.
But it's the best way to see Paris, Emma. You must come
along!"

I looked at him dubiously. "You're not pulling my leg?"
I asked.

"No, no!" he exclaimed. He dug in his pocket and
pulled out a computer printout. "Look. This is the route
for tonight. It comes out each Thursday."

He handed me the crumpled sheet, and I studied it for
a moment. It was a map of Paris that seemed to have been
colored over with an interlocking, zany design.

"That's the route," Gabe said, pointing at the tangled
mass of zigzags. "It's nineteen miles long. It's fantastic! My
baby sister Lucie and I used to go every week, but then she
moved back home to Brittany to live with our father. So
I've been going alone, but it would be perfect for you! It's
the best way to see the city!"

"Oh," I said. I didn't know what he wanted me to say.
"So . . . you're asking me to come?" I said. It sounded like
a zany idea. But I had to admit, the longer I looked at the

piece of paper, the more intriguing it sounded. I'd never considered seeing Paris on skates.

"Yes, yes, you'll love it!" he said. He was grinning like a lunatic.

I narrowed my eyes at him suspiciously. "Is this just another way to trick me into giving you information about Guillaume?" I asked. "Or are you going to try to corner me into an interview?"

Gabe looked taken aback. "No, Emma, I wouldn't do that," he said, the smile slipping from his face.

I made a face at him. "I think you would."

He frowned. "Emma, I promise," he said. "I won't say a word about work this evening."

"Really?"

"I give you my word," he said solemnly.

I hesitated. "I'm just not sure if it's professional," I said reluctantly.

Gabe looked surprised. "What do you mean?"

I blushed. "I don't know. Since you're a reporter and I'm a publicist and everything. Isn't this unethical?"

"Emma," Gabe said. "I'm not asking you to spill all your Guillaume Riche secrets or give me exclusive information. I'm asking you to go skating."

I thought about it for a moment. What did I have to lose? My alternative was spending an evening alone. And when would I have a chance to skate all over this city again? It sounded fascinating. And perhaps, if we could stay away from talking about Guillaume for a night, I could curry a bit of additional favor for KMG with Gabe.

Obviously, I'd need the extra store of goodwill for the next time Guillaume did something stupid.

"But I don't have skates," I said.

"Don't worry," Gabe said. "My sister left hers at my apartment. If they don't fit, we'll figure out a way to rent you some."

"Well . . . okay," I said after a moment. I smiled. "I guess I'm in."

"Great!" Gabe said. "Why don't you meet me in an hour and we'll eat first."

Against my better judgment, I was at the door of Gabe's apartment in an hour, dressed in jeans and a long-sleeved shirt, as he had suggested. It felt crazy to be there, but I kept reminding myself that it was for the good of Guillaume. After all, if I was friendly to Gabe, he might forgive more of my rock star's wackiness, right? He might be easier to charm the next time Guillaume did something stupid. Unfortunately, there was no doubt in my mind that there *would* be a next time.

Plus, I had to admit, I'd spent the past hour getting excited about the Pari Roller. I had looked it up online to make sure that Gabe wasn't making it up, and as wacky as it sounded, it was true. From 10 p.m. to 1 a.m. every Friday, a group of nearly twenty thousand skaters, most of them in their teens and twenties, went roaring north from the Montparnasse station into the heart of Paris, snaking their way past monuments and landmarks in one noisy stampede on wheels.

When Gabe opened the door to his apartment, which was indeed just a few blocks from mine on Rue Augereau, he was holding a pair of skates in one hand and a baguette in the other.

"My sister's," he said in greeting, holding up the pink Rollerblades. "And dinner," he said, holding up the baguette. "Well," he amended. "Part of dinner, anyhow."

"You cooked?" I asked. I'd assumed we would just grab a sandwich or crêpe on the way.

Gabe shrugged. "We'll need the energy. Believe me. Besides, it's nothing special. I'm not so great in the kitchen. But I do make a fantastic spaghetti Bolognese, if I do say so myself."

I laughed. "It sure smells good," I said. And it did. The pungent aroma of tomatoes, basil, and garlic danced down the hallway toward the door, enticing me in.

"I'll go get things ready," Gabe said. "Why don't you try on Lucie's skates?"

While Gabe set the table and chopped up lettuce for a salad, I slipped my feet into his sister's Rollerblades and was a little surprised to find that they fit almost perfectly. I stood up and wobbled a bit. Gabe came over to check on me.

"How do they feel?" he asked.

"Good," I said. He looked down at the skates and bent to press his fingers into the space just above my toes, like shoe salesmen sometimes did.

"They're a little loose," he said. "But I think you'll be okay if you wear a second pair of socks. I'll go get some for you."

Forty-five minutes later, our stomachs full of spaghetti and our arms full of skates, socks, helmets, and pads, Gabe and I left his apartment and started walking toward the Métro stop at La Motte Picquet Grenelle, about five minutes away.

"So I thought you said you grew up in Florida," I said to make conversation along the way. "How come your sister lives in Brittany?" I tried to shift the weight of the skates from one arm to the other as we walked. They were getting heavy.

"She's actually my half sister," Gabe said. He glanced over at me. "Here, let me take those," he said, coming to a dead stop in the middle of the street. "I'm sorry. I should have offered." Despite my protests that he didn't have to, he grabbed my skates and handed me his much lighter helmet and pads to carry. I thanked him, and we started walking again.

"So Lucie is your half sister on your dad's side?" I asked after a moment.

Gabe nodded. "Yes. He's still in Brittany. My mother, of course, still lives in Florida. I spent every summer with my dad, so I'm close to Lucie."

I absorbed this for a moment. Then I realized something. "So when you said in the UPP story that Guillaume had grown up in Brittany, you knew that because you spent summers there as a kid? You knew who he was from when you were younger?"

"Yes," Gabe said quickly. "That's right. But I thought you said we weren't going to talk about work tonight." We had reached the Métro entrance, and before he could say more, we had to scramble to get our tickets out with our hands full. By the time we were through the turnstiles and had boarded the *Nation*-bound 6 train, Gabe was already on to another subject, asking me where I had lived in college. I let the whole Brittany issue go. After all, he had answered my question; it had been bothering me for days how Gabe had known so much about Guillaume's background.

The Pari Roller was, without a doubt, the craziest thing I had ever seen.

We joined thousands of other skaters in the Place Raoul Dautry, between the train station and huge Montparnasse tower, just in time for a brief lecture, in French, from the roller organizers about safety and road rules. Gabe quietly translated for me as I pulled on my knee pads, the extra socks he had loaned me, and his sister's skates. He helped me fasten Lucie's helmet on my head and grinned as he adjusted the strap.

"Why, you look beautiful, Emma," he said, patting the top of my helmet once he had tightened it on. I made a face at him.

"Yeah," I said. "I'm sure I'm really hot with my hair squished into a mushroom shape under a big, hard helmet." I rolled my eyes.

"You *are* hot," Gabe said, looking surprisingly serious. I opened my mouth to say something smart in return, but before I could, the whistle blew and we were nearly run over by a sudden onslaught of skaters descending on Paris.

"Let's go!" Gabe grinned down at me. He put a hand on my arm and helped steady me as we made our way into the crush of bodies on wheels. "You ready?" he shouted over the noise that came from twenty thousand sets of wheels grinding over the pavement in unison.

"Uh-huh!" I nodded nervously, and off we went, swept away in a tide of skaters.

For the next hour and a half, we barely said a word to each other, although Gabe kept looking down to make sure I was with him. I was—and I spent the entire skate in awe. It was the fastest and the hardest I'd ever bladed, but it was next to impossible to fall behind with a tide of thousands to sweep me forward every time my energy faltered. My rib cage vibrated with the gentle, steady roar of the thousands of wheels around us, and I marveled as we made our way toward the river, passing the Eiffel Tower far off to the left, then up past the impressive Opéra on the Right Bank and through the ninth up to the Gare du Nord, the station I'd be returning to tomorrow morning to take the Eurostar to London. We snaked through several neighborhoods I didn't recognize, and everywhere we went, people stood along the sidewalks, cheering and waving as we roared by. I felt like part of a parade.

By the time we arrived, breathless and drenched in sweat, in the Place Armand-Carrel, a big park in the nineteenth on the opposite side of Paris from where we'd started, it was eleven forty-five. I scooted onto the grass and, like thousands of other exhausted skaters, collapsed onto my back.

"That was amazing," I breathed to Gabe, who was standing over me, looking down in amusement.

"I'm glad you liked it," he said. "But you realize we're only halfway done."

I sat straight up. "What?"

He laughed. "This is just the halfway point. We take a break here before we skate back through the Place de la République and over to the Left Bank again."

I stared at him for a moment. "Oh," I finally said. I flopped back down on the ground and closed my eyes. I couldn't imagine another hour and a half of this.

"We can stop here and just take the Métro back if you want," Gabe said. I cracked open an eye and looked at him. He was still gazing down at me in amusement.

"I'm not a quitter," I said.

"I didn't say you were," Gabe said. "It's just pretty overwhelming the first time. I would completely understand if—"

I cut him off. "No." I sat up. "We're going to finish this course." I struggled to my feet, but my legs felt like jelly. Gabe grinned and helped me up, taking my hand in his to steady me. His fingers were rough and warm as they folded through mine.

"You sure you want to do this?" he asked.

I looked him in the eye and nodded, my heart pounding. "Yes."

We stood there for a moment, looking at each other. I was standing just fine on my own now, but Gabe hadn't let go of my hand. Nor had I pulled away. For a moment, as we stared at each other, I had the crazy feeling that he was about to kiss me. But just as he leaned a little closer, the whistle blew, and the stampede of twenty thousand skaters began again.

"Ready?" Gabe shouted over the din. He squeezed my hand, and I felt a little tingle run through me.

"Ready whenever you are!" I shouted back.

For the next hour and a half, as the tide of skaters swept us south through the eastern edge of the Right Bank, through the Place de la Bastille, over the Pont d'Austerlitz, and then for miles west along the Left Bank of the Seine before heading south back toward Montparnasse, Gabe didn't let go of my hand.

And, to my surprise, I didn't want him to.

"That was amazing," I said as we walked up to the front door of my apartment building just past 2 a.m. Every bone, every muscle, every tendon, and every joint in my body ached, but somehow I felt better than I had in years.

"Yeah, it's pretty fun, huh?" Gabe said, grinning down at me. He set our skates down on the ground and touched my left forearm with his right hand. My skin tingled. "I'm glad you came with me."

"Thank you so much for inviting me," I said. I couldn't believe this was the same Gabe Francoeur who had made my professional life tense and tenuous for the past few weeks. When he wasn't wearing his journalist hat, he was . . . normal. And very nice. Not to mention surprisingly attractive.

"I'm glad I did," Gabe said. He took a step closer. I suddenly realized that I wanted very much for him to kiss me. "You're amazing, Emma, you know that?"

In what felt like slow motion, he put both his arms around me and gently pulled me closer. Then he dipped his head and touched his lips softly to mine. A bolt of electricity shot through me; it felt perfect. His lips tasted salty and sweet, all at the same time. He lingered for a few seconds and then pulled away. He quickly straightened his glasses and cleared his throat.

"Well," he said. He coughed and smiled at me.

"Well," I echoed, feeling suddenly awkward. It had been the perfect kiss, but it had lasted only a few seconds.

"I, uh, probably shouldn't have done that," Gabe said, glancing away.

I felt my heart sink. "Oh," I said.

"I mean, I wanted to," he amended quickly. "It's just that with work and everything . . ." His voice trailed off.

Feeling foolish, I hurried to agree. "Of course. It was totally unprofessional of both of us."

"Totally," Gabe agreed. He paused and glanced down at me. "But do you mind if I say it was nice?"

I cracked a smile. "No." I felt relieved. "Not if you don't mind me saying that I thought it was nice, too."

"Well," Gabe said. "Good."

"Good," I agreed nervously.

"So, um, I'll see you tomorrow evening, then?" he said. "In London?"

"Um, right." I nodded, trying to look professional.

"Yes, definitely. We look forward to introducing you to Guillaume's music."

He smiled. "Right. Well. I'm sure I'll love it."

"I hope so."

Gabe studied my face for a long moment. Then he nodded. "Good night, Emma," he said.

Then he bent to pick up the skates from the ground, and without another word he strode quickly away.

And despite the fact that I knew I had a long day ahead of me in London for the opening day of the junket, I barely slept at all that night. I could still feel Gabe's fingers woven through mine.

Chapter Fifteen

I snoozed on the train to London the next morning. Although I was supposed to be keeping an eye on Guillaume in first class to make sure he didn't moon any passersby or go streaking through the dining car, I figured that Edgar and Richard could handle him for once. I was too exhausted to care.

"Late night, Emma?" Guillaume asked with a suggestive smirk as I settled into my seat.

"I was just skating, Guillaume," I said wearily. "Nothing more salacious than that."

He arched an eyebrow at me. "I don't know. Skating can be pretty hot and heavy."

I rolled my eyes. Clearly our definitions of *in-line skating* differed in some fundamental ways.

Every time I began to doze off, I thought of Gabe's lips pressed against mine and felt a mixture of pleasure and guilt. The kiss had been perfect, but publicists weren't supposed to go around kissing journalists, were they? I felt like I had violated some important code of ethics.

Somehow Brett was back in my mind, too, lurking at the borders of my conscience. Sure, I'd kissed a few guys since I'd been here, at Poppy's insistence. But Gabe was the first I'd actually felt anything for. Even though I knew it was crazy, I felt a little guilty, like I was being unfaithful to Brett.

Three hours later, when the limo that had picked up the four of us at the station dropped us off at the Royal Kensington Hotel, I stared in awe for a moment before letting the valet help me out. It was one of the most beautiful places I'd ever seen. Stately and enormous, lined with marble columns, its exterior was softened by lush window boxes and a bevy of flapping flags that soared over the marbled drive. Dozens of bellhops and valets in tuxedo jackets and top hats rushed around outside, opening car doors and effortlessly extracting luggage. If the journalists at the junket were half as impressed as I was, we were already off to a good start.

After I checked in, I went to see Poppy, whose room was beside mine. We did rock-paper-scissors for who would go check on Guillaume and make sure his suite was to his satisfaction (and that he hadn't managed to sneak in any teenage girls during the thirty minutes since check-in). Poppy's rock crushed my scissors, which meant that I had to go.

"I'll just be here taking a nice soak in the tub!" Poppy singsonged as I rolled my eyes and put my shoes back on. She didn't realize that I'd recently become the skating champion of Paris and would have given my left arm for a soak in a hot bath. "I'll think of you while I'm relaxing in the bubbles, sipping cava and reading *Glamour*."

"You're lucky I like you," I muttered as I slipped out the door and into the hallway.

Poppy and I were in nice enough rooms, but of course

our rock star was staying in a suite on the top floor. I couldn't imagine that it *wouldn't* be to his liking, but keeping him happy, especially prior to the press junket, was a vital part of my job. So off I went.

I knocked on his door twice before I heard a rustling inside.

"Who is it?" came Guillaume's muffled voice through the door.

"It's Emma!" I yelled back, attracting a scornful look from a bellhop delivering several Louis Vuitton suitcases to the suite across from Guillaume's. Evidently yelling didn't fit with the decorum of the hotel.

"Just a moment!" Guillaume yelled from inside. I heard footsteps, and a second later he pulled open the door. "Hi there," he said, looking down at me with a smile.

I hadn't been sure what to expect when I knocked on his door, but I'd been relatively sure that there would be some form of undress involved. To my surprise, though, Guillaume was fully clothed and actually looked relatively normal in a long-sleeved green T-shirt and a pair of dark jeans. Had I not known he was a lunatic, I might have assumed he was simply a normal, good-looking (okay, Calvin Klein–billboard-perfect) guy.

But alas, he was a crazy person. And my client.

"How are you, Emma?" Guillaume asked, stepping aside and gesturing with his arm. "Come in, come in."

"No, I think I'll just stay out here," I said. After all, I'd seen the kind of thing that went on in Guillaume's hotel suites. And I was really bad at poker.

"Whatever you want." Guillaume shrugged and moved

again so that his body filled the doorway. "How can I help you?"

It was the most normal, civil conversation I'd ever had with the guy. "I just wanted to make sure you were okay and that everything with the suite is fine," I said uncertainly.

"It's better than fine," Guillaume said. "It's perfect."

"Well, good."

"Good," Guillaume repeated.

"Is there anything I can get you?" I asked. "Or anything you need?"

"No, I'm fine." He studied my face for a moment. "But can I ask you a question?"

"Um . . . sure." I braced myself for the worst. He was probably going to ask if Poppy and I were interested in a threesome. Or if I knew where to buy good crack in London. Or if I knew of any monuments he could get naked in. I thought I'd suggest Big Ben.

But his question wasn't anything like that.

"Emma, I just want to know if you're okay," he said slowly.

I could feel my eyes widen. "What? Yes, I'm fine," I said quickly, flashing him a bright smile. "Why?"

Guillaume shrugged and looked a bit uncomfortable. "I don't know. You just haven't been yourself today. And you looked upset on the train."

I was startled. "Thanks," I said, forcing another confident smile. "But I'm fine. Really."

"Are you sure?" He looked genuinely concerned. I didn't know what to make of him.

"Yes, I'm sure," I said. I was getting uncomfortable.

Guillaume looked at me for a long time. "You know, I'm not such a bad guy," he said. "I mean, I know I can be a bother sometimes. But I'm not so bad underneath."

Where was he going with this? "I know," I said, my heart hammering a little.

"I just mean—" He paused. "Well, if there's anything you want to talk about, you can talk to me."

I think my jaw actually dropped. How could this be the same person I'd performed a death-defying duet with while hanging from a rope strung between two buildings just last week? How could this be the same guy who kept twenty-eight hundred euros in his briefs, just in case?

"Um, well, thank you," I said. "That's . . . really nice of you."

"Yeah, well." Guillaume shrugged and glanced away. "Anyhow, try to feel better. About whatever it is."

"Thank you," I said, still in partial shock. Guillaume gave me an awkward little hug and a peck on each cheek and closed the door to his suite.

I stood in the hallway for a long time wondering what had just happened.

Six hours later, Poppy and I had briefed a staff of twenty assistants, most of them from a British temp agency specializing in media and public relations. They would all be providing various functions at the cocktail reception that was due to begin in half an hour. A blond girl named Willow and a brunette named Melixa, for example, had been stationed in the lobby to help streamline media check-in. Two brunettes who looked as if they could have been sisters were upstairs in the media suite, handing out press packs, while two guys were manning the small continental buffet of fruits, pastries, sodas, water, and coffee that sat in the adjoining suite. A girl named Gillian was working as a sort of page, running back and forth between the lobby, the media suites, and the ballroom, alerting Poppy and me to any problems. (So far, knock wood, there hadn't been anything more serious than an entertainment writer from the *New York Daily News* being put in a room with two double beds when she had requested a king.) And several of the assistants were running around backstage in the reception room, making sure that everything was all set for Guillaume's performance tonight.

"I'm really nervous," Poppy said as the two of us settled into seats at the check-in table outside the reception room. In ten minutes, TV and print journalists would begin arriving for the opening-night cocktail party, which would culminate in a surprise three-song set from Guillaume. He'd open, of course, with his hit single, and he'd also be debuting two other songs, including my favorite, "La Nuit," a haunting ballad about unrequited love, sung half in English, half in French.

"Me, too," I admitted, rifling through the stack of papers in front of me until I emerged with tonight's media list. Most of the journalists on the two-day junket had arrived tonight, and although I knew that some would skip the reception in favor of wandering around London (not realizing, of course, that Guillaume would play), I figured that 90 percent of our reporters would be there, which added up to just over a hundred guests.

Poppy and I were both wearing black cocktail dresses, something we had debated about for some time last week while shopping at the Galeries Lafayette. I'd said we should wear suits in keeping with our roles as the business leaders of the evening. Poppy had rolled her eyes at me and said that it was a cocktail party, and we should dress accordingly.

"More than half of the journalists we're inviting are men," Poppy had reminded me with a wink. "There's nothing wrong with giving them something to look at while Guillaume sings his love songs, yeah?"

By seven thirty, nearly all of the journalists we'd invited had checked in at our table, where Poppy and I welcomed them warmly, made sure they had everything they needed, and then sent them inside to a room whose decor Poppy had been planning for months.

The reception room was lined with enormous photos of Guillaume in various outfits and poses, interspersed with blown-up *Riche* album covers. The lights were dim, and disco balls dangling high above cast sparks of light that almost looked like falling snowflakes around the room. Poppy had even taken care of ordering aromatherapy scents to be piped in, so the vague smell of French lavender permeated everything.

"Are you ready to go in?" Poppy asked me at seven forty-five, folding in half her list of checked-in journalists and putting it in her handbag. We hadn't had an arrival in ten minutes, and inside, we could hear enough conversation and laughter to know that the party was in full swing.

I looked at my watch. "Maybe a few more minutes out here," I said.

"But we have to go on in fifteen minutes, to introduce Guillaume. Don't you think we'd better have a glass of champagne first?"

I shrugged. "Just give it a few more minutes," I said. "Not everyone is here."

Poppy looked confused for a second. She glanced at the list. "We're only missing five people."

"I might as well wait."

Poppy looked at me strangely and shrugged. "Well, *I'm* going inside. Suit yourself."

Ten minutes later, Gabe still hadn't arrived. *Surely he's coming,* I thought in frustration. *But where is he? And more important, why is it bothering me so much?*

I sighed and got up from the table, leaving one of the PR assistants in charge in case anyone—like, for example, Gabe—showed up late.

Inside, the reception was in full swing, and it looked even more perfect than I had anticipated. I grabbed a glass of pink champagne off a tray that went by on the arm of a tuxedo-clad waiter and drank half of it down in one sip, trying to relax. There were roughly a hundred journalists in the room and, glancing around at their faces, I could see that most of them looked content. And why shouldn't they be? There were endless trays of hors d'oeuvres being carried around the room by a fleet of servers, and there were flutes of pink champagne, glasses of Beaujolais, strong mojitos, and Riche-tinis—a specialty drink of champagne, vodka, crème de cassis, and Sprite that Poppy and I had created for the event.

I shook a few hands as I made my way toward the stage to find Poppy. None of the reporters knew they were in for an impromptu concert in a few moments, and I could hardly wait to see their faces when the man of the hour took the stage.

"Were you waiting for someone in particular?" Poppy asked quietly as I slipped behind the curtains to the backstage area. She was standing by herself with her glasses on, reading over the scribbled remarks she planned to make later.

I shook my head and tried not to blush.

"You're not developing a crush on one of the journalists, are you?" she asked.

"No!" I exclaimed defensively.

Poppy looked at me carefully. "I told you to be careful with these French guys," she said. "They'll just break your heart."

I nodded and tried not to look guilty. It's not like I was *falling* for Gabe or anything. "I know."

Poppy took off her glasses and slipped them back into her case. Then she ran a hand through her hair and shoved her notes into her bag. "You ready?" she asked.

"Ready when you are."

She nodded, and together we walked out in front of the curtain onto the small stage.

"Hello, everybody, and welcome," Poppy said into the microphone. The chatter around the room quieted, and a hundred pairs of eyes came to rest on us. I smiled politely as Poppy continued. "Thank you so much for being here today for an event that we at KMG are very excited about. We're thrilled to launch Guillaume Riche to the world with the debut of his new album, *Riche*, which hits stores Tuesday."

There was a smattering of applause, and Poppy looked momentarily troubled. I assumed she'd been expecting more.

"Of course you've all probably heard 'City of Light,' the debut single from Guillaume's album," she continued. There was more applause this time, and a few whoops and catcalls to boot. Poppy smiled at this. "Of course as you all know, one-on-one interviews with Guillaume begin tomorrow. Print journalists are in the morning; TV reporters are in the afternoon. You should have received your interview time in your check-in packet. Please plan to be in the media suite thirty minutes prior, and make sure you check in with either Emma or me."

There were nods around the room, and the buzz of chatter started up again softly, as if some of the reporters had decided that Poppy wasn't saying anything of real value. I shot her a look, and she nodded.

"But before I bore you with more details," she continued. "I'd like to introduce you to the reason you're all here tonight." She paused dramatically, and the chatter faded again as the reporters looked at her expectantly. "Ladies and gentlemen . . . I give you France's greatest export, Guillaume Riche!"

There was a collective startled gasp, and then the clapping

began. A moment later, the curtain rolled back and revealed Guillaume's backup band. They started to play the first chords of "City of Light," and the room exploded into applause and cheers. Poppy grinned broadly at me as she stepped down and joined me beside the stage.

"They love him!" she whispered.

"How could they not?" I said back, watching as Guillaume, looking deliciously sexy in tight leather pants and a black button-down shirt, emerged from the other side of the stage with a wireless microphone in hand. The cheering and whistling went up an octave, and the applause thickened. Guillaume smiled at the crowd and waved.

"Welcome to London!" he said with a charming smile, eliciting even more cheers. "I can't wait to meet you all tomorrow during the interviews!"

Then he launched into the first verse of "City of Light," and the crowd went wild, which was a very good sign. In my previous experience, I'd found that journalists tended to be a particularly unexpressive lot, as they were supposed to remain objective and judge things without emotion. But this crowd was falling hook, line, and sinker for the musical bait Guillaume was casting out, and he was expertly reeling them in with his rich voice, his heartfelt lyrics, and his smoldering gazes.

After "City of Light," Guillaume and the band launched immediately into "La Nuit," and the decibel level of the crowd skyrocketed as they all realized they were getting the very first exposure to one of Guillaume's new songs.

Poppy gave me a spontaneous hug as we watched the

normally staid reporters go wild. "It's working!" she whispered. I hugged back, just as enthused.

As I gazed out contentedly over the room, I suddenly spotted Gabe toward the back of the crowd, and my heart leapt immediately into my throat. He looked perfect—and very French—in a pair of jeans, a blue oxford, a charcoal-gray suit jacket, and a black scarf, with his dark hair spiked a bit and his face smoothly shaven. He spotted me at the exact same moment I noticed him, and he grinned and raised his hand in a little wave. Then he turned his attention back to the person he was chatting with.

I took a step to my left to see who he was talking to. It was an older, gray-haired man whom I didn't remember checking in. Perhaps Poppy had met him.

"Hey." I nudged her. "Who's that Gabe is talking to?"

Poppy glanced out at the audience then back at me. "Ah, so it's Gabe, is it?"

I could feel my cheeks heat up. "What do you mean?"

"He's the journalist you fancy, is he?" Poppy was grinning at me. She didn't wait for me to respond. "He's a bit of a pain sometimes, but he *is* a good guy. And rather gorgeous to boot, I admit. Good for you!"

I looked at the floor, feeling like an idiot. "Yeah, well, whatever," I mumbled. "So do you know that guy?"

Poppy leaned to the side to see Gabe's conversation partner, and when she leaned back, she looked troubled. "This could be a problem," she said under her breath. "That's Guillaume's dad." She took a step forward to glance at them again. "Oh, bollocks! I told him not to talk to any media! What's he doing talking to Gabriel Francoeur?"

"Oh, no," I said grimly.

"You'd better go over there and interrupt," Poppy said. I nodded, gave her a worried look, and started making my way through the crowd. Just before I reached them, Guillaume's father patted Gabe on the arm, glanced at me, and turned to walk away.

"Hi, Emma!" Gabe said quietly, reaching out to kiss me on each cheek. He glanced toward the stage, where Guillaume was still belting his heart out to "La Nuit." It sounded amazing, and everyone in the room seemed to be standing in silence, transfixed by his performance. Except Gabe. Who didn't seem to care. And who'd been using the time to chat up the one person we wanted to keep him away from.

"Hi," I whispered, trying not to bother any of the other journalists. After all, I didn't want to detract from what was, so far, the perfect performance. "You arrived okay?"

"Yes, yes," Gabe said, glancing again toward the stage and then back at me. He smiled. "Thank you."

"You were late," I said. I realized immediately that it sounded like an accusation, and I felt foolish.

But he just smiled again. "You noticed."

I cleared my throat and ignored his words. I tried to sound casual. "So, um, was that Guillaume Riche's father you were talking to?"

Gabe hesitated but didn't look the slightest bit guilty. "Yes."

"I thought Poppy told him not to talk to any reporters!" I grumbled, looking crossly at Gabe.

He looked surprised and, if I'm not mistaken, a little bit

wounded. "Well," he said after a moment. "I suppose I'm not just any reporter."

I glared at him for a moment and lowered my voice. "You know, just because I let you kiss me doesn't mean you can get away with anything you want now."

Gabe looked startled. "I know that, Emma," he said.

Before I could respond, Guillaume and the band finished "La Nuit," and Guillaume began to speak.

"Thank you all so very much," he said. "You are a very kind audience. Now I will play one more song for you. This one is the third song from my album. It will be the second single. It is called 'Beautiful Girl.' Tonight, I dedicate this song to Emma, my lovely publicist, who keeps coming to my rescue. I hope you are smiling, Emma."

My jaw dropped, and Guillaume and the band launched into the upbeat song about a man who falls in unrequited love with a woman from afar. I could feel my cheeks heat up as several journalists turned to look at me with curiosity.

"Oh, great," Gabe muttered. "Now your rock star is dedicating songs to you."

I glanced at him in surprise. "He's not *my* rock star," I stammered.

"Is something going on between you and Guillaume?" Gabe asked, staring at me.

"What? No!"

"Then why is he dedicating songs to you?" It was not an unreasonable question. Unfortunately, I didn't have a good answer.

"I don't know!" I insisted.

Gabe made a face but didn't respond.

I cleared my throat and looked away, hoping that Gabe would drop the subject. I gazed around the room for a moment while Guillaume played, taking in the rapt, smiling faces of most of the journalists. His charm was so evident in a small, intimate live show. I knew half the female reporters would go back to their rooms tonight fully in love with him.

"So what time is your interview with Guillaume tomorrow?" I asked Gabe as the song wound down, hoping that we could move on to safer conversational topics. But when I looked to my left for his answer, he had disappeared. I frowned and looked around. He was nowhere to be seen.

Guillaume ended the song with a big grin, a wave, and a shouted, "I'll see you all in a little while!" He strode offstage, and I realized I didn't have time to worry about Gabe or where he had gone. I needed to go find Guillaume so I could escort him briefly through the reception room to meet journalists.

I found Poppy backstage.

"So? What did Gabriel say?" she asked.

"Nothing," I said, averting my eyes.

She gave me a funny look. "No, I mean about why he was talking to Guillaume's dad," she said.

"Oh. Right. Well, he didn't exactly explain."

"That's weird," Poppy murmured. Just then, Guillaume appeared with his guitar case in hand.

"I'm ready for the walk-through, ladies," he said with a grin. "How did you like the songs?"

"Oh, Guillaume, you were marvelous!" Poppy exclaimed.

"Merci beaucoup, mademoiselle," he said with a little bow. He turned to me. *"Et toi?* Emma, did you like the concert?"

"Yes, Guillaume, you did a great job," I said.

"And the dedication? What did you think of that?"

"Um—" I didn't know what to say. "It was . . . it was very thoughtful, Guillaume. Thank you very much."

"You *are* a beautiful girl," he said, staring at me intensely. I glanced at Poppy, who was looking intently at Guillaume.

I cleared my throat. "Um, well, thank you anyhow," I said quickly. "So, uh, are you ready for the walk around the room?"

"You take him first," Poppy piped up, making matters worse. She glanced back and forth between us then reached out her arms. "I'll put his guitar away." Guillaume obediently handed the instrument over, and I made a face at Poppy.

For the next twenty minutes, I led Guillaume around the room and tried to introduce him to the various journalists, all of whom were conveniently wearing HELLO MY NAME IS . . . stickers with their names and affiliations. I was worried at first, because this was the Get-to-Know-the-*Real*-Guillaume-Riche part of the evening, and of course Poppy and I were trying to conceal that the *real* Guillaume Riche was, at times, a raving lunatic.

But tonight, miraculously, he stayed normal. He shook hands with the men and chatted them up about soccer (if they were British), his visits to the United States (if they were American), and his love of music (if they were from anywhere else). With the women, he turned on the charm to full voltage, talking, laughing, and flirting like it was his job, which, I supposed, it was.

Eventually, after Guillaume had shaken hands with all the journalists and Poppy had wandered off to talk to a British radio host she knew, Guillaume and I made our way over to his father, who was standing near the bar in the back of the room, drinking a glass of red wine.

"Emma, have you met my father yet?" Guillaume asked as we approached. I shook my head. "I would love to introduce you. Come."

Guillaume's father was about five foot ten with a slender build, thin and trembling hands, and green eyes that looked surprisingly bright on a face that had sunken into itself with age. It was easy to see the resemblance between father and son; it was all in the brilliant eyes and the mop of dark hair, although the elder man's hair was peppered with gray. Guillaume said something to his father in French, then I caught my name.

"Oui, oui, enchanté." Guillaume's father smiled at me pleasantly and leaned forward to kiss me once on each cheek.

"Nice to meet you," I said, smiling at the older man. "We are very happy to work with your son."

"He eez, how you say, very good. Very good talent," his father said.

I smiled. "Yes, absolutely. He's wonderful."

His father nodded and smiled at me. *"Merci beaucoup,"* he said.

Father and son talked for a few moments in rapid French,

then, seeming to realize he was excluding me, Guillaume switched to English.

"So you liked the show?" he asked his father slowly.

"*Oui, oui,*" his father said. "Eet was perfect."

"Thanks, Papa." Guillaume smiled. "And this party? What do you think?"

"Very nice, very nice," his father said haltingly.

It was so strange seeing Guillaume interact with his dad. He seemed almost . . . normal.

"Guillaume," the elder man said slowly. "I talk to Gabriel during your show. He has some, how you say, concern about you."

My head whipped toward Guillaume. "Wait, Gabriel *Francoeur*?" I interrupted in surprise. "Your dad actually *knows* Gabriel Francoeur?"

Guillaume's father started to say something, but then Guillaume interrupted. "Let's just say Gabe and I go way back," he said quickly.

I looked at him in confusion. I'd realized last night that Gabe hailed from Brittany, too, but it was an enormous region. I hadn't thought they would actually have known each other. And why had neither man mentioned it before? I was about to ask more, but just then Poppy came flouncing up with a handsome, dark-haired man in tow.

"Guillaume!'" she bubbled, completely unaware what she was interrupting. "I would like you to meet Vick Vincent, London's premier disc jockey and one of the people who has been pushing your record hard. He's an old school chum of mine."

"I don't know that I like the adjective *old*, Poppy," Vick

boomed in a flawlessly deep deejay voice. "But indeed I've become one of Guillaume Riche's supporters. Good job, mate." He clapped Guillaume on the back.

"Thank you," Guillaume said graciously. He took a small step back. I knew he didn't like to be touched—unless he invited the touching. And he usually only invited touching from females, not pompous male disc jockeys.

I leaned closer to Guillaume. "You want to call it a night?" I whispered in his ear while Poppy was saying something to Vick.

Guillaume nodded. I looked around to gather his father up, too, but he had seemingly vanished. What was it with men and their disappearing acts this evening?

"Where's your dad?" I asked Guillaume.

He glanced around and shrugged. "Don't know," he said. "But he'll find his way. I'm the only one you have to worry about."

Chapter Sixteen

The interviews the next day went flawlessly. Once again, Guillaume was on his best behavior, which made me nervous. I was starting to worry that his good-guy routine was too good to be true. I found myself waiting for the other shoe to drop. But so far, so good. Poppy and I took turns sitting in on the interviews all day, so we each heard him say, dozens of times, how pleased he was to be bridging the gap between France and the English-speaking world with his music.

He sang a few verses a cappella for the TV journalists who thought to request it and flirted incessantly enough that most of the women, regardless of age or experience, were reduced to giggling schoolgirls within five minutes. He looked handsome, acted charming, and came across cool, calm, and collected. In short, he was perfect.

"He's a dream!" bubbled one starstruck reporter from the *Daily Buzz* after she emerged from her interview room.

"He's hotter than Justin Timberlake and John Mayer and Adam Levine put together!" exclaimed a reporter from the *Orlando Sentinel*. "And omigawd, he kissed me! I'm never washing this cheek again!"

"What a charmer," said a red-faced reporter for *The Advocate*. "I think I'm in love," he added.

Poppy and I celebrated the success of the day's interviews that evening in the hotel bar with a big dinner and a bottle of wine between us. Most of the journalists would be leaving in the morning, after a lavish breakfast, during which Guillaume would perform a surprise acoustic rendition of "City of Light." Then Poppy and I were to escort Guillaume back on the four-twelve Eurostar train, so as long as we made it through tonight, we'd be through the junket virtually scot-free. Neither of us could quite believe how easy it had all been.

After dinner, Poppy yawned and said she was tired; she was thinking of turning in. I was a bit disappointed; I'd hoped that now that the bulk of the junket was over, she'd feel up for a night on the town and I'd be able to see a bit of London. Poppy had given her mobile number to the security director of the hotel so that if there was any sort of problem, we could be reached anywhere. But I'd have to resign myself instead to a night of watching pay-per-view movies on TV from my king-size hotel bed.

Thirty minutes later, I sat in bored silence in my room, flipping aimlessly through muted channels on the television. I found myself thinking of Gabe and feeling disappointed that I hadn't seen more of him. He had somehow managed to change his interview time today without my knowing it, and I'd been taking a lunch break downstairs the entire time he was in the press suite.

I thought about calling him but eventually nixed the

idea. After all, what would I say? Still, it felt strange to be all by myself in an unfamiliar city, sitting alone in a hotel room at 9 p.m. when Gabe was just a few floors away. All I could think about was how much I wanted to kiss him again.

But evidently, he wasn't feeling the same way. If he was, he would have called me, right? *Perhaps*, said the little self-conscious voice in my head, *he was just using you to get access to Guillaume.* That couldn't be true, could it?

Just then, the hotel phone in my room began jangling. It startled me, and I whipped my head toward it immediately. It couldn't be, could it? Could Gabe be calling me? It had to be him, right? No one else who would want to call me knew I was here. Heart pounding, I picked up the receiver.

"Emma?" The worried voice on the other end wasn't Gabe's. It was Poppy's.

"Hi," I said, startled. "What's wrong? Are you in your room?"

"Er, not exactly. I'm actually out."

"You're out? I thought you said you were tired."

"I'm sorry I didn't tell you," she said. "I'm kind of on a date."

"A date?" I was shocked. I hadn't realized that Poppy's dating schemes extended across the Channel.

"Well, yes. I'm sorry. I didn't want to make a big deal of it."

"But I thought you only dated Frenchmen," I said, confused. "Your whole French-kissing philosophy and all."

"Er, right, well, I guess I might have forgotten to tell

you that Darren still lives in London." Poppy's voice sounded muffled.

My jaw dropped. "Darren?" I asked. "As in ex-boyfriend, voodoo-doll Darren?"

"Er, yes," Poppy admitted, her voice sounding strained. "We've sort of been, er, talking lately."

"Ah," I said, somewhat confused. "Like, talking talking? Romantically?"

Silence on the other end. "Maybe," Poppy said, her voice small.

"What do your books say about getting back with an ex who broke your heart?" I asked accusingly.

Poppy paused. "I suppose they would advise against it," she said. "But you can't always believe everything you read."

I pulled the receiver away from my ear for a moment and stared at it in disbelief. Poppy was still talking when I tuned back in. "Anyhow, I feel really badly about this, Emma," she was saying. "But I just received a call from hotel security. About Guillaume."

I groaned. "What did he do this time?"

"It seems there is some sort of party going on in his room with loud music and such." Poppy sighed. "I'm on my way back to help you out. I know it's just dreadful of me to ask you, but would you please go up and try to put a stop to things before they get out of hand? It'll be another thirty minutes till I'm there, at least."

I closed my eyes and took a deep breath.

"Yes, of course," I said finally. "I'll go right now. Don't worry."

"Emma, you're a gem," Poppy said. "I really owe you. I'm getting back there just as soon as I can."

"Thanks," I muttered. I forced a smile that I hoped she could hear through the phone. "Good luck with Darren, okay?"

Grumbling to myself, I threw the covers off the bed, disentangled myself from the sheets, and found a pair of jeans, an old Beatles T-shirt, and a pair of black ballet flats that were so worn I generally used them as slippers around the house. In front of the mirror, I swiped on some blush as well as a bit of mascara and lipstick so that I would look vaguely presentable. Then, grabbing my room key and sticking it into my back pocket, I reluctantly left and headed for the elevators.

Two minutes later, when the elevator doors opened on the penthouse floor, I could indeed hear loud music blasting from the direction of Guillaume's suite.

"Can't he control himself for *one* night?" I said aloud, throwing in a few expletives for good measure.

I had to pound on the door three times—the third time with all my strength—before the door swung open to reveal Guillaume standing there, in just a pair of jeans, holding a glass of champagne in his hand. His dark hair had gone haywire, shooting off in all directions, and he evidently hadn't shaved since earlier in the day, as he was sporting the beginning of a five o'clock shadow. I tried to tear my eyes away from his body and focus on his face, but that took considerable effort given the obvious solidity of his pecs and the impressive definition of his chest.

I took a deep breath and locked eyes with him.

"Hi, Emma!" Guillaume said with a broad grin. "You have come to join me?"

"No, Guillaume, I haven't come to join you." I fixed him with a reprimanding look. "Honestly, Guillaume, can't you keep the partying to a minimum when you're in a hotel filled with media?"

Guillaume looked confused. "Partying?" he asked, swirling around the remainder of the champagne in his glass and downing it in a big swig. "*Chérie*, it's just me in here."

I looked at him suspiciously. There was no way our hard-partying rock star was entertaining *himself* with a room full of blasting music and a bottle of champagne. "Come on, Guillaume. I'm not here to get you in trouble. But please, whatever girls you have in there, just send them home before the situation gets worse."

"Emma, I promise you," Guillaume said, looking me dead in the eye. "It's just me. I swear on my life."

I locked eyes with him, and when his gaze didn't waver after a moment, I sighed and shrugged. "Fine, whatever you say," I said, not quite believing him. "But could you turn the music down, at least? Hotel security is getting calls."

Guillaume stared at me for a long moment then shrugged and disappeared back into his suite, leaving me standing in the open doorway. I waited and waited for what felt like an eternity, but the volume never went down, and Guillaume never returned. I waited a bit more. Then, looking from side to side to make sure no one was watching who might get the wrong idea, I left the door ajar and walked into the suite and down the hallway to find Guillaume—or at the very least, to find the volume knob on the stereo, which was currently blasting an old Rolling Stones album.

"Guillaume?" I called out above the music as I made my way down the suite's long hallway and into the living room. "Where did you go?"

Just before I reached the living room, Guillaume appeared from around the corner, scaring me half to death. I jumped, startled. Guillaume grinned and thrust a full flute of champagne toward me.

"Guillaume? What are you doing?" I demanded, eyeing the bubbly warily. Inside the glass, it fizzed mesmerizingly.

Guillaume thrust the glass forward again insistently. "Drink up, Emma!" he said cheerfully. "We must toast!"

"Guillaume, I—"

"Listen, Emma," he said. "The hotel gave me two complimentary bottles of this wonderful champagne. Now, it's up to you, of course, but if you don't have a drink with me, I'll be forced to drink both bottles myself."

"Guillaume—" I began wearily, but this time he interrupted before I could even get to the frustrated eye rolling.

"We both know what happens when I drink too much, *oui*?" he continued. "So really, if you think about it, it's in your best interest to drink with me, because that's less champagne for me, now, isn't it?"

I started to say something, but the protest got lost in my throat. After all, he was right, wasn't he? I couldn't exactly argue with the more-for-me-equals-less-for-him theory, could I?

"Fine," I said, reluctantly accepting the glass. "But only if you promise to turn the music down."

Guillaume beamed at me. "As you wish, my dear." He raised his glass and waited until I reluctantly raised mine, too, in a toast. "Here's to you, my dear Emma," Guillaume said. I made a face as we clinked glasses, and Guillaume looked delighted. He waited until I took a small sip from my glass.

"The volume, Guillaume?" I reminded him.

"Ah, of course, of course!" he said. He dashed toward the living room. The moment he had turned his back, I emptied half my flute of champagne into the potted plant at the end of the hallway. Then I innocently righted the glass and put my lips to the edge as if I'd been sipping it just in time for Guillaume to return.

"Emma, you *do* drink!" he exclaimed, eyeing my glass with delight. "Very good! Very good!"

I smiled wanly at him.

"Well, aren't you going to come in?" he asked. "Or do we have to drink standing up in the hall?"

I didn't see that I had much of a choice. With any luck, I could sit beside another potted plant and proceed to get rid of as much of Guillaume's champagne as possible before he could drink it and do something stupid. I followed Guillaume into the living room. He grabbed the open bottle of champagne from where it sat in a bucket of ice, and topped off my glass.

"Have a seat, Emma," he said, gesturing to the couch. "Please, make yourself at home. My suite is your suite, my sweet," he said, laughing uproariously at his own pun.

"Thank you." I tried to stifle a yawn. It had been a long day, and I should have been falling asleep in my own bed, not playing AA sponsor to my client. This surely wasn't in my job description, although I had to admit that very little of what I'd had to deal with in the past few weeks fell under the umbrella of officially outlined duties.

I sat down on the couch, beside another potted plant, feeling a bit surprised at how comfortable the cushions were.

"So," Guillaume said, settling down beside me. "Are you going to tell me what's wrong? Or do I have to begin guessing?"

I looked at him, startled. "Nothing's wrong. What do you mean?"

Guillaume shook his head knowingly. "You were sulking today."

"I wasn't sulking!"

Guillaume laughed. "Yes, you were. You were sulking. You cannot deny it."

I sighed. "It's nothing." I took a long sip of the champagne—one sip couldn't hurt—and felt a small tingle of warmth spread over me.

Guillaume watched me closely. His near nudity was beginning to get to me.

"Could you put a shirt on please?" I asked crossly. I took another sip. After all, if I was going to have to sit here with him and dispose of half his champagne, I would appreciate us both being fully clothed.

But Guillaume only laughed. "It's hot." He shrugged. "Does my body offend you?"

No, I wanted to say. *It's making me feel attracted to you.*

"No," I said. "It just seems weird that you don't have a shirt on."

Guillaume laughed again, shrugged, and made no move to go put more clothes on. Instead he topped off my glass again. Obediently, I took another sip. I was starting to feel the alcohol, but not enough to worry about it. Just enough to relax me a little. Besides, it was all for the greater good. Every sip I drank was one less that Guillaume could consume.

After a moment of silence, Guillaume tried again. "So? Are you going to tell me what is bothering you? I want to help."

I studied his face for a moment. He certainly appeared genuine. His usual smirk was gone, and he simply looked concerned.

"Fine." I sighed and glanced away. "Look, it's just that I'm confused, you know?" I turned back to Guillaume and found him listening to me carefully. "I mean, Poppy offered me a permanent job in Paris, working with you, and I think I want to take it. I really do. But I'm just not sure it's the right decision."

"Pourquoi?" Guillaume asked, leaning forward with interest. I took another sip of my champagne and glanced away. Really, I hadn't intended to share so much.

I hesitated. "Because there's a guy at home whom I just ended an engagement with." The words came pouring out. "Well, I didn't exactly end things with him. He broke up with me. But now he thinks he made a mistake. He says he wants to try again. And we were together three years, you know? I'm really confused. But I don't know that I want to go home. I love Paris. I love almost everything about it. I even love the job, even if you make it difficult for me sometimes."

I stopped, embarrassed. What was in this champagne—truth serum?

Guillaume smiled. "I'm sorry I make your life difficult," he said.

"No, it's not that you make my life difficult," I amended. "And you will never hear me say this again. But really, I prefer working with you to working with the boy-band boys I used to deal with. There was nothing exciting about that job."

I hadn't realized until that very moment how true the words were. I *did* like working with Guillaume, despite—or perhaps even because of—the fact that I never knew what was going to happen next with him. How could it be that I preferred talking my clients down from ropes suspended in midair to making excuses for prepubescent boys gone wrong?

I looked down at my glass. Somehow it had become empty. Had I really sipped it all while embarrassingly pouring out my heart? I glanced guiltily at Guillaume. But he wasn't looking at me. He was looking at my glass. Which he was presently refilling. Why did I have the sudden sense that I was the one drinking the majority of the champagne? Somehow, my pour-it-in-the-shrubbery plan seemed to have derailed.

"Well, I'm glad I can make your life more exciting," Guillaume said, refilling his own glass as well. He upended the bottle in the ice. We seemed to have finished it all. He reached for the other bucket, which held a second bottle of champagne. "So," he continued smoothly. "Do you still love this guy back home? The one you just ended your relationship with?"

I blinked a few times and studied my glass of champagne intently, as though an answer to the question might appear on the surface courtesy of the constantly rising stream of bubbles. No such luck.

"I don't know," I mumbled. I took another sip of champagne as I contemplated the question. "I don't think I do. No. Not anymore. It's confusing. I don't think you can love someone for three years and then just turn it off."

"Probably not." Guillaume nodded supportively.

"But I don't think I've been *in* love with him for a long time," I continued, still wondering vaguely what was possessing me to confide so much in Guillaume when I had barely even admitted these things to myself yet.

Satisfied with my honesty, at least, I leaned back into the comfortable cushions and watched as Guillaume popped the cork on the second champagne bottle and poured us each a fresh glass. The liquid seemed to be disappearing with surprising speed.

"Plus," he added nonchalantly, leaning back and taking a sip from his glass, "you have a crush on a certain UPP journalist."

"What?" I sat up so quickly that I sloshed a bit of champagne onto my jeans. But I was more concerned at the moment with the fact that my cheeks felt like they were on fire. "No I don't! I don't know what you're talking about! I don't have a crush on him!"

Had I really been that obvious? I'd hardly realized it myself until just a few days earlier, although I suppose I'd been attracted to him since the moment I'd first spotted him in the Hôtel Jeremie press corps crowd.

"Yes, you do," Guillaume said simply.

I could feel the heat rising to my face. I had no doubt I was beet red.

"No, I don't!" I don't know why I felt so compelled to deny it. But I couldn't have Guillaume thinking that. I was determined to be 100 percent professional. And my idea of professionalism did not include drooling over a cute reporter who seemed determined to be my client's primary adversary.

"Yes, you do." The words were singsonged merrily at me this time.

"*No*, I don't!" I felt annoyed now. Had he lured me into his room for the express purpose of making me feel foolish? "And just what would make you think that, anyhow?" I asked defensively, realizing a bit late that my indignation perhaps wasn't transmitted as clearly as it could have been, given that I was slurring my words pretty severely.

Guillaume rolled his eyes. "Wow, I don't know. The way you look at him. The way you're always looking around for him when you can't find him. The way you're blushing now that I am asking you."

"I'm not blushing," I said quickly.

"Right. It must be that the temperature in the room has climbed. Perhaps you're overheating?"

"Don't make fun of me," I snapped. "I'm serious. It's

not like I'm even looking for a boyfriend or anything anyhow."

"Oh?" Guillaume asked with some interest.

I had the dim sense I was talking myself into a hole. But I just kept on digging. "Yes," I said triumphantly. "I'm *dating*. According to Poppy, I need to go out with as many Frenchmen as possible, but no more than one date each."

Guillaume grinned. "And you sleep with them, yes?"

I shook my head vehemently. "No, of course not!"

Guillaume looked confused for the first time. "So what is the point?"

I thought about this for a moment. "The pursuit of the perfect French kiss, I think," I said, realizing that I was slurring even more than before. I'd better stop drinking the champagne and go back to the shrubbery plan. "Can I ask you something?"

"But of course." Guillaume smiled.

"What's *with* you, anyhow?" I realized that the words sounded completely tactless, but between my frustration and the champagne, I hardly cared anymore. "I mean, do you have a drinking problem? I've never actually even seen you drink until today. Or are you crazy? Or is it like Gabe says and you just want the attention?"

Guillaume looked surprised. Then a slow grin spread across his face. "Gabe said that, did he?"

I shrugged. "Maybe I shouldn't have said that."

"No, no, it's fine," Guillaume said. He shook his head. "It's just typical of him." He took a deep breath. "Okay. So you asked whether I was crazy. No, I do not think I am."

"So it's alcohol then?" I asked.

Guillaume shook his head. "No. Can I tell you a secret?"

I nodded. "Yesh." I had intended to say *yes*, but the champagne was really kicking in.

"I actually don't drink at all," he said.

"But you're drinking champagne now!" I exclaimed.

"No," Guillaume said. "I've been pouring it in the shrubbery."

My jaw dropped. "That was my plan!"

Guillaume arched an eyebrow. "Was it? Hmm. I seem to have executed the plan better than you, then."

Okay. I had to admit that he was right.

"But why did you ask me to come in and have a drink if you weren't planning on drinking yourself?" I asked.

Guillaume shrugged. "I was lonely. And you and I never get to talk."

I stared. "I'm your publicist. We're not supposed to be sitting around bonding, Guillaume."

"I know," he said. "Still, this has been fun, right? I mean, that thing you were telling me about French kisses? That's pretty interesting."

"It is?" I couldn't figure out why Guillaume would be so intrigued.

"Indeed," he said. He scooted a bit closer and smiled. "So what is it you've discovered?"

"About French kissing?" I asked. "Well, for one, I think someone needs to tell all the women back in the United States: No one kisses like a Frenchman!"

Guillaume laughed. "Really?"

"Mais oui," I said with an exaggerated French accent, thinking how much easier it was to speak French while drinking. Hmm, perhaps I would have to begin stashing a bottle of champagne in my desk at work. "You Frenchmen have really perfected the art of the kiss, you know."

Guillaume studied my face for a moment. He looked sort of fuzzy around the edges, but I supposed that was because of the alcohol, not because he was actually disintegrating. "That's very interesting," he said softly. Then, before I realized what was happening, he leaned over and pressed his lips to mine, softly at first and then, when I didn't protest, with mounting intensity.

Wow, he's a good kisser, I thought vaguely. *And being pressed against that amazing body is incredible.* My mouth, which apparently had a mind of its own, kissed him back. *But wait,* I thought suddenly, trying not to sink into the sensation of the kiss. *He's my client! What am I doing?*

I had just started to pull away when there was a voice from the doorway.

"Guillaume, *putain de merde*! You're such an asshole!" I jerked my eyes open, pulled away from Guillaume, and whirled around, horrified.

Gabe was standing there in the doorway, fists clenched, staring at us. I felt absolutely horrible—and all of a sudden terribly sober. He wasn't looking at me; he was staring at Guillaume with eyes that flashed with anger. Slowly, I turned back to Guillaume and was surprised to see him smirking again, looking rather pleased with himself.

"Oh, Gabe, I wasn't expecting you," he said casually, as

if Gabe had just walked in on us playing bridge or sipping tea or something equally mundane.

I looked slowly back at Gabe. He looked even more furious. He glanced at me, then back at Guillaume. "That's bullshit, Guillaume," he said sharply. "You called my room thirty minutes ago and asked me to come up! You even had a room key delivered!"

"What?" I asked, startled. I whirled back to look at Guillaume, whose expression was vaguely guilty but still mostly self-satisfied. Then I turned back to Gabe, who was staring at me. He seemed about to say something, but then he shook his head and shut his mouth. His face looked sad, which made me feel terrible.

"Gabe?" I started to say. But he cast one last look at me, shook his head, turned on his heel, and strode quickly back down the hallway.

"Gabe!" I tried again, standing up and staring after him. But the only reply I got was the violent slamming of the door to Guillaume's suite. I stared down the dark hallway for a moment, feeling totally crushed.

Slowly, I turned back to Guillaume. The smirk had finally vanished from his face, replaced with an expression that I could have sworn looked a bit guilty.

"What is wrong with you?" I hissed at him. He shrugged.

"It's nothing, Emma," he said, waving a dismissive hand, as if I was being high-maintenance, in some way, for reacting to what he'd done. "Don't worry about it so much."

I could feel my head throbbing with anger—or was it

alcohol? "You are *such* a jerk!" I exclaimed. I slammed my glass of champagne down on the coffee table. I heard the glass crack, but I didn't care. With one last furious look back at Guillaume, I jumped up and dashed toward the door. I pulled open the door and looked frantically out into the hallway. But Gabe was already long gone.

Back in my room, still slightly drunk and completely ashamed, I immediately dialed the front desk and asked to be connected to Gabe's room. There was no answer. I tried three more times until the hotel operator suggested, in a tone filled with barely concealed annoyance, that *perhaps* the gentleman I was trying to reach had gone out. I hung up, feeling stupid, and wondered where he could have gone.

Checking to make sure I still had my key, I raced out of the room and took the elevator down to the lobby, willing it to go faster. I emerged on the ground floor just in time to see Gabe striding rapidly out of the hotel, pulling his suitcase behind him.

"Gabe!" I called desperately, pushing past the crowd of people waiting to climb aboard the elevator. "Gabe, wait!"

But he didn't slow down. Nor did he look back. I dashed after him, pulling up beside him just as he reached the front doors.

"Gabe, where are you going?" I asked, my voice laced with a desperation that made me feel ashamed.

"To the train station," he muttered without looking at me.

A valet appeared from outside to help Gabe with his bag. "Where to this evening, sir?" he asked, bowing slightly.

"The Eurostar terminal," Gabe said tersely. "As soon as possible."

"I will get you a taxi right away, sir," the man responded. He hurried officiously away.

"Gabe, I am so sorry," I said quickly, my words pouring out on top of each other in my desperation. "Please look at me. Please! Gabe!"

Finally, with obvious reluctance, he looked down at me, his face stony.

"Gabe, I'm so sorry!" I said again. "It's not what you think!"

"Hey, it's not my business if you want to make out with your client," he said coldly. "After all, what woman can resist a rock star?"

"Gabe, please, it didn't mean anything," I babbled. "I swear!"

He shook his head as a cab pulled up and the valet approached us with a raised hand. "It never does," Gabe muttered.

"What does that mean?" I asked. But he ignored me.

The valet began dragging Gabe's bag away, and he turned away from me to follow.

"Wait!" I exclaimed, desperately searching for any reason to make him stay. "You can't go! We're hosting a media breakfast in the morning! Guillaume's going to perform again!"

He laughed bitterly. "I think I know everything I need to know about Guillaume Riche." He got into the cab and slammed the door behind him. The valet was staring at us, but I didn't care.

"Gabe—" I pleaded.

"Emma," he said. "You're the only reason I came to this junket."

The words pierced me like a spear through the heart. "I'm so sorry," I said in a whisper.

Gabe shook his head. "No, *I'm* sorry," he said, looking away from me. "I should have known better."

Gabe said something to the driver and then turned his attention forward. As the cab pulled away, he didn't look back.

Chapter Seventeen

I thought I would die on the spot. I sank to the ground, my head throbbing, my face was flushed with shame. The valet was staring at me like I was a lunatic.

Just then, another cab pulled up, and Poppy cheerfully alighted with a tall, sandy-haired, completely gorgeous guy in tow. He had his arm slung over her shoulder, and she was giggling about something he was saying. Then, just as they tumbled onto the pavement in unison, she looked up and saw me.

"Emma!" Her eyes registered surprise as she stopped dead in her tracks. She started to smile at me then seemed to realize that something was wrong—perhaps due to the fact that I was currently crumpled on the sidewalk. "Emma?" she said again, dropping to one knee next to me. "Are you okay?"

I shook my head, and although I was biting my trembling lip and trying not to, I burst into tears. I didn't know if they were from the shame or the sense of loss or the copious amounts of champagne. I knew only that I was sitting on the ground in front of one of the nicest hotels in London, trying not to cry in front of my friend and the human incarnation of her voodoo doll.

"Oh, goodness, Emma!" Poppy exclaimed in concern, wrapping me in her arms and then pulling back to search my face. "What's wrong? What is it?"

I glanced up at the man with Poppy—presumably Darren—and flushed. "I'm sorry," I said to him. I looked at Poppy. "I'm sorry. Now on top of everything else, I'm ruining *your* night."

"No, no, not at all," Poppy soothed, stroking my hair. She glanced up at Darren, who was looking at us with concern but not, I noticed, with any sort of disdain. Poppy stood up slowly and whispered to him. He nodded.

"I'm going to head home," he said with a casualness I knew was forced. I tried to protest, but he shook his head. "No, no, it's late. I'll see Poppy tomorrow."

"Emma, this is Darren, by the way," Poppy said.

I forced a smile at him and stood up from my spot on the ground, feeling silly. I extended a hand, which Darren shook firmly. This both impressed and embarrassed me, as my hand had obviously just been on the ground—not to mention on the surface of my wet, mucky face.

"Nice to meet you," I said.

"And you as well," he said pleasantly, as if I weren't a pathetic mess. "Poppy has told me a lot about you."

"Er . . . thank you," I said, glancing at Poppy.

Darren smiled at me again and then, after a few whispers and kisses with Poppy, he got back into a cab, waved good-bye to both of us, and disappeared.

"I'm so sorry I ruined your date," I moaned as soon as he was gone.

"Nonsense," Poppy said firmly. "Now let's go inside, and you can tell me what's wrong."

She put her arm around my shoulder and guided me back to my room, where we both sat down on the edge of my bed.

"I think I've ruined everything, Poppy," I declared miserably, once she'd gotten me a box of tissues and a glass of water. Her eyes widened, but she didn't say anything. "Guillaume will have a problem with the UPP, I've lost Gabe . . . everything is just so screwed up!"

I found myself pouring out the whole story of what had happened this evening, from the champagne-in-the-shrubbery plan gone awry to the hurt-looking Gabe hurtling out of the hotel with his suitcase, slamming the cab door behind him.

"Emma, why didn't you tell me you felt like this about Gabe Francoeur?" Poppy asked when I was done.

"I don't know." I shrugged uncomfortably. "I don't think I even realized I did before the whole roller thing the night before last anyhow. Or maybe I did, but I didn't want to. It's not like it's professional of me to start falling for one of the journalists I work with."

Poppy shrugged. "Hey, we live in Paris," she reminded me gently. "The City of Love. You can't control who you fall in love with."

I shook my head. "Anyhow, it doesn't matter. I've totally ruined it. But what's even worse is I've probably ruined Guillaume's relationship with the UPP. I have no idea what Gabe will write, but seriously, Poppy, he could sabotage us. And I don't know that I would even blame him at this point."

I felt tears pricking the backs of my eyes and blinked them back. I was already pathetic enough.

Poppy put a hand on my shoulder. "It's not your fault, Emma," she said gently. "First of all, I don't know that Gabe is necessarily going to do anything. But even if he does, it's really Guillaume's fault, not yours, right?"

I paused. "No," I said after a moment. "I should have known better. I let my personal stuff get in the way. I made a big mistake with Guillaume. I should never have had a drink with him. That was really, really stupid. And then Gabe came in . . ." I stopped and closed my eyes for a moment. I swallowed hard. "And now he hates Guillaume. He's going to get bad press on the eve of his album release, and it's going to be all my fault."

"Okay, now you're just being silly," Poppy said firmly. I looked at her, surprised, as she continued. "You were trying to do the right thing. And I must say, it sounds a bit like Guillaume lured you into all of this, although I can't imagine why. Guillaume obviously planned for Gabe to walk in on you. And Emma, if Guillaume is so intent on sabotaging himself, there's not much you can do."

I thought about it for a moment. It *was* very strange, come to think of it, that Guillaume had apparently called Gabe either before or just after I'd arrived and asked him to come up in thirty minutes. Why would he do such a thing? And why on earth would he lean in to kiss me if he was expecting a reporter whom he suspected I had a crush on? Was Guillaume *trying* to hurt me? The thought startled and unsettled me.

"Whether it's all my fault or not," I said finally, "I wouldn't be surprised if Gabe totally rips him apart in print. And that's going to come down on us. On your firm." I felt like everything was on the line here, and I'd screwed it up irreversibly. "I've put everything in jeopardy, Poppy. I don't think I deserve to be here anymore."

I barely slept that night. I tossed and turned thinking about Gabe, worrying about what his next article would say, and worrying about what would happen to Poppy's company.

After I woke up, I logged on to my computer and was tentatively relieved to find that Gabe hadn't published an article about Guillaume in the past twenty-four hours. It was mildly comforting, but I feared that it was really just prolonging the inevitable. In a way, I would have preferred to have everything out on the table that day so that it could all end in a cataclysmic burst of shame instead of under a lingering cloud of tense regret, waiting for the other shoe to drop.

The press breakfast that morning was in the grand ballroom on the second floor, a spacious, soaring room with domed ceilings and smooth ecru walls. As the reporters—conspicuously minus Gabe—settled into their seats and chattered happily away, a fleet of waiters filled their water glasses, brought them orange juice, coffee, and tea, and refilled their overflowing pastry baskets. Fifteen minutes after we'd begun, nearly everyone was accounted for.

After the meal, during which Guillaume continually shot me wide-eyed, guilty glances from his table near the stage, he performed "Charlotte, Je T'Aime," a love song off his album, a cappella, to the delight of the press. Then, with his guitar, he did one final acoustic version of "City of Light," which had the crowd on its feet, applauding wildly by the time it was over. I met Poppy's eyes as Guillaume strummed his last chords. We both smiled. In the space of two days, our press plan—and the charm and talent of the crazy Guillaume—had won over a room full of a hundred journalists who were paid to be skeptical. We had somehow done the impossible.

Poppy and I said good-bye to all the reporters as they filtered out of the room. When we finally shut the doors behind us, I leaned back against the wall with a sigh.

"Well, that went perfectly!" Poppy said with a smile. She looked at me carefully. "Are you okay?"

I forced a smile. "I'm fine. You're right. It was perfect."

Just then, Guillaume slipped back into the ballroom. I looked quickly around for an escape route, but alas, he was entering through the only set of doors, and there was no conversation about rugby or cosmetics or cricket that I could join and feign interest in.

I could feel Poppy put a hand on the small of my back. "It's going to be fine," she said softly. I nodded, trying to summon some strength.

"Emma," Guillaume said as he approached. He looked shamefaced. "Please, Emma, I'm so sorry."

I could see Poppy glaring at him beside me. I averted my eyes. "It's fine," I mumbled. I dismissively waved my hand and hoped he would go away.

Beside me, Poppy took a step forward. "It is *not* fine!" she declared hotly, putting her hands on her hips and glaring at Guillaume. "Don't you dare tell him it's fine, Emma! He totally screwed you over!"

Guillaume looked uncomfortable. "In my defense, I was trying to screw with Gabe, not you."

"What are you talking about?" Poppy demanded. "Are you *trying* to destroy your career before it even takes off?"

He ignored her and continued to address me. "I, uh, didn't realize how much you liked him," he said. "I'm really sorry."

I felt mortified. Great. Not only had Guillaume ended any chance I may have had with Gabe, but now he was also under the mistaken impression that I was madly in love with the reporter he'd just scared away.

"It's fine, Guillaume," I said uncomfortably, wishing he would disappear. But quite irritatingly, he didn't. "Anyhow," I added, "it's not as though I even liked him that much to begin with."

The lie felt sour on my tongue, but it wasn't like I had a choice.

The next morning, the world came tumbling down.

After having taken an evening train back to Paris the night before, Poppy and I arrived at the office early in the morning to see what kind of an impact the junket had made.

At first glance, the coverage was good. The *Boston Globe*

ran a glowing profile of Guillaume that said his music was "like a bottle of fine French wine: smooth, delicious, and designed to make you feel good." The *New York Times* ran a piece about how Guillaume—actor, songwriter, singer, and international playboy—was the first real Renaissance man of the twenty-first century. The *London Mirror* ran a front-page story with a headline that screamed: "Prince William, Watch Your Back! There's a New Bachelor in Town!"

But there was one glaring problem.

There was nothing on the UPP wires about Guillaume. Or about the junket.

"Gabriel didn't file a story," Poppy said after a few moments of flipping through various sites. She looked at the computer screen—and then at me—in awe. "He didn't file a story," she repeated.

"Well, at least he didn't file a *bad* story," I said in a small voice, trying to look on the bright side.

Poppy gazed at me for a long moment. "Right, but there's nothing at all," she said quietly. "That means that for all the money KMG poured into this, the junket is conspicuously absent from more than two hundred newspapers around the world."

I gulped. A knot was beginning to form in the center of my stomach. "Oh," I said quietly. "Right." In a way, then, no news was even worse than bad news.

The phone rang, and Poppy reached over distractedly to pick it up. The voice on the other end was so loud that I could hear it from where I was sitting. After a moment, Poppy hung up, her face pale.

"That was Véronique," she said. "She wants to see us both immediately."

"Oh, Poppy," I said. "I'm so sorry."

Poppy took a deep breath and tried to smile. "Don't worry," she said. "Not yet, anyhow. Maybe all Véronique wants to talk about is the great coverage we got."

Fifteen minutes later, we were walking in the door of KMG, where we were promptly ushered into Véronique's office. After nodding at both of us and telling us to take seats, she sat down behind her desk, crossed her arms silently, and looked back and forth between us for what felt like an eternity.

"Poppy," she finally began in an even tone. "Do you know how much KMG spent on this junket?"

Poppy gulped. "Yes, ma'am," she said. "It was quite a lot."

"Correct," Véronique said. "And do you know *why* we spent so much money?"

Poppy gulped. "To help promote Guillaume?" she asked uncertainly.

"Well, yes," Véronique said. "And because *you* insisted that this junket was the way to do it."

Poppy cleared her throat. "We got some great coverage," she said in a small voice.

I chimed in: "The *Boston Globe* did a great piece. So did the *New York Times*. And the *London Mirror*."

Véronique glanced at me quickly, as if I was an insignificant annoyance, then focused her stare back on Poppy.

"I wondered when I got into the office this morning why, with all that money spent on this, Guillaume Riche was missing from hundreds of papers around the world where you had promised there would be coverage."

There was dead silence for a moment. Poppy glanced over at me and then back at Véronique. She cleared her throat nervously again.

"I can explain," she said finally.

"No need," Véronique said crisply, holding up a hand. "Because I already have this issue answered, you see. When I realized the omission, I thought to myself, *Why? Why is there no coverage in more than two hundred papers Poppy promised would carry news of the junket?*"

"Véronique, I—"

"Do not interrupt," Véronique said, again holding up a hand. I felt ill and sunk down lower in my chair, wondering if it would be possible to simply vanish into the upholstery.

"In any case," she continued, "I began calling around and realized that the omissions were all in papers that rely on UPP content. *But*, I said to myself, *I thought there was a UPP reporter on the list for the junket.*"

"Véronique, I—" Poppy tried again.

"Let me finish," Véronique said icily. "I checked your junket list, and indeed, there was a listing for a Gabriel Francoeur from the UPP. And according to your master billing list, he checked in and stayed all weekend. *Well, I thought to myself, perhaps he did not like the music.* So I called the Paris bureau chief for the UPP to find out."

"You did?" Poppy asked quietly. All the blood had drained from her face. I slid even farther down in the chair, feeling like the worst person in the world.

"I did," Véronique confirmed. "And do you know what I found out?"

Poppy didn't respond. She just sat there, staring. Véronique's gaze flicked to me. I could feel my cheeks heating up. I tried to keep an innocent face.

"I found out," Véronique continued, "that this reporter, this Gabriel Francoeur, *did* indeed like Guillaume's music. He's the one who has been giving us coverage so far. But his editor said that something happened at the junket that made this Mr. Francoeur return early, saying that he no longer felt he could cover Guillaume Riche impartially."

"Oh, no," I mumbled. Véronique looked sharply at me.

"Mais oui," she said. "His editor didn't understand at first, either, and he was distressed that he had spent all this money sending one of his top reporters to this junket and had even teased the forthcoming story on the wires, so that papers around the world had created space in their entertainment sections for it. So he pressed this Gabriel Francoeur for some sort of an answer."

Poppy and I exchanged worried looks.

Véronique pressed on, glaring at us. "The only information Mr. Francoeur offered was that something had happened between himself and a publicist *in the employ of KMG.* He wouldn't specify what actually occurred, but the incident was apparently so serious that it made him give up the music features beat for the time being. He has been voluntarily demoted to the international obituary department."

Véronique paused again and studied us for a moment, first Poppy, and then me. I felt like I wanted to sink into the floor.

"Would either of you care to explain?" Véronique asked. "Since you are the only two publicists in the employ of KMG who were at the junket this weekend?"

Poppy opened her mouth, but Véronique rolled right over her, gathering steam as she went. "Because"—her voice was arctic—"you realize that whatever has happened here, you have damaged a relationship with one of the most influential media outlets in the world."

"Véronique, it wasn't really such a big deal," Poppy said in a small voice.

Véronique's smirk twisted into a frown, and she glared at Poppy. "*You* do not get to decide what is a big deal to KMG," she said. "That is for *me* to decide. You are just the hired help."

Poppy was stunned into silence. I glanced at her, and my heart sank to see Poppy—so rarely at a loss for words—looking stricken. I had to do something.

"Véronique?" I said quietly. She turned and focused her flashing eyes on me. "It's not Poppy's fault. It's mine. And for the record, I don't think there's any way in the world that you could possibly accuse Poppy of failing. She got an enormous amount of media coverage for Guillaume. Far more than most record launches. She really did a phenomenal job. The junket was a huge success even if the UPP didn't carry the story."

"I did not invest so much of my company's money to have it undone by some personal problem between a publicist"—she paused to glare at Poppy—"and a journalist."

"It was my fault, Véronique," I said. Véronique turned her gaze back to me. I braced myself and continued, "I was the publicist who screwed things up. It was me, not Poppy."

"Don't do this," Poppy muttered. But I shook my head at her.

Véronique stared at me. "Go on," she said, her voice hushed, her expression unforgiving.

I took a deep breath. "I behaved in an unprofessional manner with Gabe Francoeur," I said. "There was an incident involving him and Guillaume, and I handled it all wrong. It's one hundred percent my fault, not Poppy's."

Véronique was silent for a long moment. "I see," she said finally.

Poppy and I exchanged looks.

Véronique looked down at her lap and sat there motionless for a moment, as if meditating. When she looked up, her focus was on me. "I trust I will have your resignation letter by the end of today," she said softly.

Beside me, I heard Poppy gasp. "Véronique, I don't really think that's necessary!" she exclaimed.

"As for you," Véronique said, turning to Poppy, "you will have one more chance with KMG because of the work you have done so far. But I will trust that in the future, you won't hire any more publicists who will risk our reputation. This is unforgivable."

"But—" Poppy began.

"Either Emma goes or you both go," Véronique interrupted.

"It's fine, Poppy," I said softly. Poppy opened her mouth

to say something else, but I spoke first, turning to Véronique. "You'll have my resignation by the end of the day. I'm sorry."

In a daze, I stood up and strode quickly to the door before anyone could see me cry.

Chapter Eighteen

I wasn't sure what would be harder to leave: Poppy, the friend I'd grown to trust; or Paris, the city I'd grown to love.

Poppy was full of apologies and promises to try to talk Véronique out of her decision. But I'd screwed up, and I knew it. I didn't want to cost Poppy more than I already had. I had the feeling that her own job security was hanging by a string, and I knew that losing the Guillaume Riche account would mean the end of Poppy's business. I would never do that to her. I felt terrible that I had already wreaked so much havoc. She had rescued me from my own depression back home, and I had repaid her by putting her job in jeopardy. Although Poppy kept insisting it wasn't my fault, I knew it was. It was unforgivable.

Once Poppy realized that her powers of persuasion weren't going to get me to revise my decision, she gave in and began to say her good-byes. She took me out to dinner at a different restaurant every night, perhaps to try to convince me to stay in France. But all the *crêpes complètes* and coq au vin and crème brûlée in Paris couldn't change things.

She even loosened up on the whole French-kissing

mission, which was a relief. I didn't know whether her relaxing of the rules was due to her pity for me or perhaps over some sort of change that her visit with Darren had wrought in her. Nevertheless, it allowed me to slip back to my old ways of *not* dating, which were much less disaster-prone. After all, if I wasn't dating and I wasn't thinking about kissing Frenchmen, there was no chance of anything going wrong, now, was there?

I tried calling Gabe several times that week, but there was never an answer on his work or cell phones, and he didn't return any of the messages I left. *I'm so sorry*, I said in several messages. *It didn't mean anything.* In others, I apologized for my complete lack of professionalism and told him I was leaving for Orlando on Saturday morning. They all had the same general theme: *I'm a jerk. And I'm so sorry if I hurt you.*

On my last day of work, Guillaume, who had managed, quite impressively, to stay out of trouble all week, came by Poppy's office in the afternoon for one final round of apologies.

"Look, Emma, I really like working with you," he said, sitting down at my desk and widening his already enormous green eyes at me plaintively. "I didn't mean for any of this to happen. I'm so sorry."

"It's okay," I said with a nod. And it was. Guillaume was Guillaume, and I should have known better. This was my fault, for the most part, not his. "I've liked working with you, too," I admitted as an afterthought.

This made him look even sadder. "Isn't there anything I can do?" he asked. "Talk to the people at KMG, maybe?"

"No. What's done is done, I think." I gave him a small smile. "But you are really talented. I will wish the best for you. I know you'll do well."

On my last night in Paris, after I'd packed and left one final apologetic message for Gabe, I went to dinner with Poppy at a crêperie near the Place d'Italie, where we stuffed ourselves with a bottle of *cidre*, salads, buckwheat crêpes with cheese, eggs, and ham, and massive flambéing crêpes Suzettes and *cafés doubles* for dessert. Outside the window, a parade of Parisians strolled continually by, walking little white dogs, carrying baguettes, chattering away on their mobile phones, or tending to small, impeccably dressed little children with pink cheeks and spring coats buttoned all the way to the top.

"I love it here," I murmured, staring out the window as Poppy counted out a small handful of euro bills and coins for our dinner, which she insisted on paying for.

"So why don't you stay?" Poppy asked softly.

I shook my head and gazed out on the Paris outside our window before answering. "No," I said. "I can't. It's obviously not where I belong."

After dinner, Poppy suggested heading to Le Crocodile in the fifth for cocktails, but I only wanted to be alone with the city. "No," I said. "I think I'm going to take a walk. I'll see you at home in a little while."

Poppy and I hugged good-bye and went our separate ways, her to a taxi and me underground to the 7 line of the Métro, which I took to Châtelet, seven stops away. I emerged twenty minutes later to a square full of sparkling lights lining centuries-old buildings. The Palais de

Justice, the Hôtel de Ville, the Pont de la Cité, and Sainte-Chapelle were flooded with soft light and glittered on the surface of the Seine, which was broken only by the occasional silent passing of a bateau.

I strolled toward the river in silence, pulling my cardigan close as a chill crept into the air. All around me, Paris was alive with conversations, smiles, the quiet exchanges between couples, the happy laughter of friends crossing the bridge on the way to a bar or a café in the fifth. As I crossed the Pont Neuf and saw the Eiffel Tower glowing over the river to the west, I could feel tears pricking the backs of my eyes. They blurred the searchlight from the top of the tower before I could blink them back.

As I walked farther across the Île de la Cité, the massive Conciergerie hulked in the shadows, a reminder of a time of sadness and horror when thousands were imprisoned and met their deaths during the French Revolution. To the left, Notre Dame basked in its own light across its broad, cobblestone courtyard, its many saints and gargoyles standing silent watch over the hushed clusters of tourists clutching guidebooks and speaking in whispers as they stared up at the fourteenth-century church in awe. Across the bridge on the Left Bank, the green-and-yellow cursive of the Café le Petit Pont glowed like a beacon, reminding me of my first night in Paris with Poppy and the interview I'd supervised between Guillaume and Gabe. Somehow, it all seemed so long ago.

I wandered for hours along the banks of the Seine, weaving down the Rue de la Huchette in the Latin Quarter then across the Petit Pont and Pont Notre-Dame and down the Rue de Rivoli on the Right Bank. The quaint cobblestone of the Marais gave way to the Pont Marie and then, as I wove back, to the regal buildings of the Place des Vosges, where Victor Hugo once sat and created a hunchback named Quasimodo to ring the bells of Notre Dame. By the time I had strolled back to the Pont Neuf to take one last look west down the Seine toward the Eiffel Tower, it was past midnight, the tourists had disappeared, and I felt like I had the city—or at least the tip of the island—all to myself. The ripples of the Seine kissed the embankment in a soothing tempo, and the moonlight reflected in the river mixed with the light cast from the buildings that had been host to kings and saints and history in all its forms.

I would miss it here. I would miss it a lot.

I took the RER from the Saint-Michel stop back to the Pont de l'Alma and walked up Avenue Rapp to our street. As always, the moment I turned right onto Rue de Général-Camou, the Eiffel Tower loomed enormous at the end of the short lane. Usually, it was a thrill to see it. Tonight it just felt hauntingly sad. In Orlando, the only thing that loomed at the end of my street had been a big traffic light. Here, one of the most beautiful monuments in the world sat just feet away, shining with golden light in the darkness.

I didn't sleep that night. I couldn't. I crawled into bed and closed my eyes, but I couldn't bring myself to spend my last hours in Paris that way. Eventually, I got up and walked to the living room window, where I sat with a bottle of Beaujolais and a crusty baguette, gazing at the Eiffel Tower long after the lights had gone out and it was just a dark silhouette against the distant rooftops of the city.

It was dawn before I realized that there were tears rolling down my cheeks. I wondered how long I'd been crying. As the first birds of the morning began to chirp and the sky turned gradually from inky blue to a blend of sunrise pastels, illuminating the steel of the tower, I got up from the window, took a shower, brushed my teeth, and went out for a walk. By the time Poppy and I had finished the *pains au chocolat* I'd brought home from the patisserie on the corner, along with the espresso she silently made in the kitchen, I still wasn't ready to go. But it was time. Poppy walked me over to the taxi stand on Avenue Bosquet, and with one last hug good-bye, I was on my way. But I wasn't so sure anymore that the place I was going to was home.

Because Brett had moved back into our old house and because I had no desire whatsoever to see any of my three so-called best friends in Orlando, I had nowhere to go when I got back to the States but to my sister Jeannie's place.

"I told you it was a bad idea to move to Paris," Jeannie said when she opened the door of her Winter Park home to find me and two giant suitcases waiting on the doorstep at 11 p.m. She'd been too busy to come pick me up at the airport, so I'd had to take a cab, to the tune of fifty-five dollars, which was not exactly the way I'd envisioned starting my life as an unemployed American. "I don't want to say I told you so, but, well . . ." Her voice trailed off and she smiled sweetly at me.

"You know the story, Jeannie," I'd answered wearily. After a grueling eight-hour flight from Paris to Detroit, a three-hour layover, and then a three-hour flight to Orlando, I was in no mood to argue with my sister.

"You have to admit, it was really immature to go to Paris on some silly whim," she said, shaking her head. "You're going to have to grow up someday, Emma." I bit my lip, figuring that things would be better all around if I didn't reply. She turned away, leaving me to drag the suitcases inside myself. "Try to be quiet, Em," she said over her shoulder. "Robert and Odysseus are in bed!"

Ah. I wouldn't want to disturb her husband. Or King Odysseus, as I liked to call her spoiled three-year-old.

Jeannie and I had never been close. After I'd turned about five (to her thirteen) and was no longer as cute to play with, she had started treating me with a general disdain.

"I'm still Mom's favorite," she used to whisper to me throughout my childhood. *"She'll never love you as much as she loves me."*

For all of our squabbles and differences, I knew that deep down we loved each other. It was just that she had an opinion about *everything* in my life. Her way was *always* the right way, and she couldn't see that she might not in fact be correct. We'd barely spoken since I moved to France, because she was so horrified that I had left Brett without trying harder to work things out.

"You have to forgive him if he's made one little mistake," she kept telling me. "It's not like Robert has always been perfect! At least Brett makes a lot of money and will provide for you. Where do you think you're going to find someone else like that when you're almost thirty?"

Now, since I'd had no choice but to come crawling back to her and stay in her guest room until I figured out what I was going to do, she had basically been proven right. As I crept into bed that night in the immaculately clean, freshly dusted, Febreze-scented room that had been prepared for me (complete with Jeannie's perfect hospital corners on the bed), I had a bad feeling about how the next few weeks would go. There was no question about it: I needed to find a job and get out of here as soon as I could.

"You know, if you had just tried to work things out with Brett, none of this would have happened," Jeannie said the next morning as I sat sipping coffee and she sat making airplane noises and "flying" little spoonfuls of Cheerios toward Odysseus's mouth; upon each landing, he would wave his arms wildly, shriek, and knock cereal and milk into the air. It was a little hard to take Jeannie seriously when she had soggy O's in her hair, milk splashed on her cheek, and a three-year-old who seemed wholly uninterested in obeying her.

"There was nothing worth working out," I said with a sigh.

Jeannie blinked at me blankly. "But you dated him for three years. And he has a *great* job."

"No Cheerios!" Odysseus screamed at the top of his lungs, sending another spoonful of cereal flying around the kitchen. "I want chocolate!"

"Odysseus, sweetie, you can have chocolate later," Jeannie said in a high-pitched baby voice that drove my crazy. At three, Odysseus was old enough to be talked to like a human being rather than a poodle. "Now it's time for Cheerios! Open wide for the airplane!"

"Waaaaaaaaaaaaaah!" Odysseus screamed, his little face turning beet red as he waved his chubby arms around. Jeannie sighed and went over to the pantry to get some Cocoa Puffs. The moment he saw the box, his screams subsided.

I rolled my eyes. "Jeannie, it doesn't matter that Brett has a great job," I said once she had commenced with shoveling spoonfuls of Cocoa Puffs into the contented Odysseus's open mouth. "*He* left *me*. Then he started sleeping with Amanda. How am I supposed to be okay with that?"

"Em, you're almost thirty," Jeannie said, spooning more chocolate balls into Odysseus's mouth. Chocolate-colored milk dribbled down his chin in little rivers. "You've got to wise up. If your fiancé's looking elsewhere, maybe there's something you're not doing at home."

"Oh, come on, Jeannie," I snapped, feeling suddenly angrier at her than I normally did. "You can't really mean that! I must not have been screwing him enough so he had to go and sleep with Amanda?"

"Not in front of the baby!" Jeannie snapped.

"Screw, screw, screw!" Odysseus repeated in delight, little globs of mushy chocolate shooting every which way.

"Sorry," I muttered, glancing guiltily at my nephew. "But seriously, Jeannie. I can't go back to him."

Jeannie sighed and put down the spoon. She turned away from Odysseus, who immediately knocked over his sippy cup and began eating fallen Cocoa Puffs off his high chair tray by picking them up with his tongue, in between muttering *screw, screw, screw* thoughtfully to himself.

"Emma, I'm just trying to help you here," she said. "God knows Mom and Dad don't have anything useful to say. I'm the only one in this family who seems to know how to make a relationship work."

I decided to change the subject before I was forced to pour the remaining milk-sodden Cocoa Puffs over Jeannie's perfectly sleek hair. "So I think I'm going to see if there's an opening at any of the restaurants on Park Avenue," I said, referring to Winter Park's shopping and restaurant district.

"You want to *waitress*?" Jeannie asked, her voice rising incredulously on the last word.

I shrugged. "I don't know. It's not like I can go back to Boy Bandz. And there's not really a music industry here, you know? I can start applying for PR jobs, but who knows if that will work out?"

"But waitressing?" Jeannie looked at me with what appeared to be disgust. "At the age of twenty-nine?"

I bit my lip. I was determined not be drawn into an argument.

"Well," Jeannie said after a moment. "I suppose it's a good way to meet rich guys. Just make sure to flirt. A lot."

I rolled my eyes. "I'm planning to waitress, not husband-hunt," I said. "Besides," I muttered under my breath, "I think I'm in love with a French guy who hates my guts."

"What?" asked Jeannie distractedly. She had turned her attention back to Odysseus, who had finished his Cocoa Puffs and was now flinging chocolate-colored milk around the kitchen.

"Nothing," I said with a sigh.

"Huband-hut! Huband-hut! Huband-hut!" repeated Odysseus, who had apparently been listening more closely than his mother.

By the end of the week, I had landed a lunch-shift job at Frenchy's, a French-American fusion restaurant on Park Avenue. The owner, Pierre, had been fascinated that I'd just returned from Paris and had given me a job on the spot.

"You know Guillaume Riche?" he asked once he looked at my résumé.

I nodded, wondering why I'd even bothered to put the miserably short-lived job on there.

"*Merveilleux!*" he exclaimed, clearly excited. "He is a huge star! You have heard his new single, *non?*"

Indeed I had. "Beautiful Girl," the second single off his album, had just been released and was heating up the airwaves. The Internet buzz was that Guillaume could have two songs—"City of Light" and "Beautiful Girl"— in this week's *Billboard* Top Ten. It was incredible.

I talked to Poppy every few days; it was the only thing that kept me mentally afloat. Despite the fact that I had spent a small fortune on international phone cards at CVS to call her, it made me feel infinitely better to talk to someone I knew was a true friend. And hearing her talk about her blossoming relationship with Darren and her increasingly infrequent crazy dates with unsuspecting Frenchmen made me laugh and forget for a moment that I was a lonely boarder in my sister's house, working at a job that just didn't fulfill me the way working with Poppy had.

Poppy attempted a few times to mention Gabe; she had seen him several times since the junket, and she said he always looked dejected. But I suspected she was just saying that to try to cheer me up.

"I can't talk about him," I finally told her. "I need to move on. I need to stop thinking about him."

Of course that was easier said than done, because everything seemed to remind me of him. Every time I turned on the radio, I heard "City of Light" or "Beautiful Girl." The second song in particular always made me feel empty inside, because the last time I'd heard it was at the junket, where everything had fallen apart.

Poppy kept me informed of Guillaume's progress, and the week after I got the new job, I was at Jeannie's one night watching the eleven o'clock news when I saw a clip of Guillaume waterskiing down the Seine with three police boats chasing him. He was, of course, wearing only his top hat and a pair of SpongeBob SquarePants boxers. I giggled a bit to myself and then groaned in empathy with poor Poppy. I thought I'd be glad that I wasn't there to clean up yet another Guillaume Riche mess. But in a way, seeing him grinning and waving at the cameras as he glided illegally down the Seine just made me miss him— and the job—even more.

"I have no idea how to get him out of this one," Poppy had confided to me when she called in a panic from her cell phone.

"Just say he was out for some exercise and the boat took a wrong turn," I advised.

"What about his underwear?"

I thought for a moment. "Say that he thought it was a bathing suit and apologizes for his error."

"Emma." Poppy laughed. "You're a genius."

"I don't think that's the word for it," I muttered.

Chapter Nineteen

Two weeks after I'd gotten back from Paris, I was sitting in the family room with Odysseus, watching Saturday-morning cartoons and trying to keep him from licking the carpet (which I suspected he did because Jeannie had started using a chocolate-scented vacuum powder to make the house smell like she'd been baking all day). He was babbling to himself in nonsense talk—a habit I thought was sort of worrisome at the age of three, but Jeannie encouraged it by babbling in baby talk right back to him.

"Use your words, Odysseus," I said, keeping my voice quiet so Jeannie wouldn't hear. She always said that criticism would wound a child's fragile sense of self-esteem. Not that it was my business, but I figured that Odysseus's precious self-esteem would be in grave danger anyhow the moment he began goo-gooing and gagaing to kids on the playground who'd left infant babble behind in their infancy.

"Goo goo blah goo ga blah," he said defiantly, then went back to licking the carpet.

Just then, the doorbell rang.

"Emma, can you get it?" Jeannie's voice rang out from upstairs. "I'm a bit busy at the moment!"

"No problem!" I shouted back, relieved that I wouldn't have to worry about Odysseus's vacuum powder consumption or lack of language mastery for at least the next few minutes. Not that it was *really* my problem anyhow. But as his aunt and his godmother—not to mention someone who loved him—I was concerned about a lot of things.

Straightening my wrinkled T-shirt and combing my fingers through my hair (when had I last washed it anyhow?—somehow I had stopped caring), I walked down the front hallway and pulled open the front door. My jaw dropped when I saw who was standing there in khakis and a button-down shirt, his brown hair neatly combed, his square-jawed face freshly shaved, and a bouquet of red roses in his hand.

"Hi, Emma," Brett said. He looked me up and down for a moment, vaguely confused. I guessed he hadn't expected a rumpled, unwashed, disheveled version of the previous me.

"What are you doing here?" I blurted out.

Granted, it wasn't the most tactfully phrased query. But really. What *was* he doing on my sister's doorstep?

"I heard you were back in town," he said. He appeared to be studying the wrinkles in my shirt with some consternation.

"You *heard*?" I repeated. I stared at him for a moment and sighed. "Let me guess. Jeannie called you."

Brett shrugged. "Yeah, well," he said. "She thought I might want to see you."

"How nice of her."

Brett paused. "I, uh, brought you flowers," he said, holding out the roses.

I stared at them. "I can see that," I said flatly. I made no move to take them. Eventually, he lowered them to his side.

"You weren't going to call?" Brett shifted uncomfortably from one foot to the other.

"I didn't think we had much to talk about."

Brett tried one of his charming smiles, the ones that used to win me over. "I don't know," he said. "I think we have a lot to talk about. Can I come in?"

I sighed and thought about it for a moment. "Fine." I turned away and let him follow me down the hallway into Jeannie's living room. Not surprisingly, she was already standing there.

"Oh, Brett!" she cooed, shooting me a look. "How very nice to see you!"

"You, too, Jeannie," Brett said. They gave each other European-style pecks on the cheeks, which made me want to laugh. What looked so natural a greeting in Paris seemed pretentious and awkward on the two of them. And they had no idea.

"Well, I'll leave the two of you alone," Jeannie chirped after a moment. "I'm sure you have a lot to talk about!" She shot me another meaningful glance and added, "I'd forgotten how perfect you look together!" She clapped her hands together gleefully and flounced out of the room, yelling "Odysseus! Odysseus! Mommy's coming!" in her ridiculous baby-talk voice.

I rolled my eyes. I needed to get out of here.

I sat down on the living room couch and gestured vaguely and unenthusiastically for Brett to sit on the love seat opposite me. Instead he sat down beside me and looked at me with baleful eyes. "I'm so glad you've come back, baby," he said. My stomach turned, and I scooted away from him. Brett looked insulted. "Emma, I've never stopped loving you. You know that."

"Really?" I asked sweetly. "Were you loving me when you were screwing Amanda?"

Brett's eyes widened and he coughed. "I was just trying to get over you, you know," he said. "It didn't mean anything."

"Ah. Of course not. How silly of me to be upset that you were screwing my best friend."

Brett looked annoyed. Evidently, this isn't the way he had expected things to go. I suspected that Jeannie had implied to him that I thought, as she evidently did, that he was the answer to all my prayers. And Brett had been dumb enough to believe that he could dump me, hook up with my friend, and come back to a blanket of full forgiveness.

"So I guess Paris didn't work out," Brett said after a moment. He looked a little smug. "You must have been unhappy there."

"Actually," I said, "it was the happiest I've been in my life."

Brett looked surprised. "What about when you were with me?"

"As I said," I repeated calmly, "being in Paris was the happiest I've been in my life."

He looked completely baffled, as if the thought that the world didn't revolve around him had never before crossed his mind. He stared for a long moment and then cleared his throat. "Look," he said. "We've both made some mistakes here. But don't you think it's time to put that all behind us?"

I was about to respond when Jeannie whisked into the room, balancing Odysseus on her hip. He was waving some sort of little plastic truck around, making *vroom-vroom* noises and smacking the back of Jeannie's head every few seconds. She didn't seem to notice.

"Oh, look at you two, sitting side by side!" she cooed. She bounced Odysseus a few times on her hip. "Look at Auntie Emma and Uncle Brett!" she said in her baby-talk voice, widening her eyes at her son. "Aren't they *so* cute together!"

Odysseus glanced at us and then went back to whacking his mother in the head with his truck. "Screw, screw, screw!" he yelled in delight, evidently recalling his breakfast-hour language lesson.

Jeannie reddened. "Odysseus!" she said. "We don't say *screw* in this family!" She shot me an evil look, and I shrugged.

"Screw, screw, screw!" Odysseus insisted.

Brett looked embarrassed. How strange, considering that he'd been more than willing to partake in the activity with Amanda.

Jeannie put a hand over Odysseus's mouth so that his babbling was muffled. "You'll have to excuse him," she said to Brett. "He hasn't been himself since Emma got here."

"No problem," Brett said uncertainly.

"Anyhow," Jeannie said smoothly, "have you asked her yet?" She looked at me and raised an eyebrow.

"Asked me what?" I said apprehensively.

Brett nodded at Jeannie and turned to me. "I wanted to ask you to consider moving back in with me, Emma," he said. He glanced at Jeannie, who nodded encouragingly. I felt like I was being ganged up on. "After all, we were perfect together, don't you think?"

"I used to think so," I muttered after a moment. "But that was a very long time ago."

"Please, Emma," Brett said. He sidled off the couch and awkwardly knelt beside me on one knee, holding the red roses up like a peace offering. I considered again the joy I would derive from beating him over the head with them. But being that I had obviously already begun to corrupt poor, innocent Odysseus with my lack of vocabulary control, I figured that attacking a man with flowers wouldn't exactly be the most responsible thing to do in front of him.

"Please what?" I asked wearily.

"Please consider getting back together with me," Brett said. "Please consider moving back in."

I stared at him with pursed lips.

He shifted uncomfortably and lowered the roses. "At least have dinner with me tonight, Emma," he pleaded. "So that I can have a chance to explain."

I opened my mouth to respond, but as usual Jeannie was way ahead of me.

"She'd love to," she said firmly. I started to protest, but she shushed me. "Why don't you pick her up at seven? I'll make sure she's ready."

"Perfect," Brett said, scrambling to his feet. He laid the roses on the coffee table and made a beeline for the door before I could protest. "'Bye, Odysseus!" he said cheerfully, stopping to give my nephew a little peck on the top of the head.

Odysseus responded by whacking Brett with his toy truck.

"Huband-hut! Huband-hut! Huband-hut!" he screamed as Brett rubbed the back of his head in surprise. "Screw, screw, screw!"

True to his word, Brett was at Jeannie's door at seven that evening, bearing a brand-new bouquet of red roses and dressed in charcoal pants, a pale blue button-down shirt, and a dark gray tie.

"You look beautiful, Emma," he said softly. Clearly a lie, as I was wearing a T-shirt, holey jeans, and flip-flops. And I hadn't bothered to brush my hair.

I smiled tightly. "Thank you." I had to admit, he looked good. He always had. But I couldn't say that to him.

"This restaurant we're going to in Thornton Park just opened," he explained, breaking an uncomfortable silence as he drove. "I think you'll like it. It's like Ruth's Chris, but nicer."

I bristled at the mention of the upscale steak restaurant

where we'd had our first date three years ago. Unexpected tears pricked the outside corners of my eyes, and I blinked them back quickly.

Forty-five minutes later, we had ordered—medium-well filet mignon for him and medium-rare for me, with asparagus, garlic mashed potatoes, and creamed spinach to share—and the waiter had uncorked and poured a bottle of Pinot Noir for us before disappearing into the kitchen.

Brett raised his glass in a toast. "To us," he said, looking straight into my eyes.

I hesitated and lowered my glass. "I can't toast to that."

Brett stared for a moment, took a long sip of his wine, and then set his glass on the table, too. "Why not?" he asked carefully.

"Are you kidding?" I asked. "Do you seriously not have any idea why I'd basically hate your guts?"

Brett sighed. "Emma. You don't *hate* me. Do you?" His eyes were sad, and his regret looked almost genuine. He took another sip of his wine. "Look, I know how much I hurt you. I know I will always regret it. More than I could ever tell you."

I shook my head. "I don't think you regret it at all."

Brett looked upset. "That's not true, Emma," he said. He stared at me. "Look, it was the biggest mistake I've made in my life."

"Yeah, well, maybe it was for the best," I muttered. I took a long sip of my wine and wished I was anywhere but here. Why had I agreed to this?

"Please, Emma, you need to listen to me," Brett said. He

reached across the table and put a hand on my arm. "I am so sorry. More sorry than you can possibly imagine. I love you, Emma. I do. I always have. I just got scared, that's all."

I considered his words. It was the same explanation Jeannie had given me, and in a way, it made sense. "But if you were scared," I said slowly, "why didn't you talk to me? Why didn't you ask to postpone the wedding or something? Why did you dump me and throw me out of our house?"

Brett looked miserable. "Geez, Emma, I don't know," he said. "I've been through this a thousand times in my head. There's just no excuse. All I can say is that I've regretted it every day since. I didn't think I was ready to get married yet, but I am, Emma. I am. Losing you made me realize that."

I could feel the ice beginning to melt on the outside of my heart. I couldn't forgive him—how could I?—but maybe I could find a way to accept his apology and move on. After all, this was my life now, wasn't it? It wasn't like Gabe Francoeur was going to come walking through the door to sweep me off my feet. I was stuck living in my condescending sister's guest room, estranged from every friend I'd made in this city. That was no way to live.

Our food arrived, and we ate in silence for a few minutes. I could feel Brett watching me between bites.

"Why Amanda?" I asked softly after a while.

Brett swallowed hard but didn't look surprised. He had to have known the question was coming.

"I can't tell you how much I regret that," he said carefully, his voice soft. He looked straight into my eyes. "There is no excuse, Emma. I freaked out, and she was right there, and I fell into something I shouldn't have. It was all my fault, and it was a huge, huge mistake."

"It wasn't *all* your fault," I mumbled, thinking that it takes two to tango, as the saying goes.

"Well, I should have known better," Brett said. "Especially with one of your best friends. I'm so ashamed."

I took another sip of wine and considered his words. Despite the fact that I'd only taken three bites of my steak, I wasn't hungry anymore.

"I'd like to go now," I said.

Brett looked up in surprise. "But we're not done eating," he said.

"I know," I said. "I just don't want to be here anymore."

He studied my face, then nodded. "Okay," he said. "I know this is hard for you. I appreciate you even giving me the opportunity to explain myself."

I nodded. I was surprised by how genuine he seemed, and the hatred and anger I'd been clinging to for the past two months were beginning to seem pointless. Yes, he'd hurt me more deeply than I ever would have imagined. But he seemed genuinely sorry and repentant. And it wasn't like *I'd* never made a mistake. If I didn't at least consider his explanation and his apology, wasn't I being just as blind as Gabe?

Thinking of the French reporter—and his refusal to take my calls after the whole incident with Guillaume—made me feel suddenly ill. I excused myself and made it to the restaurant bathroom just in time to throw up what little I had eaten.

Chapter Twenty

That week, I went out twice more with a repentant Brett, and he even stopped by Frenchy's one day at lunch to bring me white lilies, my favorite. There was no doubt that he was doing everything he could to win me back. I just hadn't made up my mind yet.

After all, on the one hand I'd been so sure little more than two months ago that he was The One, I'd been gleefully planning a wedding with him. Had he not freaked out on me, I probably never would have considered leaving him. Our wedding would be mere weeks away.

On the other hand, his leaving me had forced me to look at all the things that were wrong with our relationship. He was, at times, condescending and overbearing. He often didn't listen to me and sometimes treated me like a child. But all in all, our relationship hadn't been bad. I knew he loved me—or at least he had, for a time. He seemed to be genuine in his proclamations of love for me now.

Maybe he *had* just made a mistake. Maybe he *did* deserve another chance.

"Are you seriously considering getting back together with him?" Poppy demanded the day after I'd been out with

Brett for the third time. I had finally called to sheepishly tell her, knowing that she wouldn't react well to the news.

"I don't know," I mumbled. "Maybe he deserves another chance."

"Emma," she said slowly. "Perhaps you don't remember. He cheated on you. With your best friend."

"No," I protested. "He didn't exactly cheat. He didn't get together with her until after we broke up. Besides, maybe he just made a mistake. You should see how hard he's trying."

Poppy made a snorting sound.

"Besides," I added, "you've forgiven Darren, haven't you?"

Poppy had been seeing her British ex regularly since the London junket, and I knew that she was beginning to think more seriously about calling off her whole mission to date as many Parisian men as possible.

She was silent for a long moment. "Emma, it's a different situation," she said quietly. "Darren and I both did a lot to hurt each other. We both made mistakes. And who knows what will happen now? We haven't made any decisions. We're just seeing where things go."

"Maybe that's all I'm doing, too," I said defensively.

"But, Emma," Poppy said, "it's different. Brett moved on by *sleeping with your best friend*. And you weren't just dating, you were engaged. He kicked you out of *your* house."

"So?" I asked in a small voice.

"So," Poppy said gently. "Don't you wonder what's motivating him now? Why has he changed his mind so quickly? It just doesn't feel right to me."

★   ★   ★

The day after I talked to Poppy, Brett took me out to dinner again, this time to Seasons 52, a restaurant I loved down on Sand Lake Road. He booked my favorite table alongside the lake out back, and he ordered a bottle of my favorite wine—a smooth Petite Syrah—and the artichoke and goat cheese flatbread I adored.

"See, babe?" he said after we had started sipping our wine. "I remember exactly what you like. We just *fit*."

But Poppy's words had been gnawing away at me for the past twenty-four hours.

"Why?" I asked slowly.

Brett looked confused. "Why what?"

"Why do we fit?" I asked slowly. "Why do you think we're so perfect together? And why are you so intent on getting back together with me?"

"Because I love you," Brett answered promptly. "Because I made a huge mistake. C'mon, Emma, we've been over this. You know how much I care. You know how I feel."

I thought for a moment. "What about your parents?" I asked. "They never thought I was good enough for you, did they? They wanted you to marry some Ivy League girl or something."

"That's not true," Brett said.

"Yes, it is," I said. "I know it is. They've always acted like I was a disappointment. Like you could do so much better."

"Well, then why are they so eager to have me get back together with you, then?" Brett asked triumphantly.

I stared at him in surprise. "Your parents *want* us to get back together?" I had just assumed that Operation-Win-Emma-Back had been a secret from them.

Brett nodded vigorously. "Yes! They've even invited you over to dinner this week. They're thrilled about us."

"They are?"

Brett nodded again. "They were mortified when we broke up," he said. "They said it made the family look bad. They even stopped paying me my allowance."

"Your *allowance*?"

Brett blinked a few times and turned scarlet. "Um, yeah," he said. "I guess I never told you. But they gave me some money every month. Something about a tax write-off."

"How *much* money?" I asked slowly, thinking of all the times Brett had insisted we split the check fifty–fifty when we went out to eat.

Brett paused. "Five thousand dollars."

I dropped my fork.

"A *month*?" I asked, my voice cracking as it went up several octaves.

Brett nodded and had the decency to look embarrassed.

I digested this for a moment. "And they've stopped paying you this allowance?" I repeated. I was starting to feel a little sick. "Until you can get me back?"

Brett nodded again, not seeming to realize he was talking himself into a hole. "They called it their grandbaby fund." He chuckled. "They're ready for us to get married and start having kids, Emma. I mean, if that doesn't prove to you how much they care about you, I don't know what will."

"Brett," I said patiently, "that doesn't mean they care about *me*. That means that they care about how our broken engagement made *them* look. And they care about being grandparents. I'm just the quickest route to that."

Brett tilted his head to the side. "That's not true. They love you, Emma. Just like I do."

"Do you really?" I asked flatly. "Or are you just trying to get me back so that you can win back your allowance?"

Brett opened and closed his mouth, fishlike. "I can't believe you'd even ask that," he said after a moment.

Just then, my cell phone rang. Grateful for an excuse to escape the conversation momentarily, I dove for it.

"You're going to answer your phone in the middle of dinner?" Brett made a face.

"Yes," I said. I checked the caller ID. UNAVAILABLE. It could be a sales call, for all I knew, but at least it would give me a temporary escape. "It's an important call."

I stood up and walked away from the table toward the outside bar area. Knowing that Brett was watching me, I sank down into a lounge chair with my back to him and pressed SEND to answer.

"Emma?" It was Poppy, and she sounded excited. "Where are you?"

"Out to dinner with Brett," I mumbled.

"What?"

"Don't ask." I sighed. "So what's up? It's late over there, isn't it?" I did the mental math. If it was eight thirty in

Florida, that made it two thirty tomorrow morning in Paris. "Is everything okay?"

"Everything's fine," Poppy said. I could hear the smile in her voice. "I'm not in Paris, actually. I'm in your time zone."

I sat up straight in my lounge chair. "What? Where?"

"In New York!" Poppy said gleefully.

"In New York?" I repeated. "What are you doing there?"

"Turns out that Guillaume's waterskiing incident was a success after all," Poppy said. "We got calls from all sorts of American media outlets. We just got in tonight, and we're scheduled to do *Today with Katie Jones* tomorrow and *Good Morning America* on Friday!"

"You're kidding!" I exclaimed. "Poppy, that's wonderful! Why didn't you tell me sooner?"

"I wanted to surprise you," she said.

"Surprise me?"

She paused. "I was hoping you would come up and join us."

My heart sank. "I'd love to, Poppy. But I can't afford the trip up there now. You know that!"

"Well," she said, "let me put it this way. I've already booked an airline ticket in your name, and you have a room at the Hyatt Grand Central. You'd fly up tomorrow morning, so you'll only have to take a day off work. Frankly, you'd be silly not to come."

"Poppy—"

"Guillaume paid for all of it out of pocket," she cut in. "He still feels terrible about what happened—as he well should. So you might as well get a free trip on his dime!"

I thought about it for a moment. She *did* have a point. And if the ticket was already purchased . . .

"All right," I said slowly. "I guess I'll be there, then."

"Brilliant!" Poppy exclaimed. "Be at the Katie Jones studio on Broadway and Fifty-third at noon tomorrow. I'll leave a ticket for you. We'll have dinner after the show!"

"That sounds wonderful," I said warmly. "I don't know how to thank you."

"I know how you can thank me," Poppy said.

"How?"

"Come to your senses and walk away from Brett before you get sucked back in," she said. "I know you feel like you're lonely and stuck there, Emma. But don't fall back into that. Please."

I thought about it for a moment. "You're right," I said softly.

"Good girl," Poppy said. "I'll see you tomorrow, Emma. *Au revoir!*"

I sat there for a moment after I hung up. What was I doing? How had I come to a place where I once again thought Brett was the answer to everything? Three weeks' worth of Jeannie's get-back-together-with-him-you-idiot diatribes had turned me into someone different, and the hopelessness of my situation had made me desperate and needy.

But I'd become someone else during my brief time in Paris. Or, more accurately, I'd looked inside for the first time and gotten in touch with *me*. It wasn't the job or the meaningless dates, or even the self-destructive crush I'd had on Gabe. It was that, for the first time in more than three years, I'd learned that being alone really wasn't so bad.

I took a deep breath, stood up, and walked back to our table.

"That was really rude, Emma," Brett said, shaking his head. "I never answer calls during dinner."

I looked at him funny. "Brett, you used to answer your phone all the time while we were eating."

"That's different," he said. "Those were work calls."

"Well, actually, this was a work call, too."

"What, the restaurant was calling you?" Brett smirked. "Important waitress business?"

"No, Poppy was calling," I said. "About Guillaume Riche."

"I thought you were fired from that job."

I nodded. "But maybe it's time to fight for what I deserve," I said. I paused. I was still standing beside the table, and Brett was beginning to look uncomfortable.

"Aren't you going to sit back down, Emma?" he asked. "People are looking."

I ignored him. "I need to ask you something," I said. "*Why* do you want to get back together with me?"

Brett looked confused. "Because I love you."

"Why?" I persisted. "*Why* do you love me?"

"I don't know." He looked uneasy. "I just do."

"Why?" I persisted. "I mean, why me? Why me instead of Amanda?"

"Let's not bring her into this," he mumbled.

"I think you already brought her in," I said with a shrug.

Brett had the decency to look embarrassed. "I don't know, Emma," he said, sounding exasperated. "I love you because you've always been there. I love you because you know me and put up with me. I love you because I know you will be a good mother to our children. I love you because we're perfect together. I don't know what else you want me to say."

I looked at him for a moment. None of his reasons for loving me had anything to do with *me*. They never had, had they?

"You were right," I said finally.

Brett nodded, as if this was a given. "About what?"

"About us."

Brett smiled. "Good. Finally! You've seen things my way. So do you want to move back in? Or should we take things slow?"

I shook my head. "No, I mean you were right the first time."

"What?"

"When you said we weren't right together. When you kicked me out."

"Now, wait a minute, Emma." Brett held up his hand impatiently. "You're being ridiculous here."

"No," I said. I shook my head sadly. "I was being ridiculous to even consider getting back together with you."

Brett gaped. "Emma, you're making a huge mistake. Do you know what you're saying?"

"Yes, I do," I said slowly and calmly. "I don't want to be with you."

He just kept staring at me, as if he couldn't understand

what he was hearing. "You're not going to find anyone better than me, you know. Not at your age."

For some reason, I thought of Gabe, whom I quite possibly would never hear from again.

"You know, I think I already have," I said softly.

I took a cab home, and the moment I walked in the door, Jeannie cornered me in the front hallway.

"Brett called," she said, putting her hands on her hips and glaring at me.

"Did he? How nice. Did you have a nice chat?"

Jeannie ignored me. "Do you know what you just did?" she asked, her eyes wide. Upstairs, Odysseus began wailing something unintelligible. Jeannie didn't seem to hear.

"Yes, I know exactly what I did," I responded calmly. "I told Brett I didn't want to get back together with him." I wasn't sure why a recap was necessary, as Jeannie had clearly been filled in already.

"Emma!" Jeannie exclaimed with dismay. "Why? He's perfect for you!"

I looked at her blankly. "Why do you say that?" I asked finally. "Why do you think he's so perfect?"

Jeannie looked a bit caught off guard. "I don't know. Because he's hot and he makes good money?" she said after a moment. "And he's a pretty nice guy. I mean, really, what more can you ask for?"

I nodded slowly, feeling deeply grateful that although we'd come from the same set of parents, somehow I'd grown up with a completely different set of values. "Yes, Jeannie," I said softly. I looked her right in the eye. "But he's not capable of loving me even remotely as much as he loves himself," I said. "And I want to be with someone who loves me and wants what's best for me. Brett will never be that person, because all Brett cares about is Brett."

Jeannie pursed her lips. "You are making a *huge* mistake," she said. "One of these days, you're going to have to learn that adulthood is about not always getting what you want, you know." Then, as if my decision not to give Brett another chance was a personal affront to her, she spun on her heel and stormed out of the room.

Chapter Twenty-One

Poppy had booked me on the 7:20 a.m. to LaGuardia, and thanks to traffic, it was nearly noon when I arrived at the Katie Jones studio for the 2 p.m. taping. By the time I was seated, my nerves were fully on edge, but I couldn't explain why. It unsettled me to think of seeing Guillaume again. I'd been trying hard to put what had happened behind me, but he was, of course, at the center of it all.

I felt conspicuously alone as I waited for the show to begin.

"You all by yourself?" asked the overweight man to my right, who was so large that he was sitting in both his seat and half of mine, wedging me against my left armrest. Thankfully, I was on an aisle, so at least I wasn't squashed against a person on the other side, too.

I forced a smile. "Yes."

"A pretty girl like you?" he asked, the words pouring out in a syrupy drawl. Beside him, his wife giggled and looked at me. "You don't got no friends?"

I gritted my teeth. "They're just not sitting with me," I said.

The man snickered and said something to his wife. I

rolled my eyes. It seemed the whole world was in cahoots with Jeannie to remind me of the error of my lonely ways.

The show began at two, and I settled in to watch as Katie Jones opened with a monologue that the Texan next to me found so funny, he shook the whole row of seats with his chortles every few seconds. I was relieved when the jokes were over.

The second half of the show opened with an interview with movie star Cole Brannon, who was starring in the most anticipated release of the summer. When Katie finished talking to the tall, handsome actor, she turned to the camera.

"Hang on, because after the break, we have France's craziest export, Guillaume Riche, who will be playing his Top Ten hit 'City of Light,'" she said, reaching one hand up to smooth her perfect brunette bob. "And maybe if we're lucky, he'll tell us what it's like to water-ski down the Seine River in SpongeBob SquarePants boxers and a top hat!"

The crowd laughed, and the house lights went up as the show went to commercial break. I scanned the room for Poppy, but couldn't find her. On the darkened stage, a crew hurried to set up a drum kit, mics, and amps that would be used for Guillaume's performance in a moment. I caught sight of Jean-Marc, Guillaume's drummer, and my heart leapt into my throat. I missed those guys more than I had realized.

After the break, the spotlight shone back on Katie Jones. She grinned into the camera and said dramatically, "Ladies and gentlemen, Guillaume Riche!"

My heart began to thud wildly the moment the stage lights flashed on, revealing Guillaume standing there. He looked even more handsome than I'd ever seen him. He was wearing a button-down shirt with the sleeves ripped just above the biceps to show off his impressive arms, and his tight jeans clung perfectly to the sculptured curves of his legs. His hair was professionally tousled into little wayward spikes; he looked like he had just gotten out of bed looking clean-shaven and perfect. The guitar he was currently strumming was the final touch; it was emblazoned with the French flag, and his Jodi Head strap read RICHE down the front in bold, Swarovski-crystal letters.

As the crowd went wild with screams and whistles, I smiled. Guillaume Riche had crossed the pond for his first American appearance as a ready-made superstar. The crowds loved him. In fact, there was a girl in front of me who was screaming so loudly that I was fairly sure she was about to hyperventilate. Although I was no longer working with KMG, I felt a little swell of pride for the small role I'd played in his career. This felt better than all the boy bands I'd ever helped unleash on the world.

The band started playing, and when Guillaume started in on the first verse of "City of Light," I was stunned to hear a chorus of voices throughout the auditorium join in. Guillaume looked surprised, too, but he grinned broadly and turned the enthusiasm up a notch. Around me, scores of girls were still on their feet, singing in unison with Guillaume. It was an incredible thing to see. In that moment, I missed working with Poppy so much it hurt; I missed KMG; I missed the buzz and excitement of working on a project that was bound for such success. I even missed Guillaume.

"City of Light" ended with a standing ovation from the crowd, and then Katie Jones joined Guillaume at the mic and promised the audience they'd be back after the commercial to talk to Guillaume about his breakout success and his penchant for getting into crazy situations.

After the brief break, the house lights faded again, and the spotlights swung toward Katie's interview area, where Guillaume was sitting, one leg crossed over the other, holding a coffee mug, and looking very French. I felt another pang that I tried to dismiss.

The crowd went wild again while Guillaume laughed and waved with his free hand. Finally, the screams quieted.

"That's quite a reaction you're getting," Katie said with her signature slow, toothy grin.

Guillaume smiled back. "I'm a lucky, lucky man," he said. A few girls in the audience screamed, and Guillaume obliged them with another wave.

"Some would say it's talent and not luck," Katie said. She glanced at her notecards. "Okay, so it looks like your album is really doing great in the United States, right?"

"Yes. It's such a thrill," Guillaume said. I smiled. They sounded like words right out of Poppy's mouth—and I suspected they were. "I'm really grateful that everyone is listening to my music. I've always wanted to be a big hit with the American girls."

The crowd erupted in still more screams, and Guillaume blew a few kisses. "I love American girls, Katie," he said over the din. "Too bad you're married."

Katie smiled again and shook her head. "So I have to ask you," she said. "What's with all these crazy stunts? You were arrested for skiing on the river in Paris last week? And you've gotten locked in the Eiffel Tower? Is that right?"

Guillaume glanced offstage, where I suspected Poppy was standing, shooting him death looks. "Well, Katie, the Eiffel Tower thing was a mistake," he said. I breathed a sigh of relief. Good; he was sticking to the story. "It was all a misunderstanding. But yes, I admit that the waterskiing thing was a little crazy."

The audience laughed and Guillaume made an embarrassed face. "I guess I just felt like having a ski, you know?" he said, widening his eyes into that same puppy-dog look of innocence he had tried with me. The audience seemed to eat it right up.

They talked for a moment more about the next single on the album, the inspiration for his songs, and his plans for a US tour in the fall. Then Katie peered down at her notes.

"So, Guillaume, I've been told that you have some sort of public apology to make tonight?" she asked.

My heart skipped a beat and I sat up a little straighter in my chair (which was hard to do with the Texan sharing my seating space).

"Yes, Katie," Guillaume said, pulling a slightly sheepish face that I suspected he had practiced in the mirror to achieve maximum cuteness. It worked. "I'm afraid I've been a bit of a fuckup."

The audience laughed, and Katie reminded Guillaume that he couldn't talk like that on American TV. "I guess that'll be bleeped out," Katie said with a smile, glancing at the camera.

"Sorry, sorry," Guillaume said, not looking sorry at all. "Anyhow. The thing is, I had this great publicist, Emma, for a month."

My jaw dropped and time seemed to slow down around me.

"She was the only one who seemed to be able to get me out of scrapes without getting too mad at me," Guillaume continued. I could barely hear him over the rushing sound in my ears. I knew that my face had turned beet red, although of course no one in the audience knew that I was the person he was talking about. Guillaume went on: "Somehow, she always made it so I came out looking good."

"Okay, she sounds perfect," Katie said. "I need a publicist like that." The audience laughed lightly, and she added, "So, what's the problem?"

Guillaume cast his eyes down. "Well, the thing is, she liked this reporter named Gabriel, and I *knew* she did," he said.

"Oh, no," I muttered to myself, prompting a strange look from my Texan seatmate. I barely noticed. My face felt hot, and my palms were suddenly sweaty. Had Guillaume really just announced to *the entire country* that I had an inappropriate crush on a journalist? And this was supposed to make me feel *better*? I wanted to shrink into my seat and disappear.

"Oh, really?" Katie prompted, leaning forward with some interest.

"Yes," Guillaume said, the sheepish expression across his face.

"Please stop talking," I muttered under my breath. "Please stop talking." But Guillaume apparently wasn't listening to me. The only one who seemed to respond to my words was the Texan, who finally scooted an inch or two away from me and gave me a look as if he was afraid I was insane.

Onstage, Guillaume continued, undeterred by the *please shut up* mental messages I was furiously sending him. "See the thing is, I've been basically trying to screw with Gabe for the last thirty years," he said.

Wait. What? Thirty years? What was he talking about?

"I'm a bit of a jerk," Guillaume continued. "But the thing is, this time, it actually mattered. It wasn't just harmless. I actually effed things up with Emma and Gabe."

"Why is it you've been trying to screw things up with this Gabe for the last thirty years?" Katie prompted. *Good question, Katie,* I thought.

Guillaume shrugged, a mischievous expression playing across his perfect features. "Ah, it's silly really," he said. "It's our stupid brotherly rivalry."

I gasped. "Huh?" I said aloud. I couldn't understand what Guillaume was talking about.

"See, he's my half brother," Guillaume continued onstage.

"What?" I breathed.

Beside me, the Texan was staring at me with alarm. "You crazy or something, lady?" he asked. He scooted even closer to his wife. I barely noticed.

"But he grew up in the United States with his mom," Guillaume continued. "He's a year and a half older than me. So when he'd come spend summers with our dad and me, all the girls went for him since he was bigger, stronger—and half American. Even all those summers he spent teaching me to speak better English, I was still just the boring French kid next door."

Guillaume paused and grinned. "It's why I had to join a band," he quipped. "It's the only way I was ever going to get laid with Gabe around every summer."

The audience laughed at his joke, but all I could do was stare, my jaw hanging open. "They're *brothers*?" I whispered to myself. How could it be? How had Gabe never mentioned any of this to me? But it certainly explained a lot—like how Gabe knew so much about Guillaume's background, how he always seemed to know what Guillaume was doing, and how he was the only one who seemed to effortlessly see through my lies about Guillaume's odd behavior.

I thought about it for a moment. Although I never would have put two and two together, it made so much sense. They *did* look alike. But while Guillaume wore his dark hair spiky and sexy, Gabe wore his combed and professional. Guillaume's green eyes were framed by thick, dark eyelashes, Gabe's were hidden behind his omnipresent wire-rimmed glasses, but they were more similar than I'd ever realized. Where Guillaume flaunted his body in curve-hugging rock-star wear, Gabe tended to be more professional and reserved, but I suspected that their builds were more similar under those clothes than I had considered. Even their accents when speaking English were identical, although Guillaume's was thicker. Obviously, this could be explained by the fact that they shared a father and that much of Guillaume's English had come from Gabe's tutelage.

Katie was talking as I tuned back in, still riveted by the revelation. "So," she was saying, "I hear from producers that this brother of yours is actually here backstage right now. Can we bring him out?"

I could feel my eyes widen as Gabe, looking even more handsome than I remembered, came striding reluctantly out from stage left, looking embarrassed. He was dressed casually in dark jeans and a gray T-shirt that actually showed off contours of his arms and chest I'd never noticed before under his stiff, button-down shirts. He had never looked better to me.

A producer guided him to the chair beside Guillaume's and quickly clipped a little microphone on his collar before scurrying away.

"Hi, big brother," Guillaume said. Gabe just glared at him. "Gabe, I'm so sorry. I really am."

I held my breath as the cameras zoomed in on Gabe's face. Overhead on the monitors, I could see his jaw set. His eyes darted nervously around. I knew he didn't like being the center of attention, and he was obviously uncomfortable on the stage.

"It's fine," Gabe muttered.

"No, Gabe, it's not," Guillaume said. The cameras

zoomed in on his face, and he looked genuinely upset, although I wouldn't have put it past him to have practiced his remorseful face in the mirror for hours before his TV appearance. "Emma's a great girl. And I screwed it up for you, before you even had a chance to make a move on her."

"Yeah, thanks for telling the world that I didn't make a move," Gabe said, rolling his eyes.

The audience laughed a bit, and Gabe's face reddened. I felt terrible for him. I couldn't shake the feeling that this was largely my fault.

Guillaume grinned devilishly. "Speaking of that, Gabe, you have to learn to stop being so shy and actually ask out the women you like."

The studio audience laughed again, and Gabe blushed as deeply as I suspected I was currently doing myself. I felt suddenly short of breath.

Gabe grimaced. "You're not helping your case here, Guillaume." He looked down at his lap, a grimace playing across his features.

Guillaume shrugged. "Look, I just wanted to apologize to you. You won't take my calls, so this was my last resort. Listen, no matter how it looked, nothing happened between me and Emma. She was actually in my room talking about *you* when I leaned over and kissed her. It was my fault, not hers."

Gabe looked up at him, and for the first time, there was something in his expression that wasn't embarrassment or anger.

Guillaume continued. "And, Emma, wherever you are—" He looked directly into the camera. I sat up in my seat and stared at the monitor above me. "I owe you an apology, too. Now, listen to me. I want you to give my brother here a chance, okay? And once you two have worked things out, I need you to come back and be my publicist again. I'll fix everything with KMG. I can't seem to stop getting myself into trouble. I need you."

The audience laughed again, and I sat stunned, frozen to my seat.

Katie, an eyebrow arched, interjected, "Okay, Gabe. Is there anything you want to say to this Emma?"

Gabe turned even redder and shook his head. The audience groaned, and Guillaume looked delighted at his brother's discomfort.

"Come on, big brother, you're on national television in America," Guillaume urged. "It's the perfect opportunity to finally make that move on the girl, for once in your life."

I felt mortified for poor Gabe. But at the same time, I hoped he'd say something. After all, I had no idea how he felt. Would he forgive me? Or was he just as angry at me as he had been?

"Okay," Gabe said, taking a deep breath. I leaned forward in my seat, my heart pounding. "I'd just like to tell her . . ." His voice trailed off, and he paused for a moment. Then he looked straight into the camera, and above me on the monitor, it looked like he was talking directly to me. "I'd like to tell her that I'm sorry I didn't take the time to listen and realize that this was just Guillaume being a jerk again." He paused and looked at his lap. When he looked up again, his cheeks were a little flushed. "And also, I think I might be in love with her."

There was a collective *"Awwwww!"* from the audience. I felt like I couldn't breathe. He *loved* me?

"Hey now, watch it, big brother!" Guillaume said with a grin.

"All right, guys, you can kiss and make up over the break," Katie said with a grin. She turned to the camera and added, "Stay right here to see Guillaume perform 'Beautiful Girl,' the second single off his album, when we come back."

The Katie Jones house band played a few chords, and the house lights came back up. I watched, rooted to my seat, as Gabe unhooked his mic, said something to Guillaume, and strode offstage.

"Emma?" said a voice above me. I looked up slowly to see Poppy there, smiling down at me. "Gabe is backstage. Come on."

I stared up at her.

"You . . . you knew about this?"

Poppy nodded and grinned.

"Guillaume has been planning it for the last week," she said. "He really does feel bad. He even made sure that the UPP took Gabe off the obit desk for the week to fly him over for an exclusive on his trip to America! But it went even better than I thought! Did you hear Gabe? He said he loves you!"

I felt like I was in a fog as I got silently to my feet and followed her. The Texan next to me shifted, looked up at me, and muttered to his wife, "Where does she think she's goin'?"

It wasn't until Poppy had shown her pass and we had slipped through a backstage door that I finally found my voice again.

"Poppy," I said, still feeling very confused. "Does Gabe know I'm here?"

"No." Poppy's grin widened. "But he's about to find out."

She led me to the area behind stage left, where I could see Guillaume and his band onstage, getting ready for the show to come back from commercial break so they could launch into "Beautiful Girl." Between me and Guillaume, only ten feet away, stood Gabe, with his back to us, watching Guillaume from the wings. I wished I knew what he was thinking. I studied his broad back for a moment, my heart pounding as I tried to think of what to say to him. I felt suddenly terrified. I stopped dead in my tracks, rooted to the spot.

Just then, Guillaume, who was adjusting his mic stand, glanced over. "Emma!" he exclaimed. He grinned and waved.

Gabe whipped his head around and stared. "You're here," he said softly after a moment, shock playing across his features.

Before I could respond, the lights came back up and I could see Katie Jones standing on the stage.

"Here he is again, ladies and gentlemen, Guillaume Riche!" she said enthusiastically. Guillaume's band immediately launched into "Beautiful Girl," and, still grinning, Guillaume turned his attention away from me and began singing. Gabe continued to stare at me for a moment, then shoved his hands in his pockets and took a few steps closer.

"Hi," he said softly. Onstage, Guillaume glanced over and gave us the thumbs-up sign before he went back to the song.

"Hi," I said nervously. We both stood there in silence for a moment. I was dimly aware that Guillaume was playing, but suddenly everything around me—the music, the bright lights, the people who were beginning to whisper and stare—faded into the background. I felt as if I were in one of those films where everything is fuzzy and blurred except for the characters in the middle of the scene.

Gabe and I stood looking at each other for what felt like an eternity. A lump had risen in my throat, and I could feel tears pricking the backs of my eyes. My cheeks were hot, and my heart was pounding. I felt like everything was suspended. Then Gabe reached out and touched my arm.

"I'm sorry," I blurted out, the spell broken. "I'm so sorry, Gabe. I never meant to do anything to hurt you."

Gabe studied my face for a moment while my heart pounded double-time. I didn't know what he'd say. Was he trying to decide whether he could forgive me? Whether he could forget what had happened? After all, even though it seemed that Guillaume had conjured the whole situation to get under Gabe's skin, the fact remained that I *had* kissed his brother.

"No," Gabe said after a moment. "*I'm* sorry. I'm sorry I didn't give you a chance to explain." He glanced toward the stage for a moment, where Guillaume was playing his heart out to a backdrop of screams from the audience. "I'm so used to Guillaume getting the girl—for the last ten years, at least—that I just assumed it had happened again."

"But it didn't," I whispered.

Gabe gave me a small smile. "I know," he said. "I mean I know that now. But he and I are pretty competitive, and, well, let's just say that the rock star usually trumps the reporter in situations like this."

I smiled. It didn't take a rocket scientist to figure out that most girls would be more attracted to a flirtatious rock star than a quiet journalist.

But I wasn't most girls.

"I'm sorry, too," I said. "I never should have let Guillaume kiss me. I . . . it's a lousy excuse, but it was the champagne, not me."

Gabe nodded and touched my arm again softly. I knew he understood. We looked at each other for a moment and then we both turned our attention to Guillaume, who was still making his way through the verses of "Beautiful Girl" onstage. After a moment, he glanced over at us, smiling.

"So doesn't this violate some sort of professional ethics?" I asked carefully. "You covering your brother for the UPP, I mean?"

Gabe shrugged. "Maybe. But my editor has known about it since day one. The thing is, I've been the chief music reporter for the UPP in Europe for the last five years, way before Guillaume signed a record deal. It wouldn't make sense to take me off a big story like this one."

"Even if you have an obvious bias?" I persisted.

Gabe smiled. "If you've noticed, I've been nothing but fair in my articles," he said. "Even when I wanted to kill my brother, I stuck to the facts. As for the reviews about his album, my editor wrote all that. We *did* decide it wasn't fair for me to pass judgment on him."

I nodded slowly. "So what now?" I asked as Guillaume launched into the chorus.

Gabe studied my face. "Will you move back to Paris?" he asked softly. "Guillaume will make sure you get your job back. I'll fix things between KMG and the UPP. You can pick up where you left off." He paused, and I could see his cheeks turn a bit pink. "And maybe," he added in an embarrassed mutter, "you and I can give things a try and see what happens without my brother getting in the way."

I gazed up at him for a moment. There suddenly wasn't a doubt in my mind that I'd do it. After all, I'd left Paris because I'd been sure that my own professional error had led to bad press for the star I was being paid to promote. But now that I knew it hadn't been my fault—or at least that it had been only about 10 percent my fault—I could take the job back in good conscience.

Suddenly, for no reason at all, Brett popped into my mind. Not because I had any interest whatsoever in him but because the fact that he had always refused to leave Orlando—and his comfort zone—remained for me an open wound.

"What if I want to stay in Orlando?" I heard myself asking Gabe. It was a stupid question; staying in Orlando wasn't even a consideration. But somehow, I needed to hear what Gabe would say.

He looked startled. He thought about it for a moment. "Well," he said finally. "I suppose there's a UPP bureau there I could find a job with."

I stared at him. "You would leave Paris?"

He considered this for a moment. "Paris is my home," he said. "But it will always be there. And you might not be. I want to see where things can go with you. And if you want to stay in Orlando, well, I guess I'll see about moving to Orlando. We could figure something out."

I felt breathless. Gabe, whom I'd known for only a couple of months, was saying the words I never would have heard in a million years from Brett, whom I'd been so sure loved me.

"No," I said finally. "I'll come back to Paris."

"Good." Gabe breathed a sigh of relief and grinned. He glanced at Guillaume. "Because my idiot brother clearly needs you to keep him out of trouble."

I laughed. "That's true. Plus, Paris *is* the most romantic city in the world."

Gabe rolled his eyes. "Yes," he said. "Guillaume told me all about how you and Poppy are on the hunt for the perfect French kiss."

I could feel myself blushing. It sounded pretty stupid when he put it that way.

"But do you know who kisses better than Frenchmen?" Gabe continued.

"No," I said, startled. Why would Gabe be suggesting

that there was someone out there who kissed better than his countrymen?

Gabe grinned. "French-American men," he said. Then he leaned down to touch his lips lightly to mine. Everything in my body began to tingle.

If I'd thought that the rest of the world had been fuzzy when we were staring at each other a few moments ago, this was a whole new ball game. Everything faded away as my lips parted and Gabe's kiss grew more passionate. It was, in fact, the perfect French kiss, the one I'd been searching for high and low at Poppy's insistence. It had been right here, with Gabe Francoeur, all along.

Gabe pulled me to him, and the whole rest of the world disappeared. That is, until I heard Guillaume whooping from the stage.

"All right, Gabe!" he was cheering into the mic. "Ladies and gentlemen, that's my brother!"

Mortified, I pulled away from Gabe and realized that not only had Guillaume and the band stopped playing while we had been lost in kissing each other, but now a camera was trained on us, capturing our every move. The audience was cheering, and I could see our faces on every monitor overhead. I suspected it wasn't just the lighting that made both of us look bright red.

"Kiss her again, Gabe!" Guillaume encouraged. The audience cheered, and I could hear a few shouts of "Kiss her! Kiss her!" Gabe and I looked at each other for a long moment.

"I guess we don't really have a choice," he said with a little smile.

I smiled back. "I guess not," I said. Then slowly, with the cameras trained on us and all of America watching, Gabe pulled me into his arms and leaned down. The cheers, the shouts, and even the refrain of "Beautiful Girl," which Guillaume had started playing again, faded into the background as our lips met in the perfect French kiss.

Epilogue

It should have been one of the most beautiful moments of my life.

As the sky deepened to a sunset of pink-streaked royal blue, Gabe and I were floating above Paris in a hot-air balloon, something I had always dreamed of doing. However, as you might suspect with Guillaume in the picture (and Guillaume *always* seemed to be in the picture these days), things weren't quite as idyllic as they sounded. For instance, apparently hot-air balloons were not supposed to move into the airspace directly above Paris—probably for fear of some sort of disaster involving a balloon impaling itself on the Eiffel Tower. But we weren't concerned about the rules at the moment.

We were more concerned about the fact that Guillaume, who was single-handedly manning a second balloon a hundred yards away, was floating to his certain death.

Below us, Paris rose up around the ribbon of the Seine, a gentle sprawl of cream-colored, centuries-old apartments, little chimney tops, quaint bridges, and geometric green parks. We were just west of the city, so the Eiffel Tower jutted gracefully into the sky right in front of us, and had I not been in such a state of panic, I would have marveled at just how beautiful it was as it loomed, all thousand feet of iron gridwork and graceful symmetry, over the glorious green ladder of the Champ de Mars, which spread out in a neat rectangle to the foot of the dark-domed École Militaire.

The Arc de Triomphe, the stone masterpiece Napoléon had commissioned two hundred years ago, looked palatial in the waning sunlight as it sat across the river in the center of the busiest roundabout in Paris, twelve avenues radiating like points on a star from its center. The Avenue des Champs-Élysées, lined with trees and sparkling lights, marched away from us toward the center of Paris, ending in the octagonal Place de la Concorde, where I could see the tall, slender, thirty-two-hundred-year-old Egyptian obelisk that pointed at the sky, framed by two fountains.

Beyond that, the perfectly geometric Jardin des Tuileries was an emerald expanse toward the enormous Louvre, which hulked on the Right Bank, long and limber around I. M. Pei's famed glass pyramid. On the Île de la Cité, the island in the middle of the Seine, I could just make out the twin towers of Notre Dame beyond the Palais de Justice and the spires of the Sainte-Chapelle cathedral. All along the gently winding river, which sparkled bright blue in the fading daylight, bridges looked like rungs of a ladder from the air.

Yet there was hardly time to take in any of the incredible beauty. Instead I was in a state of panic as Gabe and I, with the help of a hastily hired balloon operator, chased

Guillaume through the clouds above Paris. Gabe had called me an hour ago to tell me tersely that Guillaume had taken a hot-air balloon and was currently floating solo above the city. My stomach had twisted into knots, and I'd asked Gabe if he could arrange for another balloon so that we could go up and try to talk Guillaume down before he killed himself. After all, hot on the heels of the success of "City of Light," Guillaume was just finishing recording his second album and was due to embark on a world tour the week after next. It would be a little difficult for us to fill auditoriums if the headliner was in a body cast or, heaven forbid, splattered across the Paris pavement. I shuddered at the thought.

Now Guillaume was floating high above Paris, all by himself, without a balloon operator, in a green, yellow, and red balloon that he'd evidently somehow stolen from a field just outside Paris. He was cheerfully firing up the propane tank every few minutes, making his balloon rise and gently fall as our balloon, which Gabe had scrambled to hire from a tour site outside the city, floated close enough to put me in shouting distance. I didn't even want to think about the legal trouble we'd all be in when we landed; we were currently much closer to Paris than we were allowed to be.

"Hi, Emma!" Guillaume's voice wafted over, faint over the wind and the periodic gentle hiss of the propane burner heating the air inside our balloon.

"Guillaume!" I shouted back, fearing that my voice wouldn't carry far enough. "What on earth are you *doing*?"

I'd just been counting myself lucky, too. I should have

known better. But it had been two whole months since a major incident with Guillaume. Sure, he'd done dumb things here and there—swimming in the fountain in the Place de la Concorde (along with his favorite rubber ducky, no less) one afternoon two weeks ago, for example—but nothing life threatening. Until now. And of course Guillaume wasn't just my insane rock-star client anymore. He was also the brother of the man I loved, which made me that much more worried about how this situation would play out.

"Emma!" Guillaume shouted. He sounded surprisingly chipper for someone who was all by himself in a hot-air balloon that could plummet earthward at any moment. "I thought you'd never get here! And you've brought Gabe with you? How fantastic!"

"Guillaume!" I shouted back. "You're going to get yourself killed!"

I turned to Gabe, feeling panic rise inside me. "We have to help him get down," I said urgently. "We have to have our balloon operator tell him how to land."

Gabe nodded, but he made no move to help or to yell across to Guillaume.

"Gabe!" I exclaimed in exasperation. "Why aren't you doing anything? Aren't you worried?"

Gabe shrugged. "Guillaume always manages to get himself out of things," he said.

I groaned. Sometimes Gabe was infuriating. Every time I'd been called by my office to respond to a Guillaume emergency, Gabe had acted like it was no big deal. One of these days, he was going to be wrong. I wished he'd stop acting like his charmed brother had nine lives—although I had to admit that so far, that had proven to be the case after all.

In the ten months I'd been back in Paris, everything had gone relatively smoothly up until now. Véronique had reluctantly given me my old job back, as it appeared that I did, somehow, have the ability to get Guillaume out of the many disastrous scrapes he routinely got himself into. I'd moved back to my old desk at the office and back into the spare room in Poppy's flat, which had relieved her to no end, because it meant she had someone to share the rent with. For her part, she was still going out with random Frenchmen occasionally. But Darren had been visiting her every few weeks, and she had confessed just a few days ago that despite herself, she thought she might actually try to have a relationship with him. I'd even seen a stack of her self-help books in the trash can, under some used coffee grounds, one day last week.

As for me, my string of random Parisian dates had ended, as I was fully absorbed with Gabe. The more I got to know him, the more compatible I knew we were. We had even taken a trip back to the States last month so that he could meet my parents and I could meet his mother, who still lived in Tampa. Jeannie and King Odysseus had even liked him; Odysseus had temporarily ceased the launching of milk-sodden breakfast cereals to play some sort of complicated French patty-cake game that Gabe patiently taught him.

But now, no matter how well things were going, I half wanted to push Gabe out of the balloon. He wasn't exactly helping matters.

"Guillaume!" I yelled across. "Our balloon operator is going to tell you how to float west out of Paris and then lower your balloon into a field. You *have* to listen!"

I nodded at the operator, who gave me an incredulous look and turned to Gabe. Gabe shrugged and said something to him in French. The balloon instructor spoke rapidly back. In the ten months I'd been in Paris, I'd enrolled in French classes and was picking up the language of my new home. But my education hadn't progressed enough to allow me to understand the quickly spoken words of someone with a thick country accent who was currently speaking over the hiss of a propane burner.

Gabe said something else in rapid French to the operator and then added, *"Allez-y."* Go ahead.

The balloon operator heaved a big sigh then shouted several unintelligible sentences to Guillaume, who grinned, waved, and yelled, *"Merci, monsieur!"*

"Guillaume!" I exclaimed in frustration a moment later when it became evident that he was making absolutely no attempt whatsoever to land his balloon. "What's wrong with you? Do you know how hard it's going to be for me to get you out of this, if you don't wind up killing yourself first?"

"Oh, Emma, you worry too much!" Guillaume yelled back cheerfully. He fired up his burner again, and his balloon rose a little higher. Our operator shrugged and followed him, trying to stay at an even altitude so that I could scream at him adequately. Not that it was doing any good. At this rate, Guillaume would be floating toward the upper atmosphere within the hour.

"You'll probably wind up in jail if you don't get killed!" I shouted. "Do you have any idea how much trouble you're in?"

"Not really!" Guillaume yelled back. He came to the edge and leaned over to look at the ground. I almost had a heart attack as his basket wobbled back and forth. He looked back over at us and grinned. "Hey, Gabe!" he yelled. "Don't you have anything to say?"

There. Finally. Maybe my boyfriend would actually step up and try to talk some reason into his lunatic brother for a change.

"Come *on*, Gabe!" I urged softly without turning around. I was still watching Guillaume wobble in his basket. "Say something!"

"As a matter of fact, there is something I'd like to say!" Gabe finally yelled across to his brother.

"It's about time," I muttered, still watching Guillaume.

"Okay, Gabe!" Guillaume said cheerfully. "Let's hear it! What is it?"

"I'd just like to ask Emma if she'll marry me!" Gabe shouted back.

It took me a second to register what he'd said. "What?" My response came out in a gurgle.

"Would you marry me, Emma?" Gabe asked.

I turned slowly and saw Gabe kneeling awkwardly in the

wicker basket of our balloon, holding a little jewelry box with a silver diamond ring inside. My jaw dropped, and my eyes filled with tears. But I quickly blinked them back.

"Gabe," I said softly. "This really isn't the time, I don't think."

My heart was thudding as I looked down at my boyfriend, who was still kneeling, ring outstretched, smiling at me. It would have been the best proposal I could have imagined, had I not been so sure Guillaume was floating speedily deathward a few yards away. I couldn't believe that Gabe had chosen *now*, of all times, to ask me the most important question in the world.

"Emma!" Guillaume shouted. I whipped around, feeling guilty that my attention had been distracted from him for a moment.

"What, Guillaume?" I shouted back. "Are you okay?"

"Did Gabe forget to tell you that I was a hot-air balloon operator for nine months the year I turned eighteen?" he yelled. "I'm still licensed, you know!"

I stared, uncomprehending. "Wait, what?"

"This is my balloon!" he yelled back. "Do you like it?"

"*Your* balloon?" I repeated. I stared at him for a moment. "Do you mean that you planned this whole thing?"

"Maybe!" he shouted cheerfully.

"You didn't steal the balloon?" I asked incredulously. "You're *not* about to float into the atmosphere or crash-land on the Eiffel Tower?"

"No!" Guillaume grinned. "But it was worth it to see the expression on your face! Sorry to disappoint you, Emma, but I've paid for these balloons, fair and square. And on top of that, I've even gotten permission from the French government for us to be in this airspace. It's amazing the doors that open for you when you're a rock star."

"Wh . . . what?"

"Yes!" Guillaume looked triumphant. "And much as I'd like to stick around to see what my idiot brother has to say to you, I suppose I'll leave the two of you alone. *Au revoir.* See you back on earth!"

With that, he turned off his burner, and his balloon began to float back toward the ground. He waved once more, blew me a kiss, and then turned his back to me. Slowly, feeling like I was in a daze, I turned around. Gabe was still kneeling in the basket, holding up the ring.

"So?" he asked softly after a moment. "Will you? Will you be my wife?"

I smiled at him, completely overtaken by emotion. I blinked a few times. Then I threw my arms around his neck and laughed. "Of course I will!" I exclaimed. I leaned back and grinned at him. "Yes! Yes, I'll marry you!"

Gabe breathed a sigh of relief. "I was hoping you'd say that." He grinned at me and took the ring out of its box. "May I?" he asked, holding it up.

I nodded, and he slipped it onto my left ring finger. It fit perfectly. We both watched for a moment as the princess-cut diamond sparkled in the late-afternoon sun.

"*Felicitations.*" Our balloon operator, whom I'd nearly forgotten about, congratulated us.

"*Merci.*" I beamed at him.

"Your accent is really getting quite good," Gabe teased. I rolled my eyes.

"I think I still have some work to do," I said. "I'm not French yet."

"Oh, I don't know," he said with a sly smile. "You have the kissing part down at least."

He touched his lips to mine, and I kissed back, feeling the breeze in my hair as our balloon began to descend. Gabe slipped his arm around my shoulders and pulled me close. As the sun began to set and Guillaume's balloon drifted gently downward below us, we held each other tightly and looked over the edge of the basket as darkness fell on the City of Light.

About the Author

Six years ago, I moved to Paris on a whim, just like Emma, the main character of this novel. I didn't speak French. I had been there only once before, on a family vacation. I had never imagined living there. It was the most impulsive thing I'd ever done, and it changed my life.

That summer was a turning point for me in terms of everything. It's hard to explain, but I think that along with encountering delicious pastries, curious cheeses, incredible wines, and charming Frenchmen, I also somehow stumbled upon the best, most authentic version of myself. I wrote every day in the Champ de Mars or along the Seine River, I shopped with my roommate Lauren, picnicked in the park, experimented with cooking French food in our tiny kitchen (which, unbelievably, overlooked the Eiffel Tower), sampled wines beyond my wildest imagination, and fell in love with the city and its people. I started writing my first novel there, and I formed a lifelong friendship with Lauren, who is also a writer. That summer in Paris changed my life.

In this book, you (along with Emma and Poppy) can visit some of the places that meant the most to me. Emma's apartment, beside the American Library on the Rue de

Général-Camou near the Eiffel Tower, for example, was based loosely on the apartment that Lauren and I lived in. Café le Petit Pont, where Emma and Poppy go on Emma's first night in Paris, was one of my favorite restaurants in the city. The Long Hop and Bar Dix were two of my favorite bars. Le Refuge des Fondues is, just as Emma finds out, a crazily wonderful fondue restaurant where patrons actually *do* sip wine out of baby bottles.

I thought for a long time that it was Paris itself that had changed me and instilled in me a new sense of freedom and self-confidence. But I've realized in the years since then that my summer in Paris simply served to bring those things to the surface because, for the first time in my life, I let go and gave myself permission to simply be *me*. You don't need to go to Paris like Emma and me to become a better version of you. You simply need to open your mind, to step out of your comfort zone, and to believe you can do anything you set your mind to. As the French say, "*À coeur vaillant rien d'impossible.*" Nothing is impossible for a willing heart.

As Emma discovers, the "art of French kissing" isn't about the kisses themselves (although they are, admittedly, nice!); it's about letting go and giving yourself permission to live and love without fear and without preconceptions about what you *should* be doing. That's the piece of my Paris summer that I try to keep with me always, and every time I see a picture of the Eiffel Tower or hear the beautiful music of a French accent, I can't help but smile.

You can find out more about me and my other novels (*How to Sleep with a Movie Star* and *The Blonde Theory*, both from 5-Spot, and *When You Wish*, a novel for teens) at my Web site, www.KristinHarmel.com, or on my page at www.myspace.com/krisdh54. I'll also post some photos of life in Paris on my site so that you can see for yourself the world that Emma and Poppy call home. Please drop by and say hello!

Kristin

Five Places YOU MUST VISIT ON YOUR NEXT TRIP TO *Paris*

Sure, you know you have to go to the Eiffel Tower and the Louvre, and you're planning to take a little cruise up and down the Seine. But to get a taste of Paris behind the scenes, follow in Emma's footsteps and check out these perfectly Parisian locales:

1 *Rue Cler:* This cobblestone pedestrian market street, overflowing with colorful flower stalls, produce stands, bakeries, cheese shops, butchers, and wineries, is the perfect place to practice your *bonjours* and *mercis*, soak in the atmosphere of Parisian daily life, and pack a picnic to enjoy in the nearby Parc du Champ de Mars, which sits in the shadow of the Eiffel Tower.

2 *Montmartre:* This bohemian Paris neighborhood sits on a hill overlooking the city and is full of mysteriously beautiful winding streets and alleyways, some of which suddenly dead-end in breathtaking vistas over the sprawling city below. Buy a *crêpe au sucre* at the base of the hill and climb up the picturesque steps leading to the glistening Sacré-Coeur basilica, where you can perch on a step and overlook all of Paris spreading out below you.

3 *The Latin Quarter:* Perhaps my favorite neighborhood in Paris, this area, enveloped by the Seine River and the beautiful Luxembourg Gardens, overflows with little shops, relatively inexpensive restaurants, and some of my favorite places, including the Long Hop pub (located at 25–27 Rue Frédéric Sauton—a favorite of Emma, Poppy, and lots of English-speaking expats) and Café le Petit Pont (located at 1 Rue du Petit Pont), the perfect place to settle with a bottle of wine and a great meal while overlooking Notre Dame.

4 *Some Favorite Places to Eat:* One of the most famous cafés in Paris, Café Les Deux Magots (at 6 Place Saint-Germain-des-Prés), was a favorite haunt of Ernest Hemingway, Simone de Beauvoir, and Jean-Paul Sartre. It's a great place to enjoy a kir or a rich hot chocolate while watching the world go by. On the other end of the spectrum is the Cockney Tavern (at 39 Boulevard Clichy), in the heart of the fascinatingly seedy Pigalle area that is also home to the famed Moulin Rouge. Owned and managed by my friend Jean-Michel Colin, it is, to me, the quintessential Parisian eatery. Drop by and say hello to Jean-Michel!

5 *Great Places Overlooking the Seine:* There's something intensely beautiful and peaceful about finding your own way along the river that runs through the city. Take a book to the Square du Vert-Galant, a tiny triangular park that juts into the river from the tip of the Île de la Cité, just west of the Pont Neuf, or plan a sunset picnic on the Pont des Arts, a pedestrian bridge that spans the Seine from the Louvre on the Right Bank to the Institut de France on the Left. Enjoy!